The Surprising Spring
of
Cyndarria Rose Thornwell

Mary McInnis Roessler

ISBN: 1732258007
ISBN 13: 978-1-7322580-0-6
Library of Congress Control Number: 2018905020

MKMR Publishing
Dimondale, MI 48821

For Michael

My best friend

My hero

My much, much better half

Acknowledgments

I am blessed with family and friends who have encouraged and supported me throughout the writing of this novel. To my good friends Polly Brown, Jean Bahle, and Sharlene Goodemoot, my heartfelt thanks for reading, critiquing, and cheering on my efforts. I owe an extra debt of gratitude to Shar who, wisely, had reservations about the original version of Chapter 15, which inspired me to change it and thus introduce what turned out to be a very important subplot. Shar also gave me the cookie recipe which is credited to Grandma Rose. I'm sure everyone who tries it will be appreciative of that particular contribution!

I owe special thanks to my daughter Kate and granddaughter Lola for the book cover. Kate took shot after shot and Lola very patiently ran, jumped, and pumped her fists till we all agreed that we had just the right image to evoke Cyndarria celebrating her "surprising spring."

Social media plays an important role in communicating to the larger community, and I am sadly ignorant in that regard. Fortunately for me, my former student and now good friend Rachel Eldridge volunteered to be my social-media guru, and she has been invaluable in spreading the word about this book. I can't thank her enough.

Finally, all writers credit their spouse for their support, but my husband Mike deserves particular praise. He encouraged me endlessly and was my true savior when it came to the technological expertise necessary to successfully get the book into print. In working with me, his expertise is exceeded only by his patience! I don't know what I would have done without him.

Foreword

I was inspired to write this novel in a very odd way: by the name of an NBA player, Sendarius Thornwell, a wonderful, young guard for the Los Angeles Clippers. I was watching a game one night, heard his name, and immediately thought, "Wow! What a great name! It should be in a novel." And with a few changes, Cyndarria Rose Thornwell and her family were born.

Much to my surprise and delight, they soon took on a life of their own, as did the other characters in the book. I found I very much liked most of them. Some made me laugh; others actually made me cry. As a writer, I can't really take the credit for that; the characters developed their own personalities, their own voices, and I simply transcribed what they said and did.

Even though this is a young-adult novel, I decided from the get-go not to simplify the vocabulary—instead, just to write as the language naturally came to me. Because of that, I created "Cyndarria Rose Thornwell's Mini-dictionary for the Conscientious, the Curious, and the Lover of Words" for when you are stumped by the meaning of a particular word or cultural reference and would like to look it up. There are over 160 words in that mini-dictionary, many of which you will likely already know, but if you come across one that is unfamiliar, just turn to the back of the book and you'll probably find it.

Also in the back of the book is a section entitled, "Some Things to Think About." Obviously, that part is not required reading! ☺ However, if you like to extend your understanding of a book or think about some of the "big ideas" it touches on, you may enjoy looking over that part and choosing a few topics that interest you that you would like to think about further.

As a special treat for those of you who like to bake, I've included Grandma Rose's recipe for oatmeal-peanut butter-chocolate chip cookies. Maybe you'd like to try it out and surprise your family or friends. I can pretty much guarantee that they're going to love them. My family and friends sure do! They're yummy!

Finally, if you are a teacher reading this novel and decide to purchase multiple copies in order to use it with your class, turn to the last page of the book and you'll find a list of supplementary materials which you are eligible to receive free of charge.

I wish you happy reading. I hope you become as fond of Cyndarria, her family, and friends as I am!

What's Inside

CHAPTER 1

THIRTEEN-YEAR-OLD Cyndarria Rose Thornwell sat in her room at the old oak desk she had inherited from her Grandma Rose and thought. She was supposed to be writing an essay for her English teacher Mrs. Wackenstein, known by her students as Mrs. Wacko.

Cyndarria's mind wandered. "What do you want to be when you grow up?" Ugh! What a boring topic!

She pushed back from her desk and felt the fresh spring air waft through her window. From the woods behind the house came the sound of sleigh bells. The spring peepers were back. She was happy about that and figured they were as well. After all, that jingling chorus meant they were mating and had lots of new, little peepers to look forward to.

The phone rang, and a moment later Cyndarria's mother Belle called up the stairs. "Cyndarria, it's Henri." She pronounced it "On-ree," as the French did.

Henri Rousseau had been Cyndarria's best friend ever since kindergarten when he had informed their teacher Mrs. Belden that Cyndarria's name was not Rose, which Mrs. Belden had persisted in calling her, it was Cyndarria. After that, Mrs. Belden called her Cindy, which was even worse than being called by her middle name.

"Thanks, Mom. I'll take it in your bedroom."

"Don't even think about inviting him over until you finish that essay."

Cyndarria rolled her eyes. Her mother was such a slave driver sometimes.

"'I know, Mom. I'm almost done."

Actually, that wasn't exactly true. She had the title written at the top of the page and had filled the margin with doodles. A wrinkled, witchy-looking woman brandishing a ruler and representing Mrs. Wackenstein was her favorite.

A cartoon bubble above her teacher's head admonished, "Children, we must maintain (which she pronounced 'm'ntain') high standards." It was her mantra—and an excuse to give a lot of C's and D's on student essays.

The best Cyndarria had ever done was a B-, and that was on the one Toad had helped her with. Toad was her father Reginald, who had been called by the name of that warty amphibian ever since he had collected them as a child.

When Cyndarria had shown him the paper with a big red B- scrawled on it, he had raised his eyebrows and said simply, "Well, it's better than I ever did when I was in her class, and better than the D you got last time." Which it was. Still, Cyndarria felt a bit cheated. Mrs. Wackenstein never made comments. Her job, she insisted, was to issue grades indicating the level of student achievement, not begin a conversation.

Cyndarria plopped down on her parents' bed and picked up the phone. "Hi, Henri," she said.

"Hi, Cyndarria. Did you finish the essay Mrs. Wacko assigned?"

"I'm working on it now, but all I've come up with so far is a doodle of her. It's pretty good, if I do say so myself."

Henri chuckled. "I think I'm going to say that I want to be a chicken farmer. I found this great poem which talks about different animals by a guy named Oliver Herford in an old book of my dad's. I have no idea where he got it. Listen to this. It ends, '*No wonder, Child, we prize the hen whose egg is mightier than the pen.*' "

Cyndarria giggled. "Oooo, she's gonna hate that! She doesn't want us to think that anything is better or more important than writing. Especially not a chicken egg!"

"I know. I'm going to volunteer to read mine aloud. I can't wait to see her reaction!"

"Cyndarria!" Mrs. Thornwell called from below. "J.J. and Toby are home. Will you please fix them a snack? I have to make a quick trip to the store."

"Okay, Mom. I'll be right down. Gotta go, Henri. See yah. If I finish my essay tonight, do you want to come over tomorrow?"

"Sure. See yah."

Cyndarria hung up and went downstairs, where her younger brothers awaited their snack. They had been at the neighbor's house playing and now claimed to be starving.

J.J., Jackson Johnson, was eight. He was named after some ancient relatives her father admired, though Cyndarria had never understood what made them so admirable. Tobias, who was generally called Toby, was six and finishing kindergarten. He was shy and didn't like to talk to adults, which made school very challenging for both him and his teacher.

"So what do you guys want to eat?" Cyndarria asked.

"Pizza!" shouted Toby, whose reticence didn't extend to ordering food at home.

"Spaghetti-O's," said J.J.

"Those aren't acceptable snacks, you guys. You know that. Mom would have a cow if I gave them to you. There are some grapes and apples in the fridge."

13

"You're supposed to *fix* us something," argued J.J. "If we can't have pizza or Spaghetti-O's, can you at least make us a sandwich?"

"I suppose," said Cyndarria. "How about I fix you a yummy peanut butter and jelly and you split it?"

After dinner, Cyndarria headed back up to her room to work on the dreaded essay. She had been inspired by Henri's idea and hoped she might come up with something that would be equally appalling to Mrs. Wackenstein. She mulled it over as she climbed the stairs. Maybe a cheerleader for some football team like the Dallas Cowboys. Mrs. Wacko had made it very clear how she felt about the "inappropriate attire" of those "misguided young women."

Or she could always kiss up and say she wanted to be an English teacher. Cyndarria almost laughed out loud as she imagined Mrs. Wackenstein's reaction. She could hear her now, "Yes, well, Cyndarria, given your somewhat limited writing skills, you probably should consider something else. I'm sure you could find a job which doesn't require you to write."

Cyndarria closed the door to drown out the television from below and sat down at her desk. She looked for the paper on which she had started her essay, but it wasn't there.

"I must have taken it into Mom and Dad's room," she thought. She got up and went to her parents' bedroom, but she couldn't find it there either.

"What the....." Cyndarria returned to her room and searched everywhere she thought the paper could possibly be, as well as some places that didn't seem at all likely, just in case.

She sat back down at her desk and thought. "It's got to be here somewhere."

A few weeks before something similar had happened. Her comb had temporarily disappeared. She had set it down on her

14

bed and gone downstairs for a couple minutes to ask her mom a question, and when she had returned to finish combing her hair, the comb was nowhere to be found. She had interrogated both of her brothers at the time, certain that they were the culprits, but they had finally convinced her that she was wrong. She had forgotten about the incident till she discovered the comb a few days later stuck inside her tennis shoe.

"This is really strange," she had thought. "I know I didn't put my comb in a shoe."

She could think of no possible logical explanation for the occurrence. It didn't make sense. She hadn't told anyone about it because it was so strange, she figured they would pooh-pooh it and make up some silly reason for why it had happened.

Now this. She was sure her brothers weren't to blame because neither of them had been upstairs either before or after dinner. Who then, or what?

"Something's going on," Cyndarria thought. "I don't know what it means, but it's definitely weird."

CHAPTER 2

CYNDARRIA TURNED ON her radio and tuned to her favorite station, hoping to settle down and write. *Bette Davis Eyes,* one of the top hits of 1981, was playing. She was especially fond of the song, the best one of the year, in her opinion. She hummed along, then sang, imitating Kim Carnes' gravelly voice, "She's got Greta Garbo's standoff sighs, she's got Bette Davis eyes…" Bette Davis? Greta Garbo? Who the heck were they, anyway? Cyndarria realized she was becoming distracted so turned off the radio.

Two hours later she sat at her desk staring at the page of writing she had managed to complete on her hopes for a future career. She had made several false starts, largely because she really didn't know what she wanted to do when she grew up. She had opted against choosing anything too outrageous; she was already on Mrs. Wackenstein's black list for passing notes in class. And chewing gum. And falling asleep twice during "free reading time," which wasn't really free or reading, but usually a very boring grammar exercise.

Starting to feel a little desperate just to get it over with, she decided on being a baker. The truth was she actually liked to bake and often made the family dessert. She had learned a lot from her Grandma Rose before her grandma had died a year ago.

Grandma Rose had lived close by, and Cyndarria often spent Saturday afternoons there doing what her grandma referred to as "baking up a storm." Growing up poor, her grandmother was the oldest of seven children, and when her mother had died at the age of 42, Rose was left in charge of caring for her younger siblings and feeding the family. She had learned to cook and bake out of necessity, not choice. Still, she had come to love baking and particularly enjoyed teaching her youngest granddaughter.

Cyndarria was an eager student and had become quite skilled at baking cookies and pies and cakes. Her favorite recipe was a fancy dessert called a *tarte soleil* in French, or golden sunburst tart, which tasted really good and looked just as pretty. It had a cookie crust the size of a pizza, a cream cheese layer, then was covered with fresh fruit and a pineapple glaze. Everyone in her family except J.J., who was a chocoholic, asked for it on their birthday.

Much to her surprise, Cyndarria had warmed to her topic as she wrote. Maybe becoming a baker wasn't really a bad idea. To finish off her essay, she included her favorite cookie recipe and decided it would be fun to take some in to share with her class. How could Mrs. Wackenstein resist? Cyndarria imagined actually getting an A on the assignment.

Much relieved and quite content with herself, Cyndarria went downstairs to join her family. The boys were involved in a big Lego project with her father, which covered a good part of the living room floor. Her mother sat at the kitchen table making lesson plans for her ESL, English as a Second Language, class the next day.

"Guess what, Mom," Cyndarria said. "I finished my essay on what I want to be when I grow up."

"And what did you decide to write about?" asked Mrs. Thornwell.

"A baker. I thought maybe I'd make some cookies to take in to share with the class."

"Do you think it might be a good idea to check with Mrs. Wackenstein first to make sure it's okay?"

"Nah. She has a real sweet tooth. She's always sneaking candy during free-reading time. I figure I might even get a few extra points that way."

"Well, I'm glad you finished, honey."

"Me too. Hey, Mom, is it okay if I invite Henri to join us for Sunday dinner? His dad usually just orders out. He still doesn't cook much since Mrs. Rousseau died."

Emmanuel Rousseau, Henri's father, had immigrated to the United States from Haiti several years before, a brilliant young college student and refugee from the oppressive Papa Doc regime. It took him more than a decade of financial and emotional struggle, but he had finally managed to earn his doctorate in Comparative Literature and now taught at Midwest State, a small college in a neighboring city. His wife Janine, whose family was also Haitian, had died in an auto accident two years before. Emmanuel Rousseau was both the smartest and the saddest man Cyndarria had ever known.

"It would be fine to invite Henri, Cyndarria. Your father's going to make pot roast. If there are leftovers, we can send some home with him."

The Thornwells were half-owners of a local family restaurant called Toad and the Frog's, and Toad was the lunch chef. He also cooked every other night during the week and once a month did the restaurant's Sunday brunch. He and his partner, Pierre "the Frog" Beaumont, had purchased the restaurant five years before. Pierre handled the business end of the restaurant and Toad, along with Pierre's son Antoine, did most of the cooking. It had been a struggle the first year, and they almost gave up; but with a few adjustments to the menu, the addition of the popular Sunday brunch, and with Pierre's daughter Juliette as the personable new hostess, the business slowly turned around and was now quite successful.

Although he cooked for a living, Toad still enjoyed cooking at home, and Belle welcomed his willingness to give her a break from the kitchen. One of his favorite dishes was pot roast.

"I should probably remind you that your Aunt Agnes will be coming for dinner as well," added Belle. "We haven't invited her in quite a while. She called and was talking about how much she missed us, so it just seemed like the right thing to ask her to join us."

Agnes was Belle's step-sister and had never married. She was about as different from Cyndarria's mother as black was from white. While Belle was quite tall and slender with brown hair just starting to streak with gray and deep blue eyes, Agnes was short and round. She was a decade older than Belle and had short bluish-white air done in tight little curls. Her eyes were a watery gray behind wire-rim glasses. Cyndarria found her mother to be pretty, even beautiful when she got dressed up. Agnes, on the other hand, seemed perpetually displeased with others and life in general, which caused her to frown a lot and pretty much destroyed any semblance of beauty.

"Mom," Cyndarria groaned. "Did you have to invite her? All she ever does is criticize us. She's as bad as Mrs. Wacko."

"Cyndarria Rose Thornwell! I do not want to hear you referring to your English teacher as wacko! It's completely inappropriate. And yes, I felt I had to invite her. She lives by herself, and I know she gets lonely."

"If she was a little nicer, she'd have some friends," Cyndarria muttered.

"That's enough, young lady. Just be nice, that's all I'm asking. She'll be here around 10:00 tomorrow and will spend the day. Oh, and why don't you make a lemon meringue pie for dessert? That's Aunt Agnes's favorite."

"Mom!" Cyndarria almost shrieked.

"Cyndarria!!" Her mother had that look in her eye which brooked no argument.

"Oh, all right. I'm going to bed now and read for a while."

"Thank you, sweetie. I do appreciate it, and so will Aunt Agnes. Sleep tight."

Cyndarria wasn't so sure about her aunt appreciating anything, but she knew it meant a lot to her mother. She kissed her mom, then went to say good night to her father and brothers.

"Cyndarria," J.J. crowed. "Look what we built! Isn't it cool?"

Cyndarria eyed the huge Lego construction. "Umm, I guess so. But what is it?"

"Oh my gosh, it's a castle! Can't you tell?"

"It's a castle," repeated Toby, "where the king and queen live. Do you like it?" He looked hopefully at his sister.

Cyndarria smiled at her little brother. He didn't talk much, and when he did, she never wanted to disappoint him.

"Of course I do, Toby. It's, umm, very unusual and, umm, clever. What part did you make?"

"The moat. A castle needs a moat. Dad helped me, but just a little." Toby looked at his father for acknowledgment.

Toad patted his youngest child on the head. "You did a great job, Tobe. It's a really good moat."

Toby grinned, satisfied with his father's praise.

"Well, I'm going to bed, you guys. See you in the morning."

Cyndarria kissed her father and J.J. Toby jumped up and wrapped his arms around his sister's waist.

"G'night, Cyndarria. I love you."

"I love you too, Tobe. Sweet dreams."

Cyndarria went up to her room, changed into her "Don't moose with me" pajamas, and brushed her teeth. She studied herself in the bathroom mirror, which she found she was doing with surprising frequency lately. She wasn't sure she liked what she saw.

She was 5'4" and desperately hoped she would grow another three or four inches. She had sandy brown hair and her mother's blue eyes. From her father, she had inherited a square chin and high cheekbones, which she liked rather well. There was a spray of freckles across her nose, which annoyed her, and a space between her two front teeth that she didn't like at all. She had wanted braces, but without dental insurance, the family couldn't afford them, so the space remained, taunting her.

Cyndarria grimaced and stuck out her tongue. "Good night," she told her reflection. The reflection stuck its tongue back out at her.

"My, my," Cyndarria said. "Aren't we charming!" She turned out the bathroom light and went back to her room.

She hopped in bed, propped her pillow up against the headboard, and took up the book she was reading. She heard a funny crackle as she moved the pillow. She picked it up and was stunned at what she saw. It was the missing paper which had the doodle of Mrs. Wackenstein.

She let out a little gasp. "This can't be," she thought. But it was.

"How could it happen?" she wondered. Had she absent-mindedly put it there before and then forgotten? That just didn't make sense. Why would she put the paper under her pillow? To make herself start over? No, for sure she would have remembered if she had done such a thing.

"There has to be an explanation," she thought. "Paper and combs don't just move themselves." But what...or who...had done it?

Cyndarria turned her attention to her book but found it difficult to concentrate. Her mind kept returning to the mystery of the disappearing and reappearing paper. The more she thought about it, the more she felt that there might somehow be a message there that she simply didn't understand. But if that were the case, who would have sent her that message? It couldn't have been anyone in her family. None of them had been upstairs. Certainly Oliver, their black Lab, wouldn't have done it!

But something or someone did. Cyndarria peered around her room, almost expecting, half-nervous and half-hopeful, that whatever it was would suddenly reveal itself, so she could understand what was happening and why it was happening to her.

No such luck. Everything was the same as always: her desk with her schoolbooks piled on one side, a lamp on the other; her dresser with a snow globe which she kept out year round, a small jewelry box, and some family pictures; her nightstand with a clock radio; and a rocking chair which, like her desk, had belonged to her Grandma Rose. In the rocking chair sat Sebastian, her teddy bear, a gift from her parents, which she had snuggled with as a child and still, occasionally, talked to because he was such a good listener.

She hadn't closed her window. It was cooler now, but the spring peepers were still singing, so she left it open and listened. The sound of the peepers relaxed her a little. Until this moment, she hadn't realized how tense she'd become. She closed her eyes and breathed in the fresh air.

When she opened them, she found herself staring at her rocking chair and thinking about her grandmother. They had been very close, and more than anyone else in the family, Cyndarria missed her. Right now she wished she could talk to her. Grandma Rose was very wise and very spiritual. She seemed to understand and accept things that others didn't. What would she say about what had happened? How would she explain it?

Cyndarria didn't know, but she knew she needed to confide in someone. She resolved to talk with Henri about it. Maybe he would have an idea.

CHAPTER 3

THE NEXT MORNING at ten o'clock sharp, Aunt Agnes arrived. Cyndarria could never figure out how she managed to be so punctual. It was almost scary. Aunt Agnes drove a very old VW bug, which she had purchased for $500.00 some years before. It was very loud and rattled when she drove.

Belle worried that it would just give out on her one day in the middle of nowhere. Toad reassured his wife that such an occurrence was very unlikely, as Agnes rarely, if ever, drove to the middle of nowhere or even the middle of somewhere. She confined her road trips to the grocery store, the beauty shop where she had her hair done, her church, and her doctor's office, which, conveniently for Agnes, was in the same building as her dentist. The 25-mile trip to visit the Thornwells was about as far as she ever drove.

Agnes rang the doorbell, and when Cyndarria, ordered by her mother to do so, opened the door, she found her aunt somewhat breathless. Cyndarria wasn't sure if it was because of her lack of exercise, which caused any physical effort to leave her virtually gasping for breath, or her supposed excitement at visiting them.

"Cyndarria, dear," Agnes gushed. "So nice to see you."

"It's nice to see you too, Aunt Agnes. Come in."

"Well, yes, of course. Here, I brought this for your mother. Just a small gift for the hostess."

Agnes forced a little smile, which looked very uncomfortable on her face, and handed Cyndarria the plant. It was yellow daffodils, which looked as though they had seen better days and now were starting to droop.

"Uh, thanks, Aunt Agnes. I'll, umm, give them a little water. They look like they might be thirsty."

Agnes raised an eyebrow but said nothing. She brushed past Cyndarria into the living room. Belle came out of the kitchen, where she had been peeling potatoes and carrots for the pot roast, wiping her hands on a dish towel. She smiled.

"Agnes, it's so good to see you. Here, let me take your coat."

"Thank you, dear. It is a bit chilly today, so I had to bundle up. I found this coat at a new shop that just opened up down the block from the grocery. What do you think?"

Belle looked at the coat as though she wasn't sure what to say. It was a bright orange with large purple buttons, which seemed like they might pop when the coat was forced to encircle Agnes's rotund shape.

"I'm down a couple sizes," she whispered confidentially to Belle. "I've lost a little weight, you know."

She fluffed her curls with her hand. "I noticed that Cyndarria looks as if she's been gaining weight. You really need to get after her, Belle."

"Yes, well, she's a growing girl," Belle said. "Come and have a seat in the kitchen. We can catch up a little while I finish peeling the potatoes."

"I'm surprised you don't ask Cyndarria to do that," Agnes sniffed. "She's certainly old enough to take some responsibility in the kitchen."

"Actually, she's going to make dessert. Lemon meringue pie—your favorite. It was her idea," Belle fibbed.

"Hmm, well, yes. How nice. I do love lemon meringue pie, although I need to be careful how much I eat, of course. I have to watch my waistline."

24

Cyndarria played Chutes and Ladders in the living room with Toby until her mom finished in the kitchen. Toad was still working over the stove browning the pot roast when Belle and Agnes came and sat down on the couch.

"I'll get started on the pie," Cyndarria said and took refuge in the kitchen with her father.

"Mmm, smells good, Dad," she said, sniffing deeply. "I imagine Aunt Agnes told you how much she appreciated you making such a nice dinner."

Toad eyed his oldest child with a look that suggested he was only half-teasing. "I've noticed," he said, "that you seem to have developed the smart mouth of a teenager."

Cyndarria felt only slightly chastened. She met his gaze. "Well, did she?"

Toad finished cutting up an onion on top of the pot roast, then covered it with beef broth. He added a bay leaf and pepper, some garlic, a can of tomatoes, a half a cup of wine and fresh parsley gleaned from Belle's small herb garden, which she kept in pots in the kitchen window.

"She said she wasn't sure how much she would eat because she has to watch her weight."

Cyndarria looked more closely at her father and saw a smile starting to form on his lips. "I see. She probably won't want any pie then. It's pretty fattening."

Toad looked up from the pot roast. This time he grinned. "I suppose she won't. It's a good thing Henri is coming. He's a big eater."

Cyndarria gathered the ingredients for the pie crust, mixed them carefully, formed a ball, then rolled it out. She popped the crust in the oven just as the doorbell rang again. "I'll get it," she called. "It's probably Henri."

25

Oliver, their pet Labrador, barked and accompanied Cyndarria to the door. "Don't worry, Ollie, it's just Henri. Nobody is doing to attack me." She patted the dog's head.

Henri grinned when Cyndarria opened the front door. He had a great smile, and his white teeth looked even whiter against his dark skin. Cyndarria envied him. Despite her best efforts, her teeth remained kind of a cream color. That, combined with the space between her front teeth, made her a bit self-conscious when she smiled.

"Hello, Cyndarria," he said. "How are you this beautiful day?" Henri's greeting was always the same, and Cyndarria could hear the echo of the Haitian Creole that both his parents had often spoken at home. It was language that was somewhat formal, almost musical, and seemed to inspire a certain courtesy in the speaker.

He was always cheerful and upbeat, but today Henri's excessive cheeriness annoyed her. "It's chilly and looks like it's about to rain. It hardly qualifies as a beautiful day."

"Hmm," responded Henri. "I see you are grumpy today." He gave Ollie a friendly pat. "Hello, Oliver. I hope you are in a better mood than Miss Cyndarria."

Cyndarria gave a little snort. "Sorry, Henri. It's just that my Aunt Agnes is here, and she's enough to ruin anyone's day."

As the two friends entered the living room, Belle and Agnes interrupted their conversation. Agnes raised an eyebrow as she so often did when she was about to feel insulted.

"Why don't you introduce Henri to Aunt Agnes, Cyndarria?" said Belle quickly. "I don't think they've met."

"Actually, we met last summer," said Henri, still smiling. "It's nice to see you again."

Agnes pursed her lips and touched her curls. "My, what a polite young man you are. Such a good example for Cyndarria."

26

"Yes, ma'am, thank you." His grin got bigger. "I do try to be a good example for her."

Belle coughed to hide a chuckle. Cyndarria glared at Henri and looked as though she wanted to whack him one.

"I have to finish making a pie," she said through clenched teeth. "Why don't you make yourself useful as well as courteous and help me out?"

"Of course, Cyndarria." Henri pretended to make a little bow. "I am always happy to be helpful...as well as courteous."

The oven timer dinged as they entered the kitchen. Cyndarria grabbed a couple holders and removed the pie crust. She set it on the counter beside the stove.

"And what kind of pie are we making today, my dear Cyndarria?" Henri asked with an innocent smile.

"Oh, Henri, stop it," Cyndarria snapped. "You're ticking me off."

Henri looked contrite for a moment, then said sincerely, "I'm sorry, Cyndarria. I was just teasing."

"I know, Henri. Aunt Agnes just sets me off. Anyway, the pie of the day is lemon meringue. I don't suppose you can guess why I'm making it."

"Umm, Aunt Agnes's favorite?"

"Bingo. Mom asked me. I think she kind of feels sorry for her."

As Cyndarria prepared the lemon filling for the pie, Henri, with her instruction, worked on the meringue.

"So what did you end up writing your essay about?" he asked.

"Being a baker. The more I wrote about it, the more I realized that it was actually something I might like to do. I enjoy it, and I learned a lot from my Grandma Rose, so I already know quite a bit."

"Hmm. That's cool, but I'm kind of surprised you chose something sort of normal. I thought you might try to come up with a more outrageous topic to, you know, kind of get a reaction from Wacko."

"Shhh! Mom doesn't want me to call her that. She says it's not appropriate."

Henri nodded. "I guess maybe your mom's right. I don't really think she's nuts anyway. More mean than crazy. But it's still kind of fun to call her," he lowered his voice to a whisper, "you know, Wacko. I just sort of like that word."

Cyndarria chortled. "I do, too. Wacko, Wacko!" she whispered.

They both burst out in laughter.

"What are you guys laughing about?" asked Toad, who had come back in the kitchen to check the progress of the pot roast.

"Oh, Henri just told me a silly joke," said Cyndarria, hoping her father wouldn't ask Henri to repeat it.

"Oh yeah? I like silly jokes. Let's hear it." He looked at the two friends skeptically.

"Umm, ahh, it was just an old knock-knock joke I heard," said Henri.

"Knock-knock joke? I remember a few of those. So tell me yours."

"Right, okay." Henri hesitated. Oh, oh, he was trapped. Finally he said, "Knock knock."

"Who's there?" said Toad.

"Tangerine."

"Tangerine who?"

"Tangerine the bell instead of knock knock all the time?"

Toad nodded and smiled, then said quietly, "Good save, Henri."

Henri look relieved. "Thanks, Mr. Thornwell."

28

"So have you two about finished that masterpiece you're concocting?"

"Yessir, Mr. Thornwell. We're just about done."

"Actually, we're all done," said Cyndarria. "All we have to do is bake it. She poured the lemon mixture into the pie crust, then Henri piled the meringue on top. Cyndarria used the back of a spoon to make fancy curls in the meringue as her grandma had taught her, then placed the pie in the oven.

"Fifteen minutes to lemon-meringue-pie heaven," she announced, flourishing the spoon.

"Yum," said Henri. "Can't wait."

CHAPTER 4

FIFTEEN MINUTES LATER, as Cyndarria was taking the pie out of the oven, Belle came into the kitchen.

"Sugar!" she exclaimed.

"What's the matter, Mom?" Cyndarria asked.

"I forgot I was going to make Bobby's salad for dinner. It's another favorite of Aunt Agnes. Why don't you and Henri go join her and your father while I make it?"

"Mom, do we have to?"

"I'll tell you what. I'll make a deal with you. Either go visit with Aunt Agnes while I make the salad, or you make it and I'll go back to the living room."

Cyndarria glanced at Henri, who nodded quickly. "We'll make it," they chorused.

"Make what? Can I help?" Toby asked, entering the kitchen. "I can cook good."

Cyndarria smiled at her little brother. "Sure, Toby," she said. "How about if you help me stir the Jello?"

"Okey dokey,"

Bobby's salad was a longtime favorite of the Thornwells. Grandma Rose had learned how to make it while serving as a maid to the wealthy Ford family when she was a young woman. Bobby, their only child, requested it for Sunday dinner every week.

Bobby had been born with Down syndrome, which was very little understood at the time. The Fords had chosen to raise him, but Mrs. Ford was not a strong woman and herself suffered from depression, so the care of Bobby fell largely to Rose. He often helped her make the salad, grating the cup of carrots called for in the recipe while Rose chopped the celery and drained the pineapple. Together, they would add all three to the lemon gelatin after it was partly set.

Every time they finished, Bobby would exclaim, "Yummy! This is going to be so good!"

Grandma Rose had told Cyndarria that story one day while they were baking together and had given her the simple recipe. It was a hit from the first time she made it for her family and now showed up frequently with dinner.

As they were finishing the salad, J.J. joined them. "I'm bored," he said. "Let's play a game."

"Hungry Hippos!" Toby shouted. "I'm good at that game."

"That's a little noisy," cautioned Cyndarria. "I'm not sure Aunt Agnes would like it."

They finally settled on Crazy Eights, their favorite card game.

Three-and-a-half hours and several different games later, Toad poked a fork in the pot roast and pronounced it done. J.J. helped his mother set the table while Toad made gravy, and soon a steaming platter of beef and bowls of potatoes, onions, and carrots, along with Bobby's salad and some warm rolls made their way to the dining room table.

Agnes consumed seconds of everything and hinted that she would love to take home some of the leftovers.

As the baker, Cyndarria also served dessert. "How big a piece would you like, Aunt Agnes?" she asked, the knife hovering over the tips of the meringue.

Agnes hesitated briefly. "Oh, well, just a teensy weensy piece."

31

Cyndarria measured out what she thought was a tiny piece. "Like this?"

"Well, maybe just a bit bigger."

Cyndarria moved the knife a little. "Is this okay?"

"Well…"

Cyndarria moved the knife again and plunged it into the pie without waiting for further instruction, then served everyone else and was left with just a small piece for herself.

Agnes peered at Cyndarria's plate. "I see you're being careful to watch your calorie intake," she said. "Under the circumstances, I think that's a very wise decision."

Cyndarria gritted her teeth. She was about to reply when Belle, who knew her daughter's outspoken nature, said quickly, "Yes, Cyndarria is very health-conscious. I'm really proud of her."

"Yeah," said J.J. "*She's* not fat at all."

Suddenly the room was silent. Cyndarria cringed. Belle closed her eyes, momentarily at a loss.

Toby looked around the table. "Why's everybody so quiet?" he asked.

"We're all just digesting our dinner," said Toad, a little too heartily. "Personally, I could go for a cup of coffee. Belle, Agnes, how about you?"

"Sounds good," said Belle, jumping up from the table. "I'll brew us a pot."

"I'll get the cups," said Cyndarria and followed her mom eagerly to the kitchen.

Belle turned as her daughter came up behind her. "Do not say a word," she whispered. "I know you're angry, but that's just how Agnes is. Ignore her."

"She always says stuff like that," said Cyndarria. "It just makes me so mad."

"I know, honey. I think it makes her feel better about herself. But you know what she's saying isn't true, so just don't take her seriously, okay?" She kissed her firstborn on the forehead.

Cyndarria blew air out through her lips, then shrugged. "I suppose," she said. "But I don't have to like it."

Agnes departed an hour later with a bag full of leftovers. Henri left shortly after that with the rest of them to share with his father. Toad and the boys plopped down on the couch to watch the NCAA regional finals basketball game between Indiana and St. Joseph's, and Belle went upstairs to take a short nap.

Like Henri, Cyndarria had decided to volunteer to read her "What do you want to be when you grow up" essay the next day, which meant she had to make the cookies she planned to share with the class that afternoon.

The recipe was another old one and had been in the family for at least five generations, as Grandma Rose had learned how to make it from her great aunt. Cyndarria studied the recipe— oatmeal-peanut butter-chocolate chip cookies. She had never known anyone who didn't love them.

Actually, the cookies hadn't originally contained chocolate chips which, her grandma had informed her, weren't invented till the 1930's, when some lady at the Toll House Inn in Massachusetts had chopped up chocolate bars and put them in cookies. A few years later the actual chip was born. It was Grandma Rose who had decided to add some to the oatmeal cookie recipe instead of raisins, with predictable results.

Peanut butter, on the other hand, had been around in some form since the Aztecs, who mashed roasted peanuts into a paste. Cyndarria had done a report on peanuts in sixth grade and learned some interesting facts about them. It took 720 peanuts to make a pound of peanut butter. And, given the fondness of her brothers for peanut butter and jelly sandwiches, it didn't surprise her to learn that the average American kid ate 1500 of them before grad-uating from high school. Considering the rate they were going, she figured J.J. and Toby might make that total before finishing middle school.

Cyndarria gathered all the ingredients for the cookies, humming to herself. "Gonna get me an A," she sang softly.

She mixed together butter, sugar, eggs, peanut butter and vanilla, then added the dry ingredients, chocolate chips, and a cup of walnuts. She put heaping spoonsful of the mixture on the cookie sheet and slid it into the waiting oven. An hour later she had three dozen extra-large, yummy cookies. She gobbled one down while it was warm and put the rest in plastic bags after they had cooled.

She wandered into the living room; the basketball game was still on. "How's Indiana doing?" she asked. The Thornwell family were all Michigan State fans. MSU had won the national championship in 1979 with Magic Johnson and Greg Kelser, but they weren't in the tournament this year. Indiana was, so Toad and the boys temporarily contented themselves with cheering on another Big 10 team.

"Indiana is slaughtering them!" announced J.J., almost gleefully.

J.J. liked basketball, but he loved baseball. He had played Tee-ball for three years and gained some batting and fielding skills. This year he hoped to play on one of the local Little League teams. Toad was delighted, as he had grown up playing baseball and had played some at the college level. He had been invited to coach one of the Little League teams that year. He was interested but a little ambivalent about having his son on the team he was coaching.

Cyndarria sat down to watch the end of the game. Oliver approached her and put his head on her knee, waiting patiently to be petted. "Good boy," she said, and gave the dog an affectionate pat.

Half-an-hour later it was over, and the result wasn't even close: Indiana 78, St. Joseph's 46. J.J. was especially pleased and gave a high five to his dad and Toby.

"How about me?" asked Cyndarria.

"I didn't think you cared that much about who won," said J.J.

"I'm glad the Big Ten team did." She held up her hand, and J.J. slapped it.

"Mmm, what do I smell?" Belle was up from her nap. "Did you make cookies, Cyndarria?"

"Yes, I'm taking them to school tomorrow to go with my essay. I think Mrs. Wack...enstein is going to like them. Hopefully, they get me an A."

"Clever girl," said Toad. "I'd give you an A if you gave me a cookie."

"Dad, you'd give me an A anyway. I'm your daughter."

"Nope, you'd have to earn it. Or bribe me with cookies." Toad grinned. He enjoyed teasing his oldest child, and although he didn't say so very often, he was extremely proud of her.

"Okay, you two," said Belle. She was usually the referee during family disagreements, even when they were in fun. "Well, since you need those cookies for your class tomorrow, what would you think about going to The Happy Cow for an ice cream?"

"Yea," shouted Toby enthusiastically. "Let's go! I want blue moon!"

"Superman for me!" said J.J., striking a super-hero pose.

"A dip of butter pecan and a dip of chocolate ripple," said Cyndarria.

"I guess it's settled then," said Toad. "Put on your jackets and let's go."

CHAPTER 5

AT 6:45 THE NEXT morning, Cyndarria's clock radio turned on and woke her from a deep sleep. She rolled over, reached out, and hit the snooze button. She was about to drift off to sleep again when her father stuck his head in the door.

"Up and at 'em, sunshine," he said cheerily.

"Go away!" Cyndarria groaned. She hated early-morning cheer.

She lay listening to the house. It was quiet upstairs. The boys didn't have to get up until 7:30 because their school started a half-hour later than hers. She knew her father would be in the downstairs bathroom shaving, and her mother would be making coffee in the kitchen. Cyndarria could usually smell it when she got out of bed. Her mom liked to listen to the radio in the morning, one that played classical music.

Cyndarria stretched and sat up. She thought about what she should wear. She wanted to dress up some, so she would look nice when she spoke in her English class. Every little bit helped, she figured, if she wanted to make a positive impression on Mrs. Wackenstein and, she hoped, get that A. She settled on a pair of black pants, which she had worn only a few times, and a light-blue blouse with long sleeves and a small collar. Finally, she fished a small heart-shaped locket that her parents had given her for Christmas out of her jewelry box.

Her wardrobe decided, she took a shower and washed her hair. Ten minutes later she was dressed and went down to breakfast—cereal and a glass of orange juice. Classes started at 8:00, and Henri always stopped by her house at 7:30, so they could make the fifteen-minute walk to school together.

"Toad, will you please check on the boys?" Belle called. "They should be up by now."

J.J. was generally good about getting ready on his own, but Toby was purposely slow in the morning. He didn't like school because his teacher, Miss Jamison, was always trying to "trick" him into talking, and he just didn't want to. Belle and Toad had had more than one conference with her in an effort to solve the problem, so far to little effect. However, this was her first year of teaching, and she was determined not to be defeated by a stubborn little six-year-old.

"He's very bright," she had told them, "particularly in arithmetic. Sometimes he figures things out in his head that are surprising, and that's one time when he's willing to speak up. I think he's curious to know if he's right and also maybe likes to show off a little."

"That sounds like Toby," agreed Belle. "He often announces that he's good at things, so he obviously doesn't lack confidence. He's just uncomfortable talking to adults."

"I understand," Miss Jamison said. "I hope with time I can win him over. I try to talk with him one-on-one every day, but so far I'm afraid I haven't had too much success. He tends to give me one-word answers, and not much more."

That had been way back in October, and things hadn't changed a whole lot. Toby still resisted going to school in the morning. Fortunately, J.J. loved school and was also very good about encouraging his younger brother to get out of bed and get ready. Their elementary school was farther away than the middle school, and Belle saw them off on the bus every morning, since her ESL classes in the local library didn't start until 9:00.

Sycamore Creek, where the Thornwells lived, was not a large city, just over 25,000 souls, as Grandma Rose used to say, but had a fairly sizable refugee population, in large part because there was a local company that welcomed workers from other countries. They had found that such employees were very reliable and could be counted on to work hard. Because of that, many refugee families moved away from Lansing, the nearby state capital, to live in a smaller community that offered more job opportunities.

Over the years, Belle had taught adult students from many different countries, among them Cuba, Syria, Nepal, and several from Haiti. One of her favorites was an older woman named Gessma from Sudan, who lived with her daughter and son-in-law. Gessma was illiterate in her own language, Arabic, which made learning English particularly challenging for her, so Belle had learned a few words in Arabic to help her feel more comfortable.

Each time Belle greeted her in Arabic, Gessma's face would light up with delight and she would cry, "Wah, Belle, Arabe, Arabe!" which she pronounced AH-dah-bay. Belle admired the fact that, at 75, Gessma was still willing to take an English class, and did her best to teach her.

In the summer, adult classes were suspended, and she worked in the vacation program for the children of Mexican migrant laborers.

The area around Sycamore Creek was primarily farmland, producing corn, wheat, and soybeans, but also an abundance of fruit: strawberries, cherries, peaches, blueberries, and apples. The migrant laborers picked fruit, beginning with strawberries in June through apples in September. The migrant children who didn't work in the orchards attended the summer program, where they learned a little English, but also played games and, more importantly, were given a nutritious snack and lunch.

Cyndarria's Spanish teacher, Señor Paniagua (literally, Mr. Bread and Water, which the students liked to call him), worked in the summer program with Belle, as did her friend Lovelie, who was, indeed, lovely, Belle said. A few years ago, Lovelie had been Belle's first Haitian student and, over the period of the year she had been in Belle's class, they had become friends.

Lovelie was in her late thirties and had never been married, a fact that mystified Belle, because her friend was not only beautiful but also gentle and kind. She was generous to others and wise in a way that Belle admired. Once when Belle had asked her why she had chosen to migrate to the United States, Lovelie had shaken her head and said simply, "I had a very bad experience with a man. I could not stay in Haiti. He would have found me."

Belle loved her job as an ESL teacher and especially enjoyed working with the migrant children in the summer. She had told Cyndarria she could help out the next summer, if she wanted to.

"You'd be a volunteer," she said, "so you wouldn't get paid, but it would be a great opportunity to practice your Spanish a little."

"I'll think about it," Cyndarria had replied. She had just started babysitting and liked working with children, but she wasn't sure she wanted to give up her mornings in the summer.

Cyndarria sat at the kitchen table thinking, but not about her summer plans. She was deep in thought about the mysterious disappearance of things which had occurred recently. She definitely wanted to talk with Henri about it.

She finished her cereal and rinsed out her bowl just as the front doorbell rang. "It's Henri," she called out to her mother. "Gotta go."

She grabbed her book bag, which held her books, her notebook, and the cookies, and opened the door to see Henri standing there with his usual morning smile. Cyndarria found it hard to understand how anyone could be so cheerful that early in the day.

"Good morning, Cyndarria," Henri said. "How are you this beautiful morning?"

Cyndarria looked her friend over, then nodded her approval. "My, my, my, aren't we fancy this morning," she grinned. "Got a hot date?"

"You might say that," said Henri. "With Mrs. Wackenstein. Do you like my new bow tie?" The tie was a bright lime green with orange and yellow polka dots.

"It's, um, very citrusy. Looks good with your pink shirt. Very bold."

"Do you think that our lovely English teacher will be impressed?"

Cyndarria pretended to ponder the question. "Hmm, she does like it when students dress up. That tie alone might be enough to earn you an A."

"Exactly as I thought," agreed Henri.

The two friends arrived at school just in time to go to their lockers, then headed to their first-hour English class. Mrs. Wackenstein sat taking attendance when they entered and looked up to see them scoot to their desks just as the tardy bell rang. She looked vaguely aggrieved at their almost-late arrival.

"I have to say," she observed, looking down her nose over her glasses, "in my experience, the most successful students arrive in class early, ready to go. They're generally much more, shall we say, ardent in their pursuit of learning."

"What's that mean?" asked Joey Bellow, a heavy-set kid who loved asking questions, especially if he thought they might annoy the teacher.

Mrs. Wackenstein directed her gaze in Joey's direction. "What, exactly, does what mean, Mr. Bellow?"

"You know, ar….," he stopped, apparently unable to remember the word.

"I can hardly tell you the meaning if you can't tell me the word, Mr. Bellow."

"Ardent," a voice from the back said. It was Henri.

"Well, thank you, Mr. Rousseau. I'm sure Mr. Bellow appreciates your assistance."

"Yes, ma'am," said Henri. "I try to be helpful."

Cyndarria covered her mouth to keep from bursting out in laughter.

Mrs. Wackenstein hesitated for a moment, then nodded. "Yes, well, helpfulness is certainly a laudable quality."

Joey looked as though he was about to open his mouth and ask another question, but then seemed to think better of it.

Mrs. Wackenstein stood up and wrote the word "ardent" on the board, then turned to the class. "Ardent," she said, articulating the word with particular care, "to put it in the simplest terms, means eager or enthusiastic, as in ardent learners, which I hope all of you are. Including you, Mr. Bellow."

She gave Joey a skeptical look, then returned to her seat.

"Now then," she continued, "today your 'What do you want to be when you grow up?' essays are due, and we will listen to a few of them. Would anyone like to volunteer?"

The room was silent. A few of the students, including Joey Bellow, sank lower in their seats.

Mrs. Wackenstein looked around the room. "How disappointing," she said. "I thought surely there would be a few students who wanted to share their work with us."

"I'll go," said Henri, and the entire room seemed to breathe a sigh of relief.

"Very well, Mr. Rousseau. Please come forward. Remember to speak up. You can't impress us with your thoughts if we can't hear them."

"Yes, ma'am," said Henri, a bit too loudly. "I will certainly do my best."

"That's all any of us can do, Mr. Rousseau. I certainly encourage all my students to do so. We must m'ntain high standards, you know."

"Yes, ma'am. I couldn't agree more."

Cyndarria put her head down on her desk to muffle a giggle.

Mrs. Wackenstein was on her with the same eagerness Oliver showed when she was throwing him the Frisbee, except her teacher was not a dog and this wasn't a game. Nothing was a game to Mrs. Wackenstein.

"Miss Thornwell," she almost barked, "is there something wrong? Do you need to go to the principal's office to talk about your problem?"

"Umm, no, Mrs. Wackenstein. Sorry. My, umm, my stomach is just a little upset this morning, but I'll be okay."

"I certainly hope so." She looked at Henri with what could almost have passed for a smile. "Proceed, Mr. Rousseau."

Henri took a deep breath, cleared his throat loudly, and prepared to read.

CHAPTER 6

HENRI SMILED AND looked around the class. "The title of my essay is, 'I can see chicken feathers in my future.' "

The class snickered. Mrs. Wackenstein raised her eyebrows and pursed her lips but remained silent.

"When I was given the topic of what I wanted to be when I grew up, I wasn't sure what to write," Henri began. "To tell you the truth, it's not something I had thought about very seriously. Sure, when I was little, I dreamed of being an astronaut or maybe a star football player, but deep down inside I guess I knew that would never happen.

"So Mrs. Wackenstein's assignment was a real challenge for me, but I like challenges, so thank you, Mrs. Wackenstein."

Henri nodded in his teacher's direction and gave her what he hoped was his most winning smile. Apparently it worked, because once again a brief flicker of upturned lips appeared on her face. Encouraged, Henri continued.

"I considered various options; after all, this was my future, and I didn't want to screw up."

A loud clearing of throat emanated from Mrs. Wackenstein's desk. "Diction, Mr. Rousseau, diction."

"Uh, yes ma'am, I mean I didn't want to make a mistake."

Mrs. Wackenstein nodded. "Proceed," she said.

"Thank you. Umm, okay, let's see, where was I?"

"Options, Mr. Rousseau. You considered various options."

"Right, thank you."

Henri found his place and went on. "I thought about being a fisherman because I like the water, and our state is surrounded by the Great Lakes, which have a lot of fish. The problem with that is I get seasick on a boat. So then I considered being a doctor. I love helping other people, but, honestly, I don't think I could stand staying in school that long.

"A chemist? An actor? A plumber? A musician? There was something wrong with all these possibilities. Finally, I was looking at one of my father's old books, and it hit me. I had what my dad calls an epiphany."

"My, what a good word," said Mrs. Wackenstein, nodding her approval.

"What's an epiph....?" asked Joey Bellow. "It sounds like something you get when you're sick, like when you puke." Joey smiled slyly, looking for Mrs. Wackenstein's reaction out of the corner of his eye.

"That's quite enough, Mr. Bellow. You are demonstrating your ignorance entirely too often this morning." She stood up and wrote the word "epiphany" on the board.

"Mr. Rousseau, would you like to enlighten the class as to the meaning of this word?"

"Umm, yes, ma'am. My dad says it's a moment when something comes to you sort of out of nowhere, and you just know that it's the right answer to a problem you've been thinking about. Like in the Bible, what happened to Paul on the road to Damascus, when he suddenly understood that he should become a follower of Christ."

Mrs. Wackenstein looked almost dumbfounded. She certainly hadn't expected such an erudite answer from one of her students, even from Henri, who was very intelligent. She was not a teacher who looked for pleasant surprises from her students, generally expecting the opposite, so when one did occur, she was quite taken aback.

"Yes, Mr. Rousseau. That's a very good explanation. Thank you. Please continue with your essay."

"Yes, ma'am," Henri said, feeling more confident. Mrs. Wackenstein almost never complimented a student. He once again found his place in his essay.

"The book was called, *Child's Natural History,* by an Englishman named Oliver Herford. It has poems about a lot of different animals, like the seal, the ant, and the cow. At the end of his poem called *The Hen*, he wrote, '*No wonder child, we prize the hen, whose egg is mightier than the pen.*' "

Mrs. Wackenstein gasped and opened her mouth to speak, but nothing came out. In the end, she simply closed her mouth.

"Home free!" he said to himself, and a satisfied smile played on his lips. "I think I've outwitted old Wacko! She doesn't know whether to cry or wind her watch!" Somehow that corny old saying seemed to fit the occasion. Encouraged by his teacher's silence, he continued.

"It seemed like that was a sign. If the egg is even mightier than the pen, think about what it would mean to be a chicken farmer! I'm sure you would all agree that feeding people is a lot more important than writing to them. And just think of all the food we make with eggs! The more I thought about it, the better the idea seemed to me. I was hooked!

"I talked to my dad, and he said I could order an incubator, so I can start to hatch chicken eggs. As you can see, I'm very serious about my future career. I can't wait to get started!"

Henri stopped and waited for the class's reaction. At first there was silence, and then Joey Bellow began a slow clap. He was gradually joined by others, and soon the entire class was on their feet applauding. Joey whooped, which was enough to move Mrs. Wackenstein to action.

"Enough, students!" she fairly shrieked.

Cyndarria was always amazed at the lung power of such a skinny woman. When she was angry and shouted, you could hear her in every other classroom in her hall.

"That is quite enough. You will all resume your seats immediately!" She looked at Henri with a gimlet eye. "You too, Mr. Rousseau."

"Yes, ma'am," said Henri, doing his best to look serious. He walked to the back of the room and sat at his desk.

"Oh my gosh, Henri, that was really cool," whispered Cyndarria. "Everybody loved it. Wacko doesn't know what to think."

Mrs. Wackenstein's voice rang out again. "Miss Thornwell, was there something you wanted to share with the rest of the class?"

Cyndarria hesitated briefly. "I was just telling Henri that I wanted to go next."

Mrs. Wackenstein looked surprised. "Very well. Come forward and speak up. Remember, you can't impress us....."

"Yes, ma'am, I know. I can't impress you with my thoughts if you can't hear them."

Mrs. Wackenstein eyed Cyndarria over her glasses, seemingly unsure if her student were sincere or just being what she thought of as a smarty pants. She opted for sincerity. "I'm certainly glad you understand that, Miss Thornwell," she said. "You may proceed."

Cyndarria grabbed her essay and the cookies from her book bag. She approached the podium Mrs. Wackenstein had ordered placed at the front of the classroom, putting the bag of cookies on the shelf beneath the top.

As Henri had done, she cleared her throat, smiled at the class, nodded to Mrs. Wackenstein, and began.

"The title of my essay is, 'The Inspiration of my Grandma Rose.'

46

"Thirteen is a pretty young age to know what you want to be when you grow up. My mom said she wasn't really sure until she was 30. She's an ESL teacher, and she truly loves her work, so, in her case, I guess it was worth waiting.

"I've always thought I'd like to be a singer, but Mr. Leavenworth wouldn't even let me in the choir this year, so I figured that was probably out. I really don't have a lot of talent, but one thing that I like a lot and am actually good at is baking. And that's because of my Grandma Rose. She's gone now, but even when I was little, she would invite me to come over and we would bake together. At first, I went because I really loved my grandma and liked spending time with her, but after a while, I found that I really enjoyed baking too.

"We made all kinds of goodies—cookies, cakes, pies, breads, and she would always give me most of what we made to take home, so my whole family could enjoy it. Of course, that was a big hit because it seems like all the Thornwells have a sweet tooth.

"After my grandma passed away, I started baking things on my own. I most always am the one who makes dessert for my family. I'm not sure if I'll ever be a baker. I know I'd have to learn a lot about running a business if I wanted to have my own bakery. That would be hard. Also, there's an awful lot of time before I'm actually an adult and might be able to think seriously about something like that. But right now, it seems like a pretty good idea—better than being a singer who can't carry a tune, for sure!

"I thought everyone might like to try one of my homemade cookies, so I brought some. Tell me what you think. If I get enough encouragement, maybe I really will become a baker some-day."

Cyndarria reached for the bag containing the cookies. There was a stir of eagerness in the class. She was about to start passing them out when Mrs. Wackenstein spoke.

"Miss Thornwell, you seem to have forgotten it's against school rules to eat in class unless special arrangements have been made ahead of time. Did you speak with Principal Johansson to get permission?"

"Umm, no, Mrs. Wackenstein. I didn't know I was supposed to."

"Ignorance of the rules is no excuse, Miss Thornwell. All students are responsible for reading our handbook, and that rule is very clearly stated. You certainly should have known."

"But I…"

"There are no buts about it. We simply can't allow students to break the rules willy-nilly. Where would the school be; indeed, where would civilization be, if we did that?!"

Cyndarria felt a tear welling up, and she blinked hard to keep it from rolling down her cheek. She would not give Mrs. Wackenstein the satisfaction. She didn't know what else to say. Cyndarria was certain that if she said what she was actually feeling, she would get an even lower grade. She walked back to her seat and just as she was about to sit down, the passing bell rang.

"Everyone, put your essays on my desk before you leave. We'll hear a couple more of them tomorrow, and then we'll continue our study of direct and indirect object pronouns."

"Miss Thornwell," she continued. "Please see me a moment."

Cyndarria picked up her book bag, steeled herself, and went up to Mrs. Wackenstein's desk. Henri waited loyally beside her.

"You are excused, Mr. Rousseau," said Mrs. Wackenstein.

"Yes, ma'am," said Henri. He looked at Cyndarria. "See you in Spanish class."

Cyndarria nodded, then looked directly at her teacher. She didn't want to show her how scared she was.

"Miss Thornwell, this is not the first time you have ignored school rules."

"I didn't mean to, Mrs. Wackenstein," Cyndarria said.

"Well, be that as it may, I think it's time that you had a serious talk with Mr. Johansson. Perhaps he can inspire you to become more aware of the rules and impress upon you the importance of following them. I will contact him and tell him to expect to see you after school today."

"I'm supposed to go home right after classes, so I can watch my little brothers," objected Cyndarria.

"I'm sure your mother will be able to make other arrangements."

"But….."

"Good day, Miss Thornwell."

Cyndarria turned and left the room. What she had hoped would be a triumph had turned into an embarrassing defeat. She would probably get another D on her essay, and, on top of that, she had to talk to the principal. This was starting out to be a really awful day.

CHAPTER 7

WHEN CYNDARRIA GOT to Spanish class, Henri and their friend Stevie were waiting for her outside the door.

"You okay?" asked Henri.

"I have to go see Mr. Johansson after school."

"You're kidding!" exclaimed Stevie. "Because of some cookies?"

"Wacko thinks I break too many rules. Here I thought I was doing something nice." She held out the bag of cookies. "You guys want one?"

"Yum! Sure!" Stevie reached eagerly for the bag. He was small for his age and always trying to gain weight. He had bright red hair, and his face was covered with freckles. Today he wore a T-shirt that said, "Save the whales!"

"These are really good, Cyndarria," said Henri, as he took a second huge bite. "I'll bet Bread and Water would like one. He might even let you pass them out to the class. He's pretty loosey-goosey about the rules when it comes to food."

If there was one teacher who could cheer Cyndarria up, it was Señor Paniagua. His family had immigrated to the United States from Mexico when he was a child, and he had long since become a naturalized citizen. He often talked about how much it meant to him to be an American.

"You kids were born American," he would tell them. "You have no idea how much that really means, how lucky you are."

Henri had told Cyndarria that his father said the same thing. He said he was so happy when he was finally sworn in as an American citizen. He still carried a small copy of the constitution around with him in his jacket pocket and sang the national anthem so loudly that it embarrassed his son. Still, Henri knew his father was sincere and truly was proud to be an American.

The tardy bell rang, and the three friends scurried to their seats. Señor Paniagua finished what he was writing on the board, then turned to face the class. He rubbed his hands together vigorously and grinned at the students.

Señor Paniagua was short and balding and always wore dress pants, a shirt and tie, and a cardigan sweater. Nobody knew how old he was, but he had been at Sycamore Creek Middle School as long as anyone could remember. He was the polar opposite of Mrs. Wackenstein in the way he treated his students. He actually seemed to like them and was pretty fun. He was Cyndarria's favorite teacher.

"*Buenos días, jóvenes,*" he said. "*Cómo están Uds. hoy?*"

"*Muy bien, maestro,*" the class chorused. "*Y Ud.?*"

"*Gracias por preguntar,*" Señor Paniagua said with a little bow. "*Hoy me encuentro maravillosamente bien, gracias, y muy contento de verlos a todos, como siempre.*"

"Uh, Señor Paniagua," said Joey Bellow, who once again had planted himself in the front row, "you kind of lost me with that one."

"Ah, *pues, Pepito,*" Señor Paniagua replied with a smile. He looked around the class. "Can anyone help *nuestro amigo Pepito* out with what I said?"

"You said you were fine and happy to see us," volunteered Sara Greene. Sara was the best student in the class and also the prettiest and was happily aware of it. Cyndarria thought she was obnoxious and phony. Henri was more forgiving. Stevie just wanted to grow a few inches, so maybe someday she would notice him.

"*Gracias, Sarita*," Señor Paniagua gave an approving nod. "*Tienes razón.* You're right."

Cyndarria raised her hand.

"*Sí, Rosita*," Señor Paniagua said, calling her by her Spanish name.

"Señor Paniagua, *tengo*....." Cyndarria stopped, not knowing how to say cookies in Spanish. "Uh, *tengo* cookies," she said finally. She shrugged, helpless to go on in Spanish. "And I was wondering if I could share them with the class."

"*Galletas,*" said Señor Paniagua. "*Fantástico! Me encantan las galletas.* I love cookies! *Pero...*let's leave them till the end of class, okay? *Está bien?*"

"*Sí,*" said Cyndarria, pleased. "*Está bien.*"

The class reviewed some vocabulary in preparation for a quiz the next day, then did a short reading and answered questions aloud.

After that, Señor Paniagua said, "*Hoy,* today, we're going to talk a little bit about the suffix *–ito* in Spanish. It's what is called a diminutive, and it's one of my favorites. Some of you have it on the end of your name. Cyndarria does, for example. *Rosa* becomes *Rosita.* It's like in English—Rose becomes Rosie. Bill becomes Billy. Sam becomes Sammie."

"So *–ito* is more or less the same as -y or -ie on the end of a word in English," offered Sara.

"Very often," said Señor Paniagua. "*Muy bien, Sarita.*"

Sara smiled smugly.

"It's used a lot with names to show a certain closeness or affection for the person."

"Like me," said Joey. "Joe to Joey. *Pepe* to *Pepito.* Guess you must like me, huh?"

Cyndarria rolled her eyes, although the truth was she did like Joey. He kept things lively in class. Sometimes he acted dumb, but she knew he was actually very smart. He made her laugh.

Señor Paniagua nodded. "*Claro que sí, Pepito*! Of course we do, and your name is a perfect example," he said, clearly pleased that the students were understanding the concept.

"-*Ito* is not used just for names, though, but for other things as well. For example, in Spanish you might refer to your little brother as *mi hermanito*. The suffix -*ito* is used instead of the word little. But lots of times it just takes the place of a –y or an –ie. Pretty handy, huh?

"So," he continued, warming to the subject, "a *libro* is a book, but a *librito* is one that is short, or, since the –*ito* can indicate affection as well, even with things, it might be a book you're especially fond of."

"Sooo," Joey said, "a *librito* could mean a small book that I like, or…it could mean bookie, right. Like, that guy is my bookie, *mi librito*." Joey chortled, obviously delighted with his cleverness.

Señor Paniagua hesitated, and then a huge grin spread across his face. "*Pepito*, you have just made a cross-linguistic pun. *Me encanta*!"

"Well, I'm not sure what that means," said Joey, "but I'm glad that you like it."

"It means you made a play on words, but you did it across two languages. I'm impressed!" He stood thinking. "Hmmm, I wonder if we can come up with any others. Let's see. What about the word *tienda*, which means store. What if we say, *tiendita*?"

The class was silent for a moment, still not sure of what their teacher was asking. Suddenly, Henri laughed. "Oh, I get it! If a *tienda* is a store, then a *tiendita* is a story! It's not really, but if you just do a literal translation, that's what comes out. I guess it shows that knowing a foreign language goes beyond simply translating word for word."

"That's correct, *Enrique*. Accurate translation is very challenging. The Italians have a saying—*Traduttore traditore*, which means translator traitor, and that kind of applies here. An incorrect or careless translation betrays the true meaning of what is being communicated."

The class groaned. "Okay, okay," said Señor Paniagua, holding up his hands as if in defeat. "I get it. You're B-O-R-E-D. Let's do one more, though. You know, just for the fun of it." He looked around the class. The students returned his gaze stoically. Señor Paniagua was just too sincere and too nice not to cut him some slack. Besides, there were the cookies at the end of class to be considered.

"So, let's see, if a *silla* is a chair, what's a *sillita*?"

The silence was deafening.

Finally Sara spoke up. "C-H-A-I-R-Y? What's a chairy? It doesn't make sense."

"Oh my gosh, I get it!" Cyndarria practically shouted. "It's cherry, like the fruit, you know? You just have to listen to the sound and not think about the spelling."

Señor Paniagua was delighted. *"Correcto, Rosita. Bravo!"*

"I think it's time for cookies," said a voice from the rear of the class. It was Stevie, who had managed to survive the hour without being called on, his main goal every time he entered Spanish class. "I'm just no good at it," he had told Henri and Cyndarria, "and I hate it when I don't know the answer. It's em-barrassing."

Their teacher checked the clock on the wall. *"Gracias, Esteban,"* he said. "You are absolutely right. *Sólo cinco minutos nos quedan!* Five minutes till the bell. *Rosita*, would you like to do the honors?"

"*Sí, maestro*." Cyndarria grabbed her bag and began passing out the cookies, giving two to Señor Paniagua.

"*Muchas gracias, Rosita. Estoy seguro que estas galletas están deliciosas.* I'm sure these cookies are delicious."

"*Sí*," agreed Joey enthusiastically. "*Deliciosas!* Umm, you got any left?"

"Just a couple," said Cyndarria, "but I need them for later."

The bell sounded.

"*Hasta mañana, jóvenes*," said Señor Paniagua. "*Que les vaya bien.* See you tomorrow. Have a good day."

"*Hasta mañana, maestro*," the students echoed.

CHAPTER 8

THE REST OF the day passed uneventfully—a science class, which could have been called Introduction to Creepy-Crawlies, given her teacher's fascination with insects, plus social studies, P.E. and Community Service, a class Cyndarria particularly liked because it gave students the opportunity to get out into the community "to do some good," as their teacher liked to say. The best part, students agreed, was that the "good" sometimes got done during school hours.

Mr. Johansson was often seen walking the halls between classes. He was hard of hearing and spoke like a Yooper, a resident of the Upper Peninsula of Michigan, where his Swedish ancestors had originally settled and where he had spent his early years. Students sometimes thought they could get away with little practical jokes, or worse, but Mr. Johansson was notorious for his ingenious punishments of offenders. One of the best known had occurred a few years earlier.

Two girls had hidden in the bathroom the last hour of the day in order to avoid taking a test, certain that no one would be the wiser, and they would simply be counted absent. Pleased with themselves, they sneaked out of the building after the final bell. They were bragging about their little adventure to a friend on the way home but were overheard by another student sitting behind them on the bus. Unfortunately for the two girls, this girl disliked both of them and promptly reported the offenders to the principal the next morning.

Unfazed, Mr. Johansson had immediately ordered the girls sent to his office, and he then marched them back to the bathroom where they had taken refuge just the afternoon before.

He pointed to the ceiling tiles, which were covered with mini-holes, whose purpose he did not fully understand but which he would now use to great advantage.

"See these tiles?" he said to the girls. "You're going to count every single one of those holes before you leave this bathroom, even if it takes you all day, which means you may have to miss lunch. And you'd better be accurate, because I know exactly how many there are in every one."

"But Mr. Johansson," one of the girls objected.

"Are you familiar with the expression, no buts about it?" he asked. "That applies here, unless you want me to call your parents and explain the little stunt you pulled yesterday."

The girls looked at each other, obviously dismayed. Finally they nodded, "We'll count."

"Good," said Mr. Johansson. "I'm glad we understand each other. Oh, by the way, you will stay after school this afternoon to make up the test you skipped yesterday. I'll have my secretary call your parents to let them know you'll be delayed and ask them to come and pick you up, since you'll miss the bus."

Cyndarria hoped that she wouldn't suffer such a punishment. She had broken a rule but hadn't skipped class or smoked in the locker room, which one of her classmates had actually been foolish enough to do. She had kept the two extra cookies for a reason, hoping that Mr. Johansson had a sweet tooth and might not impose too stiff a punishment if he enjoyed a cookie while they talked.

After the dismissal bell, Cyndarria returned to her locker to get the books she needed for that night's homework. Henri's locker was next to hers.

"Do you want me to wait for you?" he asked.

"Thanks," said Cyndarria, "but I don't know how long I'll be. You should probably just go on home."

"Track practice starts next week. I'm going to stop by and talk to Coach McIntyre for a minute. I'll check back at the office before I leave."

"Okay. See you."

Cyndarria headed for the office. She was greeted there by Oraleen Jackson, Mr. Johansson's longtime secretary. Oraleen was very motherly and had a special place in her heart for students who were sent to see the principal after school, even the seemingly incorrigible ones. She made it a point to know all the kids' names and always had a friendly smile for whoever entered the office. It was her personal mission to make the school a comfortable, welcoming place.

"Why hello, Cyndarria. It's very nice to see you. Mr. Johansson mentioned that you'd be coming in this afternoon. Why don't you have a seat, and I'll tell him you're here."

"I think I'd rather stand," said Cyndarria. "I don't want to get too comfortable here."

Oraleen gave her a little smile. "I understand," she said. "I'm quite sure Mr. Johansson will see you right away."

A minute later she reappeared. "You can go in now," she said. "He just got off the phone."

When Cyndarria entered Mr. Johansson's office, he was standing by the window with his hands behind his back, intent on watching the last of the buses depart. She waited for him to turn around. When he didn't, she cleared her throat. No response. Finally, remembering that he was hard of hearing, she said loudly, "Hi, Mr. Johansson."

He turned and looked almost surprised to see her.

"I'm Cyndarria Thornwell," she said. "Mrs. Wackenstein said I was to see you after school."

58

"Hmm," said Mr. Johansson. He sat down. "Have a seat, Cyndarria." He looked through some papers on his desk. "Ah, yes, something about cookies?"

"Yes, sir," said Cyndarria, not sure how else to respond to a principal.

"I see. Hmm, cookies." He looked up from the note he was reading. "What kind?"

"They're, umm, they're oatmeal-peanut butter-chocolate chip. My grandma taught me to make them."

"Thornwell. Was your grandma Rose Thornwell?"

"Yes, sir. My dad's mother."

"I knew your grandma. I was very sorry to hear she had passed. She was quite a baker, you know. Always made something sweet for church potlucks. I loved her pies!"

Something inside Cyndarria let go, and she began to relax. "So did I. She taught me to make a lot of them, and other things too."

"So you brought some of your cookies to school and were going to share them with the class without getting permission from me beforehand?"

"I didn't know I was supposed to. I'm really sorry. I didn't mean to break a rule."

"Well, you know, I never was real crazy about that rule, though I think you should probably check with your teacher ahead of time about bringing in food—just in case, you know?"

"I guess you're right."

Mr. Johansson studied Cyndarria's face. "You know you look a little like your grandma when she was young."

Cyndarria felt herself blush. "I do? Thank you. She was a pretty lady."

"Yes, she was. And a darn nice one, too. I always liked her."

They sat in silence for a moment. Suddenly Cyndarria remembered the cookies. "Uh, Mr. Johansson, would you like a cookie? I had a couple left over."

An almost beatific smile lit up Mr. Johansson's face. "I was kind of hoping you might offer," he said. "Yes, I'd love one. If you don't mind, I'll take that other one home to my wife."

Cyndarria handed her principal the paper bag which contained the cookies, and with that motion the last bit of tension left her body. "Sure, of course," she said. "That would be, uh, that would be great."

"Then we're both happy," grinned Mr. Johansson. He stood and held out his hand. Cyndarria wasn't really sure what to do. "Shall we shake hands on it?" he asked. "I'll tell Mrs. Wackenstein that you were properly reprimanded and will never repeat the offense. How does that sound?"

"Great!" said Cyndarria, and grasped Mr. Johansson's hand. "That would be just great."

"Okay, Cyndarria, you're excused. Say hello to your father for me. He was a pretty good shortstop in high school, as I recall."

"I'll tell him you remember that. Thank you, Mr. Johansson."

Cyndarria left the office feeling as though a serious weight had been lifted from her shoulders. Henri stood waiting for her.

"How'd it go?" he asked.

"I think Grandma Rose helped me out a little. I'll tell you all about it on the way home."

CHAPTER 9

HENRI LISTENED AS Cyndarria recounted the details of her meeting with Mr. Johansson. "I always thought he was a good guy," Henri said. "He was real nice when my mom passed away."

"There's something else I kind of want to talk to you about," said Cyndarria. "You're probably going to think it's weird."

"Oh, yeah? I sorta like weird. Try me."

"This has happened a couple of times recently, and I don't know what to think. I can't really explain it. All I know is that it actually did occur."

"Now I'm really interested. C'mon! Tell me."

"Well, it started a couple weeks ago when my comb disappeared. I couldn't find it anywhere. I'd almost forgotten it had happened when the comb showed up a few days later inside one of my tennis shoes."

"No way!"

"Yup. I told you it was weird. Then last Saturday, the paper with the doodle of Mrs. Wackenstein on it disappeared. I looked everywhere, but it was gone. You're not going to believe this, but later that night I found it under my pillow. I *know* I didn't put that paper under my pillow."

Henri was quiet and looked suddenly pensive as they walked.

"Is there something wrong?" asked Cyndarria. She wasn't used to seeing Henri look sad.

"What you describe reminds me a lot of what has happened to my dad and me since my mom died. I didn't think anyone else ever experienced anything like it."

"How so? Have things disappeared and then reappeared on you like that?"

"No. It's different, but sort of related, because it seems impossible to explain."

Cyndarria studied her friend's face, wondering if he was serious. "Well, are you going to tell me?"

"Pennies," he said.

"Pennies," Cyndarria repeated. "Pennies? How are pennies related?"

"It's a little complicated, but you won't understand how they're related unless you know the whole story."

"Okay," said Cyndarria. "I'm all ears."

"So the second year my father was in this country, a good friend of his who lived in Colorado invited him to spend Christmas vacation with his family in Denver. While they were there, his friend taught him how to ski. In Haiti, my dad had never even seen snow, and he didn't especially like it until that vacation. As it turned out, he loved skiing and was pretty good at it.

"On their honeymoon, he and my mother drove out to Denver. It was January, so there was a ton of snow. Dad really wanted to teach my mom how to ski. She tried it a couple times, but she fell a lot and just didn't like it.

"The third day they were there, Dad was ready to go out and was waiting for my mother to go with him. She didn't like to disappoint him, but finally she admitted that she really preferred to stay in the hotel room. My father kind of gave her a hard time, so they decided to toss a coin to make the decision. Heads she could stay in the room, tails she would go out with my dad.

"She won. The coin was a new penny that had a 'D' on it, which meant it had been made at the Denver mint. She called it her lucky penny because it allowed her to stay warm and read all morning. She always kept that penny."

"That's very sweet, but what does it have to do with what happened to me?"

"I'm not really sure it does, but here's the rest of the story. Every once in a while, my father will find a shiny penny with a 'D' on it in the most unlikely place. I have too, a couple times."

"Like where?" asked Cyndarria.

"Like in a glass in the cupboard or in an old shoe he hasn't worn for months. The last one was in the silverware tray. I found one under my pillow, and it wasn't from the tooth fairy!"

"Whoa," said Cyndarria. "That's crazy. What does your dad say about it?"

"He doesn't seem to want to talk about it, but one time he was looking at the penny, and he sort of whispered, 'Janine.' I think maybe he senses that the pennies are some kind of sign from my mother."

"Do you think so?"

"I don't know, but I do know that I can't really explain where they come from. To tell you the truth, I kind of like thinking that they're from my mom. It sort of makes me feel better." Henri blinked hard.

Cyndarria patted her friend's shoulder. "I understand," she said softly.

They had arrived at the Thornwell house, so they said goodbye. "Thanks for sharing that story, Henri. It gives me something to think about."

Cyndarria went inside and headed up to her room. She closed her door, put her books on her desk, and sat down on her bed. No one else was home, so she figured her mother had called the neighbor and asked her if it would be okay for the boys to stay there after school until someone could pick them up. The families often did each other babysitting favors, so there was rarely a problem when something unexpected happened.

The house was completely quiet. Cyndarria looked around her room, almost expecting to see that something else was mysteriously missing. However, all was as she had left it that morning. But inside her head was different. Henri's story had started her thinking about something she had never before considered.

She looked at the rocking chair she had inherited from her grandmother. "Grandma Rose," she whispered. "Is that you? Are you trying to tell me something?"

Suddenly the silence was broken. She heard the front door slam and footsteps running up the stairs. Her mother must have picked up her brothers.

"Cyndarria! Where are you?" It was Toby. Her door burst open, and he made a beeline for her bed. He jumped on and started to bounce up and down.

"Hi, Cyndarria," he said as he bounced. "Guess what happened."

Toby was being more talkative than usual, so Cyndarria figured that whatever had happened must have been pretty exciting.

"Tobe, why don't you stop bouncing and tell me?"

Toby bounced a couple more times for good measure. "Okey dokey," he said and plopped down beside his sister. He looked at her expectantly.

"Well, are you going to tell me?"

Toby frowned. "You're supposed to guess."

"Hmm, okay, let's see. Miss Jamison brought in cookies for the class."

Toby looked disappointed in his sister. "Don't you know that's against the rules?" he asked. "No sweets except for special times, my teacher says. Like birthdays. She says it's not good for us to eat too many sweets."

He looked thoughtful for a moment. "I kind of don't like that rule."

"Yeah," said Cyndarria. "I know what you mean."

"Guess again," said Toby.

"Okay, one more time and then you have to tell me."

"All right."

"You got to play a fun game in class."

"Nope, two wrong. You're not a very good guesser."

Cyndarria looked down at her younger brother and smiled. "I suppose you're right," she said. "How about you tell me what happened?"

"Weeelllll," Toby said, purposely drawing out what he considered to be the suspense. "I figured out something in class that nobody else knew."

"How so, Toby?"

"With numbers. I figured it out." He beamed proudly at his sister, then looked more serious. "I like to think about numbers."

"Wow, Toby! That's really cool. Can you tell me more about it?"

"Miss Jamison brought a big jar of marbles to class. She said we each got four of them."

"I love marbles," said Cyndarria. "Do you get to choose them? Are there any cat's eyes?"

"Yes, but Cyndarria, I want to tell you the rest."

"Sorry, Tobe. Go on."

"Well, there are 25 kids in my class, so I thought about it, and I asked Miss Jamison if there were 100 marbles in the jar."

"Oh my gosh, Toby, how did you figure that out?"

"Miss Jamison said I did some multi...cation?

"Multiplication?"

"Maybe. I don't remember for sure."

"Wow, Toby, if you did multiplication, that's amazing! How did you do it?"

"I just thought about it, and I figured it out. But Cyndarria, I don't think it was multication. I just remembered there are four quarters in a dollar, and four quarters make 100 pennies. Miss Jamison said she was really proud of me."

Cyndarria felt her heart get bigger. "I am too, Toby. That's great."

Toby smiled almost shyly. "Miss Jamison is a pretty nice teacher," he said. "I think I like her."

"I'm sure she would be very pleased to know you feel that way. Do you think you might want to tell her that sometime?"

Toby appeared to think about it, then shook his head, hopped off the bed and headed out the door. "Unh-unh," he called. "Too much talking."

CHAPTER 10

SUDDENLY CYNDARRIA HEARD loud voices coming from below. Alarmed, she hurried downstairs.

"But, Mom," she heard J.J. almost shout, "it wasn't my fault."

It was quiet for a moment. "J.J.," Belle said softly, "that's not what Mrs. Aubrey said. She told me you started it."

Cyndarria looked at her brother when she entered the kitchen. He was obviously distraught. She could tell he had been crying.

"What's the matter?" she asked her mother.

There was a look of deep concern on Belle's face. "J.J. hit another student, a boy named Tommy."

"Tommy Aubrey?" asked Cyndarria. "He's the teacher's son."

"I don't really think that matters," said Belle. "J.J. can't be hitting other children. You know you shouldn't do that, don't you, J.J.?"

J.J. was stone-faced. He looked down at the floor.

"Why did you hit him, J.J.?" asked Cyndarria. It was so unlike her brother to do something like that. He was generally pretty happy-go-lucky and got along well with all his classmates.

"Because of....." J.J. spoke so softly, the rest of the sentence was inaudible.

"I'm sorry, honey, what did you say?" Belle asked.

"Because of Toby."

"Toby?" Cyndarria repeated, surprised. "What does Toby have to do with it?"

J.J. sighed deeply. "Tommy said Toby was dumb because he doesn't like to talk. He kept calling him 'kindergarten baby.' It just made me so mad."

Belle's own eyes filled with tears. She wrapped her son in her arms. "Oh, J.J.," she whispered, and then she couldn't say anymore.

"Are you mad at me?" he asked, his voice muffled a little because of his mother's fierce embrace.

"No," Belle said finally, releasing her son. "I'm not mad. I'm proud of you that you stuck up for your little brother. But, honey, you shouldn't hit people, even if they're being mean. You just shouldn't."

Belle looked at Cyndarria. "Mrs. Aubrey wants your father and me to go in for a meeting with her tomorrow after school. She insists that we bring J.J. along and make him apologize to her son. Either that, or he's suspended for hitting another child."

"I didn't even know that third-graders could be suspended," said Cyndarria. "Isn't that kind of extreme?"

"I thought the same thing," said Belle, "but she maintains that when there's physical violence involved, that's the rule."

"Didn't she ask why it happened? I mean, Tommy really started it by saying those things about Toby."

"She didn't seem too interested in the reason. She's very protective of her son, which I kind of understand, but still..."

"He's a bully," said J.J. "He's always doing mean stuff like that. Kids are afraid to say anything because he's the teacher's son, so he gets away with it. When anyone gets upset, he just laughs."

"Doesn't Mrs. Aubrey realize what's going on?" asked Cyndarria. She was starting to become really angry.

"It usually happens on the playground, and she's not around. There's a helper there, but she's so busy, I don't think she notices. He's pretty sneaky about it."

Cyndarria looked at her mother. "Don't you think someone should tell Mrs. Aubrey the truth? She needs to know what her son is doing."

"You're right, Cyndarria. I'll talk with your father about it. We'll figure something out."

Belle was not very good at conflict and confrontation. It made her extremely uncomfortable and reminded her too much of her father's second marriage, after her mother had died. Her stepmother was a thoroughly unpleasant woman, and Belle had wondered why her father had ever married her.

"You needed a mother," he had explained. "You were so lonely and sad, and I didn't think I could do a good enough job raising you on my own."

Unfortunately, rather than helping things, her father's second marriage had made them worse. Agnes had come to live with them along with her step-mother, and she was bossy and critical of Belle from the start. There had been so much conflict and so many tears on Belle's part that she vowed never to allow fights among her own children, and she assiduously avoided most disagreements with her husband. She was the family peacemaker. Happily, Toad was a kind and patient man and not inclined to argue much, mostly because he and Belle were of a mind on practically everything.

Later that evening, Belle and Toad went upstairs and sat on their bed to talk, which they often did when they had something to sort out.

"I'm worried that J.J. might start feeling it's okay to hit another child," said Belle. "I understand that he was defending Toby, but still."

"Well, it came out when I talked with him up in his room that he didn't actually hit Tommy, he pushed him. And that was after J.J. tried to walk away. I guess the kid wouldn't stop yammering. He grabbed J.J.'s arm and got right in his face. That was when J.J. kind of lost it and pushed him. Something happened, and Tommy tripped and fell down and started crying. As luck would have it, that's when the aide showed up and believed him when he claimed that J.J. had hit him. Of course, Mrs. Aubrey was furious and apparently didn't ask for an explanation of what had happened and why. It was kind of muddy on the playground; Tommy's pants got dirty, and that only seemed to make matters worse.

"You know," he said finally, "I think it would be helpful to have a third person in on this meeting, someone who would be neutral and listen to both sides, because I kind of doubt Mrs. Aubrey would be willing to do that."

"I guess I could call Mrs. Prescott, the principal," said Belle. "She's new, but I've talked with her a few times, and I was impressed. She seems very committed to student welfare and to providing the best possible education for the kids. I think she's a good listener."

"Good idea," nodded Toad. "I don't want to attack Mrs. Aubrey, but I also don't want my son treated unfairly. And she really needs to know the truth about her own son."

"Thanks, Toad," said Belle. She gave her husband a hug. "I don't know what I'd do without you."

He smiled, "Probably find a much richer and nicer guy."

"Yeah, well, money isn't everything, and I doubt I could find anyone nicer. Except maybe the Pope. I hear he's a pretty nice guy." Belle gave a mischievous giggle.

"Belle Thornwell, that's positively sacrilegious. I am shocked!"

70

"You're right," Belle conceded. "I take it back. I don't know what possessed me!" She smiled at her husband. "I guess I'm stuck with you."

"Lucky you," said Toad.

"Yeah, lucky me."

Just then there was a loud yell from downstairs. "Daddy, are you coming down pretty soon? We need you."

It was Toby. He and J.J. were once again consumed with building a new Lego structure and counted on their father to help them.

"Duty calls," said Toad. "Ah, the life of a Renaissance man! So many projects, so little time."

"Go get 'em, Leonardo," said Belle with a laugh.

After her husband went down to work with the boys, Belle went to Cyndarria's room and knocked on the door.

"Come in," called Cyndarria. She sat at her desk doing her homework.

"What's up?" asked Belle. She walked over to Grandma Rose's rocking chair to sit down.

"I'm working on my Spanish. Guess what Toby told me after school, Mom. He said he likes to think about numbers. He's six-years-old! When I was six, I mainly liked to think about recess and what I was going to have for snack when I got home. He may not talk much, but I think he's pretty smart."

"I think you're right," Belle agreed.

"Oh, something else," said Cyndarria. "He admitted that he likes Miss Jamison. She told him she was proud of him today for figuring out all by himself how many marbles there were in a jar."

"Well, wonders never cease. And how did your conversation with Mr. Johansson go?"

71

"Actually, he was really nice. He knew Grandma Rose. He said I kind of looked like her when she was young."

Belle studied her daughter more carefully. "I don't know why I never thought about that before, but yes, you kind of do."

"He also remembered Dad played baseball in high school. He told me to say hi to him."

"So what about the cookie incident in Mrs. Wackenstein's class?"

"He said he would tell her that I was 'properly repri-manded' and would never make that mistake again. Oh, and I gave him my last two cookies. He seemed pretty happy about that. So all in all, I guess things worked out quite well."

"I hope we'll be able to say the same thing tomorrow after our meeting with Mrs. Aubrey," said Belle.

"Me too, Mom."

Belle kissed her daughter on the forehead and left the room, leaving Cyndarria to think about mysterious shiny pennies, marbles in a jar, J.J.'s defense of his brother, and the power of Grandma Rose's cookies.

CHAPTER 11

BELLE CONTACTED THE principal's office the next morning during a break between classes and was told by the secretary, Mrs. Beach, that Mrs. Prescott was not available.

"I've checked her schedule, and it's clear after school," she assured Belle. "I'm certain she would be happy to meet with you. I'll let her know that you'll be coming in."

Toad was scheduled as the dinner chef that night. Thinking he might be late, he notified Antoine of the situation, and Antoine readily agreed to cover for him until he could get there. Toad and Belle arrived in the principal's office at 3:30 and found J.J. sitting in a chair waiting.

"Hi, buddy," said Toad. "Everything okay?"

J.J. shrugged. "I guess so. Mrs. Aubrey told me to come down here and wait. So I'm waiting."

Mrs. Beach smiled. "Have a seat. I'll let Mrs. Prescott know that you're here."

"Thank you," said Belle. She was a little nervous about the upcoming meeting with Mrs. Aubrey and looked at Toad for reassurance. He winked at her, and they sat down beside their son.

Five minutes later, Mrs. Prescott appeared. She was a middle-aged woman with short, prematurely gray hair and serious but kind blue eyes. She wore a navy suit and serviceable low heels. She smiled when she saw the Thornwells and extended her hand.

"Mrs. Thornwell, it's nice to see you again." She turned to Toad. "And you must be J.J.'s father. Gloria Prescott. It's nice to meet you. Principal Johansson tells me you were quite a baseball player a few years back."

Toad grinned. "More than a few," he said, "but thanks. I have a feeling J.J. may end up being better than I ever was." He patted his son on the head.

"I always feel that it's a good thing if our children out-achieve us. I like to think it means that we're doing our job as parents.

"Why don't we step into my office? I think there will be enough room for all of us, but I'd like to speak with you for a few minutes before I let Mrs. Aubrey know that you're here. She's already told me Tommy's version of what happened, but I've found that there are always two sides to every story, and it's helpful to me to know both sides going into any parent meeting."

There were five chairs arranged in front of Mrs. Prescott's desk. After they were seated, she turned to J.J. "So J.J., why don't you tell me what happened yesterday on the playground?"

When he finished, Mrs. Prescott looked at him seriously. "Hmm, I see. Did you push Tommy hard?"

J.J. hesitated a moment. "Kinda, I guess, but I didn't mean to push him down. I just wanted him to let go of my arm and go away."

Mrs. Prescott pushed a button on her phone. "Marge, will you please call down and tell Mrs. Aubrey that the Thornwells are here?"

A few minutes later Mrs. Aubrey appeared with Tommy in tow. Toad stood when she entered the office and extended his hand, which seemed almost to surprise her. "It's nice to meet you," he said. "I think you already know my wife Belle."

"Yes, of course," said Mrs. Aubrey and took a seat. "Sit down, Thomas," she said curtly.

Thomas sat.

"Perhaps we should start with a brief explanation from each of the boys about what happened yesterday," suggested Mrs. Prescott. "Tommy, would you like to begin?"

Tommy squinched up his face and pointed at J.J. "He hit me. I was swinging, and he wanted the swing. I told him no, that it was my turn, and he got all mad and hit me. He's mean," he added to emphasize the injustice that had been done to him.

Belle felt her back stiffen, but she resisted the temptation to say anything.

"I see," said Mrs. Prescott. "J.J.?"

"I didn't do that," he said, his voice almost a whisper.

"Speak up, J.J.," ordered Mrs. Aubrey, "and remember to tell the truth."

"We always expect J.J. to tell the truth," said Toad evenly.

"Yes, well, as parents we always hope that will be the case," said Mrs. Aubrey. "Unfortunately, we are sometimes sadly disappointed. As a teacher, I've seen that happen more than once."

Mrs. Prescott put up a hand. "Thank you, Gladys," she said. "Why don't we just let J.J. tell his story?"

"Of course," sniffed Mrs. Aubrey.

"Go ahead, J.J.," said Belle.

J.J. looked at his mother. Belle gave him an encouraging nod. When he finished, Mrs. Aubrey, who had been alternately frowning and raising her eyebrows, raised them to their highest point. She looked at Mrs. Prescott.

"Gloria," she said. Her voice rang with authority. "I've always thought J.J. was a nice boy, not always attentive, but generally obedient. However, clearly he is…" She made a dramatic pause. "Prevaricating." She looked pleased with her word choice.

"I'm wondering how you know," said Toad, his voice rising only slightly, "that it's J.J. who's lying, not Tommy."

Mrs. Aubrey glared at Toad. "Mr. Thornwell, I assure you that my son does not lie. He has been brought up properly."

Toad was about to respond when Mrs. Prescott once again raised her hand to calm the conversation. She turned to J.J. "Have there been any other children who have been treated unkindly by Thomas?"

"Mrs. Prescott!" Mrs. Aubrey exclaimed shrilly. "Surely, you can't..."

"Let J.J. answer my question," said Mrs. Prescott. The look on her face silenced Mrs. Aubrey mid-sentence.

"Lily," J.J. said. "She's poor and doesn't wear very nice clothes. Tommy calls her ugly. And Freddie. He cried one time when he couldn't understand a math problem. Tommy tells everyone that he's a cry baby."

"No, I don't! No, I don't!" Tommy was suddenly on his feet and shouting.

"Thomas!" Mrs. Aubrey's voice was stern. "Sit down and be quiet."

"He's lying," Tommy said as he sat back down.

"I know, dear," said Mrs. Aubrey. "Clearly J.J. needs to be suspended for hitting..." Again she paused dramatically. "And for lying. We will straighten this out."

"Yes, we will," agreed Mrs. Prescott. "I think we're done here for now. Gladys, please wait while I escort the Thornwells out."

Toad, Belle and J.J. left the office, followed by Mrs. Prescott.

"Mrs. Prescott," Toad said. "I hope that..."

"Don't worry, Mr. Thornwell," she said. "I think I have a pretty clear understanding of the situation." She bent down and addressed J.J.

"Thank you, J.J. I'll see you tomorrow."

J.J. looked uncertain. "Do you mean I'm not suspen-dered?"

Mrs. Prescott smiled. "No, J.J., you're not."

She turned to Belle and Toad. "Thank you for coming in this afternoon. I think you have a fine young man here. I look forward to seeing how his baseball skills develop."

On the drive home, Belle felt almost giddy with relief. Toad dropped her and J.J. off at the house and then continued on to the restaurant. Cyndarria opened the door eagerly when she saw them arrive.

"Well?" she asked.

"I'm not suspendered," said J.J.

Cyndarria bent down and gave her brother a big hug. "I'm so glad, J.J."

"Me, too. I'm kind of hungry. Could you make me a PB & J?"

"Mom walked over to the Stevensons to get Toby. How about we wait till he gets here, and you can split one?"

"Okey dokey, Cyndarria." He looked at his sister. "Do you want to play a game?"

"Sure. How about dominoes? We haven't played that for a long time."

"Goodie," said J.J. "I'll get them."

Cyndarria got out bread, peanut butter, and grape jelly to make the sandwich. Suddenly the front door burst open, and Toby came charging in, followed by Belle. "I'm hungry," he shouted. "C'n I have a sandwich? Oooo!" he exclaimed when he saw J.J. setting out the dominoes. "I wanna play!"

Cyndarria looked at her mom, who smiled. She finished making the sandwich, cut it in two, and took it to the table, where the boys were getting ready to start the game.

"I really like peanut butter and jelly," said J.J. happily as he took a big bite.

"Me too," agreed Toby. "Do you, Cyndarria?"

"I do," said Cyndarria. "And I like to play dominoes."

"With us, huh, Cyndarria," said Toby.

"Oh, I guess so." She grinned at her brothers, who both had grape jelly smeared on their lips.

Belle approached the table where her three children were playing. She took a deep breath and let her body relax. Finally, she felt, at least for a while, things were back to normal, and all was right with her world.

And it was. For a while.

CHAPTER 12

WHEN CYNDARRIA GOT out of bed the following Saturday morning, she gasped. It had snowed unexpectedly during the night—a wet, early-spring snow that stuck to every branch and twig on the trees behind her house. She didn't know whether to laugh or cry. She longed for warmer weather and summer vacation but loved the sparkly beauty of fresh snow. Her thoughts were interrupted by the sudden opening of her door and the excited exclamations of Toby.

"Cyndarria! Look! Look! It snowed! Let's build a snowman! Do you want to?"

"It's a little early for that. How about we have some breakfast first?"

Cyndarria loved looking at the snow but wasn't so sure she wanted to go out and play in it. The promise of food was always a sure distraction for Toby from anything else he wanted to do.

"I want bunny pancakes!" Toby exclaimed, his excitement about the morning undiminished.

"How about a one-eyed Egyptian?" suggested Cyndarria, hoping her little brother would settle for the easier-to-make egg fried in a frame of bread.

"Okay. With syrup."

"Tobe, people don't put syrup on eggs."

Toby looked at his sister as though she were lacking some basic understanding of free will. "Well, *I* do. It's yummy."

"What's yummy?" It was J.J., who was up and had wandered downstairs in search of breakfast.

"Syrup," said Toby with authority, "on one-eyed ejigens."

"Egyptians," corrected Cyndarria.

"Right," agreed Toby. "That's what I said."

"Okay," said Cyndarria, giving up on what she knew would not be worth a second attempt to correct Toby's pronunciation. "Do you want one too, J.J.?"

"Yes, but I want mine with ketchup."

Cyndarria cringed. "Okay, two one-eyed Egyptians coming up, one with syrup and one with ketchup."

Cyndarria made the boys breakfast, then poured herself a bowl of corn flakes and cut up a banana on top. As they sat down to eat, Belle entered the kitchen.

"Smells pretty good down here," she said.

"It's the syrup," said Toby. "It's yummy on my one-eyed ejigen."

"Cyndarria, thank you for taking care of the boys. I'm going to go see Grandpa today. Would you like to come along?"

Cyndarria hesitated, but she knew she should go. It was hard for her mother to go by herself, and she loved her grandfather, even though it was painful to see him in his current condition.

Patrick O'Brien, who was Paddy to friends, had explained to his daughter that their last name meant 'high' or 'noble' in Gaelic. Belle thought the name appropriate for her father, as she had always viewed him as an honorable man who demonstrated a certain nobility of spirit.

A few years before, he had begun to exhibit significant memory loss and confusion. His speech sometimes became jumbled, and he often forgot to eat. One terrible afternoon he had disappeared and could not be found. Finally, a family who lived a mile away from his home had discovered him sitting beside the road, unable to remember where he lived.

After a careful examination by a neurologist, he was diagnosed with Alzheimer's disease. Belle and Toad had insisted that he come to live with them, and for a year that had worked pretty well. Over the past several months, however, his condition had deteriorated to the point that they realized he needed around-the-clock care. Fortunately, they had found an excellent local facility, so it was easy for them to visit.

"Sure, Mom," said Cyndarria, "but doesn't Dad want to go? I can take care of the boys."

"I know, sweetie, but he promised to take them sledding if it snowed again. How about if we leave in an hour? They don't allow visitors before 10:00 anyway."

"Okay, I'll go up and get ready."

An hour-and-a-half later, they arrived at the Sycamore Creek Advanced Care and Respite Facility. Belle greeted the receptionist at the desk, a kind woman who had worked there for several years. She always checked in with the nurses when she came on duty at 9:00 about how the patients had done the night before. She had lost her own mother to Alzheimer's the previous year so was particularly sensitive to the needs of visiting family members.

"Good morning, Belle. I see you brought Cyndarria with you this morning. I'm sure Paddy will be happy to see both of you."

"How is he today?"

"He was very restless in the night, but Nurse said he ate a pretty good breakfast and seemed alert."

"Thank you, Norma." Belle took a deep breath and forced a smile. "Let's go, honey," she said to Cyndarria.

When they got to her grandfather's room, Cyndarria felt a moment of regret at having come with her mother. She dreaded seeing him because he was so changed. He wasn't the smiling, good-natured man who used to count her ribs to make her giggle when she was little and give her money for ice cream.

The door was open, but Belle gave it a little knock anyway. Paddy looked at her and appeared confused for a moment. Then his face brightened.

"Why, Lydie, I didn't know you were coming. Why didn't you call? Come here and give me a kiss."

"It's Belle, Dad, not Mom. Cyndarria's here too."

Cyndarria had hung back but now forced a smile. "Hi, Grandpa. It's nice to see you."

She went over and gave her grandfather an awkward hug. He looked a little surprised. "Well, aren't you a pretty little thing," he said. "Who are you again?"

"Cyndarria. I'm your granddaughter."

He looked at Belle. "Lydie, did you know that we have a granddaughter?" His gaze returned to Cyndarria. "What was your name again?"

"Cyndarria."

"Cyndarria," Paddy repeated. "Are you a friend of my daughter Belle's? That's right, isn't it, Lydie? Our daughter's name is Belle." He looked bewildered.

Belle felt a moment's discouragement. "Yes," she said. "That's right. Dad, would you like to go down to the living room? It snowed last night, and you can see all the trees from there. It's very pretty. There might be a fire in the fireplace too. You'd like that, wouldn't you?"

Paddy looked at his daughter with a frown. "Who are you?" he said. "I have to wait for Lydia to come. She said she would."

Belle tried one more time. "I'm Belle, Dad. I'm your daughter."

Paddy looked at her hard. "You're Belle? Are you sure? Belle is much younger than you are."

Cyndarria touched her grandfather's arm. "I brought you some cookies, Grandpa. They're the kind you like, you know, with oatmeal and raisins." She handed him the small bag of cookies.

Paddy eyed them suspiciously. "What are these?"

"Cookies," said Cyndarria. "The kind you like. Why don't you try one?"

Paddy opened the bag and looked in cautiously. He picked up a cookie and smelled it, then took a small bite.

"Do you like it, Grandpa?"

"Yes, they taste like Lydie's. She's my wife. She's coming to visit soon."

"I'm glad you like them," said Cyndarria.

Paddy yawned. "I'm sleepy. I want to take a nap. Good night." He rose slowly from his chair, tottered unsteadily over to his bed and lay down. He turned away from them onto his side.

Belle took Cyndarria's hand, and they stood there together waiting. A few minutes later, Paddy began to snore softly, so they turned, walked back down the hall, and left the building.

On the drive home, Belle was quiet and thoughtful. She never talked much after they left her father, and Cyndarria found she was more comfortable that way as well. Belle turned on the radio and tuned it to WKAR, her favorite public-radio station. A classical piece was playing.

"I love that piece," said Belle softly after it had finished. "I've loved it since the first time I heard it."

"What's the name of it?" asked Cyndarria. "It's pretty and, I don't know, kind of lifts you up."

Belle patted her daughter's leg fondly. "It does, doesn't it? The first time I heard it was in Chicago. Shortly after we were married, your father and I went to see *Cyrano de Bergerac*, and they played it during intermission. Neither of us was familiar with it, but we both thought it was beautiful. Coincidentally, I heard it again a week or so later on the radio."

"Did they tell the title?" asked Cyndarria.

"Yes, it's the *Canon in D*, but I didn't understand the composer's name because I hadn't heard it before. I had to laugh because I actually thought the announcer said Taco Bell."

"Taco Bell?" Cyndarria smiled.

"Well, I knew that wasn't right, but I was still confused. A few days later I was talking with my friend Irma, and I mentioned it to her. She's very knowledgeable about classical music, much more so than I am."

"Did she know who the composer was?"

"Yes, she laughed when I told her what I thought I'd heard. She said his name is Pachelbel. He was a German composer of the 17th century, and the Canon is his best-known composition."

Belle was silent for a moment. "I suppose this is going to sound kind of morbid, but I've thought that when I eventually leave this world, I'd like to have that piece playing in the background."

"It's weird to think about that, Mom."

"Perhaps, but, you know, the music is so peaceful and uplifting and kind of hopeful. Like you're on the wings of angels. I think it would be a lovely way to go."

Cyndarria had never heard her mother talk that way. She looked at Belle, who seemed to have an almost far-away look on her face. "Okay, Mom," she said gently, "but not anytime soon, okay?"

"Okay," said Belle. She took her daughter's hand and squeezed it. "I'll do my best."

CHAPTER 13

THE NEXT DAY was Sunday, and it was Toad's turn to be in charge of Toad and the Frog's Sunday brunch. He got up early and left the house by 5:30. The restaurant's doors opened at 10:00, but most people didn't come in till after church, which gave him and the wait staff time to finish setting up the serving tables.

Juliette, the hostess and his partner Pierre's daughter, was there and in charge of the flower arrangement which adorned the small lace-tablecloth-covered table near the entrance to the dining room. For today she had found beautiful peach, yellow, and cream-colored gladiolus and placed them in a silver urn.

"Very nice," observed Toad as he inspected the table.

"Thanks, Toad," said Juliette. "Glads are my mother's favorite flower, so I'm always pleased when the florist shop has them."

Juliette was a striking young woman of 21—tall and slender with her father's dark brown eyes and her mother's black hair, which she wore long and fastened in a loose pony tail. Today she was wearing a floral-print dress and black patent-leather flats. She had worked as the restaurant's hostess for the last four years and was now a senior at Michigan State University, majoring in Hospitality Business.

The summer before, Juliette had won a prized internship at the Grand Hotel on Mackinac Island, where she impressed the owners so much with her efficiency, her competence, and her charm that they had offered her a management position after she graduated. Toad hated to think of losing her but secretly hoped that a few years down the road, Cyndarria might take her place.

Toad returned to the kitchen where Antoine, Juliette's older brother, and two other college students who worked in the kitchen on weekends were hard at work finishing the preparation of the final dishes to be served today.

"About done?" asked Toad.

"We're ready to go," replied Antoine. "Just have to get everything out to the dining room."

Toad was pleased with the variety of dishes they were able to offer for the brunch. Some had been prepared the night before and some this morning. Besides various breakfast items, they always offered a fish dish, chicken, a pasta, and Swedish meatballs, a local favorite. In addition, they had recently introduced a carving station, which included prime rib and ham. There was also a salad table, plus at least two vegetables and a potato dish. Usually it was au gratin potatoes, about the only food J.J. put on his plate when his family came for brunch, which they did most Sundays that he worked. Finally, there was a dessert table, where they served fresh fruit plus two kinds of pie, a cake, pudding or custard, and a variety of cookies, all homemade.

At home, Belle and the children were getting ready to leave for the restaurant. Cyndarria had once again invited Henri to go with them, and this time Belle had suggested that she invite his father Emmanuel to come along as well. Somewhat to Cyndarria's surprise, he had consented to joining them.

At 11:00 the doorbell rang, and Oliver barked his usual doggy greeting.

"I'll get it," called J.J., who was already dressed and ready to go.

When he opened the door, he was met by smiles from Henri and his father, both dressed in their Sunday finest.

"Why hello, J.J.," said Henri. "You look very handsome today. This is my father," he added. "I don't think you have met."

Emmanuel Rousseau bent down and extended his hand. "I am very happy to meet you, J.J.," he said. His voice was deep and rich and still carried a hint of the formality and accent of his native language. J.J. liked him immediately.

The two shook hands. "Umm," J.J. said, "this is Oliver. He's our dog. He's a black Lab, and he likes to chase Frisbees."

"A black Lab is a very handsome and loyal dog," said Emmanuel. "I think you are lucky to have him."

"I think so too," agreed J.J.

Just then Belle appeared, dressed in a beautiful emerald-green dress. "Goodness, J.J., invite our friends in. Hi, Henri," she said, then smiled at his father. "It's so nice to see you, Dr. Rousseau. I'm delighted that you can join us."

"The pleasure is mine, I can assure you. And please, call me Emmanuel, and if it's acceptable, I will call you Belle."

"Of course," said Belle. "Please come in. I think Cyndarria and Toby are about ready."

Five minutes later, they left. Belle drove with Emmanuel joining her in front, and the four children squeezed together in back.

"I was surprised to see the snow yesterday," Emmanuel said. "In Haiti I never saw snow. It was quite a surprise my first winter in this country, but a friend taught me to ski, and since then I have rather liked it."

"I like looking at it," said Belle, "especially when it comes down in big flakes and sticks to everything the way it did yesterday. Toad skis, but I never learned to. I guess my favorite winter activity is sitting by the fire and watching the snow fall." She smiled sheepishly, as though she were embarrassed to admit it.

"Mine too," said Cyndarria from in back. "And hot chocolate."

"With little marshmallows floating on top," said Toby enthusiastically. "Yummy! I like marshmallows!"

"I like to build snowmen," said J.J. "And snow forts. And play fox and geese. What do you like, Henri?"

"I'm learning to ski," Henri said. "I like it, but I love to go tobogganing. I think that's my favorite."

A few minutes later, they arrived at the restaurant. Belle parked, and everyone piled out of the car. Inside, they were greeted by Juliette, who seated them. "I'll let Toad know you're here," she said.

"Mommy," Toby whispered. "I see my friend Jeremy. C'n I go say hi?"

"Okay, but come right back. We're going to eat as soon as we have a chance to say hello to your dad."

"Okey dokey, Mommy," said Toby, and he raced across the dining room to greet his friend, almost running into an elderly lady with a plateful of food.

Belle restrained a gasp. "Cyndarria, please go get your brother," she said quietly, "and make sure he *walks* back. No more running!"

"Well, if it isn't my favorite family," said a voice from behind them. It was Toad, dressed in a clean white jacket and toque, the latter a recent addition urged on him by Pierre, which he had finally agreed to wear for Sunday brunches only.

Emmanuel stood up and shook hands with Toad. "Thank you for the invitation to join your handsome family today," he said. "I have heard very good things about this brunch. I look forward to trying it."

"I hope it lives up to expectations," said Toad. "You'll have to excuse me now. I see someone is waiting to be served at the carving station."

After Cyndarria returned with a contrite Toby, the group went to the serving tables and began to fill their plates.

"J.J.," Belle said to her older son, "I want you to eat something besides the potatoes. Have a little vegetable, and I'm sure your father will carve you a small piece of ham."

J.J., whose plate was already almost filled with the potatoes, complained, "Mom! Do I have to? I don't like broccoli. Yuck!"

"Then have the corn. You like corn perfectly well. And go see your dad."

J.J. made a face but knew he had no choice. "Okay," he grumbled. "I'll eat some corn." He took a small spoonful, then went over to the carving station.

"What'll you have, buddy?" his father asked.

"Some ham, I guess," muttered J.J. "Mom's making me."

Toad hid a smile. "Well, your mother's probably right about that. This ham is real good, though. I think you'll like it."

"Okay," J.J. conceded, "but only a little piece."

Everyone had just begun eating when J.J. leaned over and whispered to Belle, "Mom, Mrs. Aubrey and Tommy are here. And some man is with them. He's really big."

Belle felt a sudden wave of anxiety. "It's probably her husband," she said without looking around.

"He's staring at us. He looks kind of mad. Oh, oh," said J.J., "he's coming over."

"Just ignore him, J.J.," whispered Belle.

Suddenly a harsh voice said loudly, "Are you Belle Thornwell?"

Belle flinched. "Yes, I am. Why do you ask?"

"Gladys told me what your son did to Tommy the other day. I want you to know that I won't stand for that kind of treatment of my son."

"Mr. Aubrey," Belle began. "I regret that there has been a misunderstanding on your part about what occurred. I assure you…"

"There wasn't no misunderstanding. My son don't lie," Aubrey said, his voice growing louder, his fleshy face beginning to turn red. "My son deserves an apology!"

J.J. looked stricken. "Mommy," he whimpered.

Belle looked at her son, who appeared close to tears. She stood up.

"Mr. Aubrey, with all due respect, I think we should have this conversation somewhere else."

"With all due respect? With all due respect, little lady?! My son wasn't shown no respect." He reached out and grabbed Belle's arm. "My wife wasn't shown no respect."

Belle looked across the room for Toad, but there was a line of people waiting to be served, and he seemed unaware of what was happening.

"Mr. Aubrey," she said. She stood firmly but there was a slight tremor in her voice.

Unexpectedly, there was another strong voice beside her. It was Emmanuel. "Mr. Aubrey, I am sure you do not want to cause trouble. In my country, it is not proper for a man to grab the arm of another man's wife. I think it is best if you release her."

Aubrey looked surprised. "Oh yeah, says who? Nobody asked you. Your country, huh? Where you come from—one of them African places? Live in a tree, did you?" He sneered, but there was a quick flicker of fear in his eyes.

A surge of anger flooded Belle. "Mr. Aubrey, you have no right…" She was interrupted by the calm reply of Emmanuel.

"My son and I are friends of the Thornwells. We are having a lovely meal together. I suggest you join your wife and son and do the same."

90

At that moment, Toad approached them. "What seems to be the problem?" he asked. His voice was steady, but there was an edge to it.

Seeing he was suddenly outnumbered, Aubrey backed off. "Your kid," he snarled. "He still owes my son an apology."

He turned and stalked off to join Gladys and Tommy. "We're leaving," he growled, grabbing his wife's arm and pushing his son ahead of him. "And we're never coming back."

"Mommy, I'm sorry," said J.J. His eyes welled with tears.

"J.J., it wasn't your fault. That man…" She began again, "Mr. Aubrey didn't understand the situation. He was…"

"Mean," said J.J.

"Naughty," said Toby.

Cyndarria was thinking words she knew she shouldn't utter in public, so she said simply, "Yes, he was."

Belle smiled ruefully. "I don't think he's a very happy man," she said.

Toad embraced her for a moment. "Are you all right?"

Belle felt her heart rate beginning to return to normal. She took a deep breath. "I'm fine," she said. "Everything's okay. Let's all just enjoy our food."

Toad looked toward the door. "I'm going to make sure that they've left. I'll be right back."

A minute later he returned to the dining room and gave Belle a thumbs up, then went back to the carving station.

"Thank you, Emmanuel," Belle said. "I wasn't sure what Mr. Aubrey was going to do."

"I have seen men like him in my own country. Mr. Aubrey is a bully and not a very brave one. I think perhaps he is also a fool."

Belle nodded. "Still, you didn't have to do it."

91

"Ah, but I did," he said. "We are all friends at this table, and we must stand up for our friends, do you not think?"

Belle gave him a grateful smile. "Yes," she nodded, "I do think."

She looked around the table at everyone, and they all looked back.

"C'n we eat again now?" asked Toby. "I'm really hungry."

"Absolutely," said Belle. "Eat what's on your plate, and then we can all have dessert."

"Yea!" exclaimed Toby. "C'n I have two?"

"Clean your plate first," said Belle, "and then we'll see."

Cyndarria felt the knot in her chest loosen. Dessert talk was good. Dessert talk meant everything was okay.

"I think I'll have the cherry pie," she said and dug into her potatoes. "It looked really good."

CHAPTER 14

CYNDARRIA AROSE AT the normal time the next morning and got ready for school. She was worried. She figured probably Mrs. Wackenstein would hand back their "What do you want to be when you grow up?" essays, and she was nervous about her grade. She had hoped to do well, but that was before Mrs. Wackenstein had scolded her for bringing cookies to class without permission and sent her to talk to the principal. Even though Mr. Johansson had been nice about it, Cyndarria doubted that his reaction would have had much effect on the grade Mrs. Wackenstein gave her.

When Henri got there, she was already waiting impatiently on the porch for him to arrive.

"Good morning, Cyndarria. Why are you out here?"

"Let's hurry. I want to be sure to get to class before the bell rings. I'm already in the doghouse with Wacko, and I don't want to make matters worse."

"Do you think she will hand back our papers today?" asked Henri.

"Probably, and I'm kind of scared about the grade I'll get. She was pretty mad at me. I think you'll get a good grade, though. She was really impressed when you explained what an epiph… What was that word you explained in English class?"

"Epiphany. It's funny, because my father had just been talking to me about that word."

"Hmm. Sounds like kind of a weird conversation. How did that come up?"

"He was talking about how he had come to the decision to migrate to this country. He had an epiphany, he said, and he just kind of knew it was the right thing to do."

"I hope I have one of those sometime when I have to make a big decision. Like what I want for dinner." She looked slyly at her friend and grinned.

"I think you are making fun of me, Cyndarria," said Henri.

"Maybe just a little," she agreed. "But seriously, I think it would be pretty cool to have something like that happen. It would make things easier."

The two friends got to school five minutes before the first bell rang.

"I'm going to class," said Cyndarria. "I want to get there a little early. You come with me, though. I don't want to go in alone."

Just then their friend Stevie came up. Today he was wearing a "Hiked it, Liked it" T-shirt that his dad had bought him when they had visited Watkins Glen in New York the summer before.

"Hi, guys," Stevie said. "Are you ready to face The Terror?" That was the way he referred to Mrs. Wackenstein, who was his sixth-hour teacher. "I'll bet she hands back those essays today. She's gonna absolutely pulverize my grade 'cuz I handed mine in late. She hates me."

"She sent me to the office for bringing in cookies," Cyndarria reminded him. "I probably won't do much better."

"They sure were good cookies, though," said Stevie. He looked at the hall clock. "Gotta go. See you guys in Spanish class."

Cyndarria took a deep breath, as though it might be her last. She looked nervously at Henri. "Ready?"

"Cyndarria, it will be okay. Don't worry so much."

"Easy for you to say. You'll probably get an A."

When they entered class, there were only two other students in their seats—Jodi and Christina, both of whom Cyndarria considered brown-nosers. Mrs. Wackenstein looked up and raised her eyebrows when she saw them.

"I see you've decided to get here on time today," she said, then returned to grading the paper in front of her.

The first bell rang, and other students began to file in. Joey Bellow assumed his usual front seat and scrunched down comfortably in his desk, letting his legs stick out.

"Mr. Bellow," said Mrs. Wackenstein, her voice dripping with disapproval, "I will thank you to sit properly."

Joey grinned, obviously pleased that he had garnered some attention even before class had started. It didn't matter that it was negative; in fact, he seemed to like that kind even more. It gave him a certain status among his classmates.

"Yes, ma'am, Mrs. Wackenstein," he said with an excessively polite smile. "Anything you say." He sat up and drew his feet in just enough to make it seem as though he were doing as he had been told.

Mrs. Wackenstein was not deceived. "Mr. Bellow," her voice crackled. "You will sit up straight and put your feet under your desk immediately, or you will be spending the hour with Mr. Johansson. I doubt he would be pleased to see you again so soon."

Joey knew when he was beaten, but he was cheerful about it. "Yes, ma'am," he said again and this time did as he was ordered. He looked around the class to see if the other students had been watching. They had. Pleased, he nodded, as if thanking them for their attention, then turned around and clasped his hands on top of his desk.

The hour crawled by. When there were 10 minutes left in class, Mrs. Wackenstein said, "We'll have free reading now. I have a story I want you to read. If you don't finish it today, it will be your homework. Also, you are to write a 100-150 word response to what you read and be ready to discuss the story in class tomorrow."

The students barely managed to stifle a groan. Joey, who always seemed to say the wrong thing at the right time, saw an opening. "Mrs. Wackenstein, if you give us the story and tell us to read it, that's not exactly free reading, is it?"

A few of the braver students nodded.

Mrs. Wackenstein, as usual, was undeterred. "Shall I require a 300-word response?" she asked, glaring at the class.

"No, ma'am," they chorused.

"Excellent," she said, pleased that she had reasserted her authority. "I will pass back your essays while you're reading."

Cyndarria's heart skipped a beat. She bit her lip and prepared for the worst. When Mrs. Wackenstein handed Henri back his paper, she uttered a terse, "Well done, Mr. Rousseau."

"Thank you, Mrs. Wackenstein," said Henri.

She turned to Cyndarria, who could almost feel herself shrink. "Here it comes," she thought.

"Miss Thornwell, I would like you to see me after class."

"Oh gees," Cyndarria thought. "She probably flunked me."

"Umm, I have Spanish then, Mrs. Wackenstein."

"I am fully aware that you have another class, Miss Thornwell. I will give you a pass if necessary."

Cyndarria nodded. She looked over at Henri after Mrs. Wackenstein had turned to go back to the front of the class. He held up his paper. There was a big red A on it.

"Way to go, Henri," she whispered. "I told you that you'd get a good grade."

"Thank you, Cyndarria. My father will be very pleased." He placed the paper carefully in a folder, then put the folder in his book bag.

Cyndarria glanced down at the stapled pages that Mrs. Wackenstein had handed out for them to read. The title of the story was *The Parsley Garden*, written by William Saroyan. She'd never heard of him but thought that a story with that title sounded pretty boring. "Ugh!" she thought. "I don't even like parsley."

She read the first couple paragraphs. They introduced a boy named Al Condraj, who stole a ten-cent hammer from Woolworth's. "He must have lived an awful long time ago," she thought, "or it was a pretty worthless hammer. A Wool-worthless hammer!" She smiled at her own cleverness.

Just then the bell rang. Cyndarria suddenly felt queasy. She put her things away slowly, so all the other students would be gone. Henri waited for her loyally.

Mrs. Wackenstein looked up as they approached the desk. "You're excused, Mr. Rousseau," she said.

"Yes, ma'am. I'll see you next hour, Cyndarria."

She nodded, then waited quietly for what she was certain would be her execution. Mrs. Wackenstein looked at her, and Cyndarria saw what she thought might be a smile. She experienced a faint glimmer of hope.

"I made cookies from the recipe you included with your essay," said Mrs. Wackenstein.

Cyndarria hardly knew what to say. "Oh, I hope they were good."

"They were. Quite good, actually. I gave one to my husband, and he ate the whole thing."

Mrs. Wackenstein hesitated a moment, seemingly unsure if she wanted to continue. "He…he isn't well, and food doesn't seem to interest him much anymore."

Cyndarria was stunned that her teacher would tell her something so personal, and for the first time she looked at her through more forgiving eyes. Mrs. Wackenstein was not a large woman, thin and standing only 5'2", but her small frame didn't make her less intimidating to students. She used no makeup and always dressed in dark colors. She kept her salt-and-pepper hair short, wore wire-rim glasses, but seemed to have a perpetual squint. It occurred to Cyndarria that her Aunt Agnes and Mrs. Wackenstein could become friends—they were kind of similar in ways.

The only piece of jewelry Cyndarria had ever seen Mrs. Wackenstein wear was a surprisingly delicate silver watch, which she checked from time to time instead of looking at the clock in the room. Cyndarria wondered if it had been a gift from her husband.

"I'm sorry," she said. "My grandpa is like that. My mom worries about it. It's difficult."

"Yes, it is. At any rate, I wanted to thank you. Perhaps I was a little hard on you last Friday. You did a good job, Miss Thornwell. Your essay was sincere and very much you, and you made a nice oral presentation. It was the best work you've done this year."

She handed Cyndarria her paper. On the top, there was an A that matched in size and color the grade that Henri had received. A wave of relief flooded through Cyndarria, and inexplicably she felt almost as if she would cry.

"I don't know what to say, Mrs. Wackenstein, but thank you. I'm sure my parents will be pleased."

"I had your father in class for a semester, you know," said Mrs. Wackenstein. "A nice young man, but not, shall we say, an inspired English student. I've heard the Sunday brunch at his restaurant is very good, though. One never knows what will happen to one's students down the road."

Cyndarria was curious. "Did you know my Grandma Rose?"

"I did. I talked to her a couple of times, if I recall correctly. She was a very impressive woman. I could tell she had high standards, and I appreciated that. I'm sure she meant a great deal to you."

"Yes, ma'am. I learned a lot from her, and not just about baking." Cyndarria looked up at the clock. "The bell's about to ring. I'd better go."

"Don't forget tomorrow's assignment," said Mrs. Wackenstein, firmly back in teacher mode. "I hope your work on that essay indicates you've turned the corner in this class."

"I hope so too," said Cyndarria. Then she walked out of the room and headed for Spanish.

CHAPTER 15

CYNDARRIA WALKED SLOWLY to Spanish class, thinking about her conversation with Mrs. Wackenstein. It was the most she had ever spoken with her, and it made Cyndarria wonder if maybe Mrs. Wackenstein was someone a little different than she had always thought, someone a little more...human.

Cyndarria remembered a story her dad had told her. It had been her impression that Mrs. Wackenstein had no children, but that was not the case. Many years before, she had had a son, Billy, who had died when he was little. Something about fireworks on the Fourth of July. By all accounts, she and her husband, who was fifteen years older than his wife, had been heartbroken, and Mrs. Wackenstein hadn't returned to work till the second semester of the following school year. A neighbor had told them that Billy's bedroom was the same it had been the day he died, his bed still unmade, his pajamas in a small pile on the floor.

Cyndarria thought about Toby and wondered how she would feel if he died. She shook her head, pushing the thought from her mind. She couldn't stand even thinking about it. It was unimaginable. It occurred to her then that maybe her opinion of Mrs. Wackenstein was changing. A little.

The bell rang. Cyndarria hurried through the door to her Spanish class. Señor Paniagua looked up and smiled when he saw her. *"Buenos días, Rosita."*

"Buenos días, Señor Paniagua," Cyndarria responded as she took her seat.

"Was it awful?" Henri whispered.

Cyndarria showed him her essay. "I can't believe it," she said. "I'll tell you about it later."

Spanish class passed pretty quickly, as it usually did, because Señor Paniagua had a way of moving things along.

"So, *mis estudiantes,*" he said with 20 minutes to go, "I have an interesting little project for you to do, *un proyecto interesante.*"

There was an uneasy shift among the students. Projects usually meant quite a bit of work outside of class, not something any of them appreciated.

"Do you see that stack of magazines?" asked Señor Paniagua, signaling a sizable pile on a table off to the side. "They're all *National Geographics,* one of my favorite publications. Every issue has an article related to the Spanish-speaking world, and each of you will read one and do a short report on what you learned. Then we will all know a little bit more about the culture of the countries whose language you are studying. *Qué bueno, no?*"

There was a collective groan from the class. "Señor Paniagua!" they exclaimed in unison. "You've already taught us lots of things!"

"Look," he said. "It's just one article, which may take you a half-hour to read. Then you'll write a one-paragraph summary of it and a list of five things that you learned. So maybe it takes you an hour in all. I'll give you till Friday to complete it. Then you'll each talk to the class for a minute or two about your article. If we don't finish on Friday, we'll do the rest on Monday. To make it fair, you're going to draw numbers to determine the order of presentation."

Señor Paniagua picked up an old hat he had sitting on his desk and walked around the room. Students made a face, then reluctantly drew a number.

When it was her turn, Cyndarria closed her eyes and grimaced, then peeked at her number. Seventeen. She breathed a sigh of relief. She probably wouldn't have to go till Monday. Henri was next. He unfolded the slip of paper and showed her. Three.

"Uh oh," Cyndarria thought. "Not good."

She glanced over at Stevie, who looked almost sick. The only thing he disliked more than doing a project was standing up in front of the class and talking about it. She showed him her number and he held up his. Twelve. Right in the middle. Hard to say if he would go Friday or Monday.

Because he sat over on the far side of the room from where Señor Paniagua had started, Joey was one of the last to draw a number. He stuck his hand confidently in the hat and withdrew a slip of paper. He opened it and his smile faded.

"C'n I draw another one?" he asked, holding out his hand.

"*Lo siento*," said Señor Paniagua. "Sorry. No do-overs."

"What'd you get, Joey?" asked the girl across from him, who had managed to draw 23, the very last number.

Joey held up his slip for the whole class to see. A big, black "1" was scrawled on it.

"Tough luck," said the girl.

"Wanna trade?" asked Joey hopefully.

"Fat chance," she said.

Señor Paniagua checked the clock. There were only 10 minutes left. "*Muy bien,*" he said. "Now I will pass out the *National Geographics.* As I do so, write your name opposite your number on this sheet of paper along with the title of your article, which I will point out, so there's no confusion."

He handed Joey the paper along with his magazine. "This one has an article on the Amazon rain forest," he said. "It's very interesting."

"I'll bet," Joey muttered under his breath.

"And this one is on the Atacama Desert in Chile," he told the girl behind Joey. "It hasn't rained in some parts of the desert for many years, but there are still some beautiful flowers that survive there, and many animals. I think you'll like this article."

The girl looked doubtful but accepted the magazine and turned to the first page. Señor Paniagua continued around the room, commenting briefly on each of the articles the students would read, hoping to encourage them.

"The Tarahumara Indians in Northern Mexico. They're the greatest long-distance runners in the world.

"The mystery that surrounds the winter home of the monarch butterfly. You'll be surprised where they go.

"Ixta and Popo—two lovers."

"I'll take that one," said a girl across the room.

"Very well," said Señor Paniagua, and handed it across to her.

"Ah, this one is fascinating. It's about the legend of the sun and the moon."

He continued.

"*Rosita,*" he said when he got to Cyndarria, "this is one of my favorite articles. It's about the history of *mole*, which he pronounced moh-lay. It's a traditional sauce from Mexico. Perhaps you would like to try making it?"

"Umm, maybe," said Cyndarria, unsure what she would be getting herself into if she agreed.

Henri's article was one on *Ullamiliztli,* the ball game of the ancient Aztecs. "I have heard of this ball game," said Henri. "I think it will be interesting to find out more about it."

Cyndarria pointed to her nose.

"No, seriously," said Henri. "I think there is some human sacrifice involved."

"Oooo, blood and gore," said Cyndarria. "Floats my boat! What did you get, Stevie?"

"St. Augustine," he said, looking mystified. "What does a saint have to do with anything? This ain't a religion class!"

"Umm, Stevie," said Cyndarria. "St. Augustine is a city in Florida."

"I believe it is our oldest city," said Henri.

"Oh," said Stevie. He grinned mischievously. "Think maybe Señor Paniagua would let us take a field trip there? I've always wanted to go to Florida."

Suddenly an ear-splitting sound filled the air. Señor Paniagua looked up, clearly surprised. It was the fire alarm, and he knew that a fire drill hadn't been scheduled for that day.

The students looked at each other, confused, unsure of what was happening.

"All right, students," said Señor Paniagua, recovering from his initial uncertainty as to what he should do. "Take your books, and go out the door at the end of the hall. Quickly."

Cyndarria felt her pulse quicken; her heart began to pound. This was not a practice, she was sure, or Señor Paniagua would have told them so. For a moment, she felt almost paralyzed.

"Oh my gosh, Henri!" She could hear a little panic in her voice.

"Take your books, Cyndarria. Let's go."

She did so, and when she got out in the hall, she could smell smoke. Penny, a small, quiet girl who was just ahead of her, stopped suddenly and seemed unable to move. Her hands covered her face.

"Oh no," she moaned softly. "Not again. Not again."

"Penny," Cyndarria spoke quickly in her terrified class-mate's ear. "We've got to go." She grabbed Penny's arm and tried to pull her along. By now, the hall was filled with students,

104

some of whom had clearly panicked from the smell of smoke and started to push and shove others out of their way.

Penny pulled back against Cyndarria. "I can't! I can't! My little sister's in the other hall. I have to get her!"

Cyndarria looked desperately at Henri, who had waited for her. "Penny," he said, trying to make his voice sound calm and reassuring, "she'll be okay. Her teacher will make sure she gets out safely."

The smell of smoke seemed to be getting stronger. "No! She needs me! I got her out when our house was on fire." Penny started sobbing. "I have to find her!"

Just then Señor Paniagua, who had waited for all of his students to safely exit the classroom, came up and put his arm gently around Penny. "*Lupita,*" he said, "I'm sure your sister is out safe. She's in Mrs. Bailey's classroom, which is right by an outside door. Come."

Penny still looked uncertain, but finally yielded to Señor Paniagua's encouragement. The four of them made their way down the hall and out into the back parking lot. The day was chilly, and there was a strong wind. The students stood shivering. They waited for the sound of sirens coming from fire engines, but none came.

A few minutes later, Mr. Johansson appeared. "Everyone can come back in," he announced. "We've managed to put the fire out. Nobody was hurt. Unfortunately, someone played a prank."

Penny began to cry again, relief flooding her face. She crossed herself, clasped her hands in front of her mouth, and whispered a prayer.

Cyndarria wondered who would have pulled such a stunt, but it wouldn't be till much later that she and everyone else found out.

CHAPTER 16

WHEN CYNDARRIA GOT to P.E., everyone was still talking about the fire.

"I was so scared," said one of the girls. "I thought we were all gonna die!"

"Oh, c'mon, Sadie," said her friend. "Don't you think that was kind of an overreaction?"

"I don't like fires," Sadie said. "They scare me. My grandpa's house burned down last year. He almost didn't get out."

Miss Davis, the P.E. teacher, let the girls talk for a while, understanding their need to release some of their feelings. Finally, she called the class to order.

Physical education was a class that Cyndarria enjoyed. It was a welcome change of pace from sitting all hour, and she liked Miss Davis, who actually preferred that her students call her Coach Sam, short for Samantha. That title reflected her favorite part of her job, which was coaching girls' track, a program she had initiated just three years before with the help of Coach McIntyre.

Miss Davis taught girls' P.E. and a health class just for girls, which she had also initiated with the approval of her principal. Having experienced some serious difficulties as a young teen, she believed that giving girls a comfortable place to talk about the changes and challenges they were, or soon would be, facing was very important to their growth and their well-being. A comfortable place meant doing it without the boys, who were dealing with their own issues, in the same class. So far the class was going well, and the girls seemed to appreciate having a safe place to ask questions and talk about personal problems without embarrassing themselves.

Miss Davis was short and trim with sandy-colored, close-cropped hair. Her green eyes sparkled with enthusiasm, especially when she talked about track. She had been a successful long-distance runner in college and still got up early enough to run five miles every morning before school.

"Okay, ladies," she said when the girls had changed to their gym clothes and were sitting before her on the basketball court. "Today we're going to play a little dodgeball. Who remembers when and where the first games were played?"

Sara, ever ready to show off her memory and impress the teacher, raised her hand. "In Africa, two-hundred years ago. But they used rocks and sometimes killed each other."

"Correct. Thanks, Sara. I think we'll avoid having that happen today," she said with a smile. "So let's choose up teams and get started."

They played a couple games each, Cyndarria's team winning one and losing one, and then Coach Sam stopped play. "We have about ten minutes left, and I want to talk to you a little about the upcoming track season," she said, "so have a seat."

The girls sat and their teacher continued. "As you may have heard, track practice starts next Monday, and I'm hoping some of you will want to join the team. We were pretty successful last year, coming in second in our league."

A few of the girls who had been on the team did a high-five.

"Several of you participated last year. I hope you'll be back, but I'd also love to recruit some fresh talent. Think about it. We have a lot of fun, and you'll finish in even better shape than you are now. Okay, go get changed, and I'll see you tomorrow."

When the bell sounded, Cyndarria and her friends headed for the cafeteria. There they sat at the same table as Henri, Stevie, and Joey. Sofia and Alison had been on the track team the year before and were trying to talk Cyndarria into joining them.

"How about you guys?" Sofia asked the boys. "Are you going out for the team?"

"I am," said Henri. "I want to try the hurdles and maybe the long jump."

"I'm going out for the high jump," said Stevie. He looked at his friends, daring them to laugh.

"Really, Stevie?" said Alison. "Wow, that's, uhh, that's cool."

"You guys!" said Stevie. "Seriously? I'm 4'10"! I'd probably be lucky if I could clear three feet!"

"So what do you really want to do?" asked Cyndarria.

"I think I'm gonna try the mile. I like to run, and I don't seem to get tired the way bigger guys do sometimes."

"How about you, Joey?" asked Sofia.

"Hundred-yard dash," Joey grinned. "This body may be fat, but inside I'm a speed demon."

Henri shook his head. "Come on, Joey, we know you don't like to run. You did pretty well in the shot put last spring. Maybe you could set the school record if you really worked at it."

"I'd settle for being the league champ," Joey said. "I came pretty close last year."

Cyndarria looked thoughtfully at Joey. She was surprised to hear him setting such an ambitious goal. In class he always seemed to be looking for the easy way out. "That would be great, Joey," she said. "I hope you do it."

"Thanks, Cyndarria. Me too. So are you going out for the team this year?"

108

"We're trying to talk her into it," said Alison, "but so far she hasn't agreed."

"C'mon, Cyndarria," urged Sofia. "Do it! It'll be fun."

"I'll think about it," said Cyndarria. "The thing is, I don't even know what event I'd do."

"Coach Sam will help you figure that out," said Alison. "She's great about helping everyone find their best events. I didn't think I would ever be a short-distance runner." She stood up and spread her arms with a big grin. "But look at me now!"

"She won first place in the 100-yard dash at the league championships last year," said Sofia. "She did awesome."

"Thanks, Sofia," said Alison. "Seriously, Cyndarria, try out. You never know what you can do till you try it."

"I said I'd think about it," said Cyndarria, "and I will."

"Think hard," urged Alison. "And say yes."

After lunch Cyndarria headed for social studies, which was, along with science, her least favorite class. Actually, it wasn't that she was totally bored with history; it was her teacher. Herman Sidebottom was an assistant football coach at the high school, and his idea of an interesting class was to lecture for half the hour, which meant that he read lists of facts from the chapter under study, interspersing them with stories of his glory days as a backup to the backup quarterback at the small college he had attended. After that, he would hand out a worksheet for the students to toil over the remainder of the hour.

By and large, Mr. Sidebottom did not assign homework, well aware that if he did so, it would be incumbent upon him to do something with it. His solution, which he considered to be brilliant, was to find a teacher's aide who would check homework answers for him, all of which were in his teacher's guide. Tests were true and false only, again checked by his aide, who also entered the scores in his gradebook, which, teachers had been warned, was strictly against the rules.

Because the school required all teachers to make at least three writing assignments a semester, Mr. Sidebottom did, although the students suspected he didn't read their essays. To verify that, Joey Bellow had once written half-way through his, "If you are still reading this, check here." When he got it back, there was a check mark at the top, but the rest of the paper was pristine, obviously untouched by human hand—at least not Mr. Sidebottom's!

Mr. Sidebottom's favorite expression was, "You can't make chicken salad out of chicken doo doo," explaining that he had cleaned up the real expression so it was "appropriate for middle-school children." Word had it that he had regularly used this expression plus many others that were X-rated on the football field. He seemed to think cussing was a manly thing to do, which annoyed the head coach so much that he finally ordered Sidebottom to clean up his language. So he did, at least when the head coach was within earshot.

Mr. Sidebottom generally showed up for class in pants, which were belted below his protruding belly, and a shirt that said, "Sycamore Creek High School Football." The toned body which he had once loved to show off in Speedos had practically doubled in size since college, much to his wife Bernadette's dismay. When she suggested that he might consider losing a few pounds, he would chuckle and say, "Just that much more of me to love, honey." Bernadette, who was not easily amused, failed to see the humor.

Today Mr. Sidebottom was absent, replaced by his favorite sub, Bradley Ratkowski, whom the students referred to behind his back as "The Rat." With his pointy nose and beady eyes, he did actually look somewhat like that rodent. Mr. Ratkowski was well into his thirties, single, and still lived at home with his parents. He had subbed for the Sycamore Creek Public School System for years, content to show up, sit, read his favorite magazine, *The Philatelist*, and collect his check. The Rat was pleased with his life—comfortable and still cared for by his mother, with modest expectations and few demands.

But then he had met Heloise, and now that comfort was shaken. The students all knew about her because Mr. Ratkowski seemed to enjoy sharing all the events of his life, major and minor, with them. He had met her at a philatelists' convention a month earlier, and they had struck up a conversation because she shared his enthusiasm for stamp collecting.

They talked about their most cherished stamps, and she told him in absolute confidence that she was the proud owner of one of the rare and extremely valuable ten-rupee Mahatma Gandhi postage stamps, produced in India in 1948. Mr. Ratkowski was flabbergasted because he knew the stamp was easily worth thousands. Heloise was tightlipped about how she had come to possess it which, along with her large hazel eyes and coy smile, made her seem utterly irresistible to him.

Mr. Ratkowski had never felt this way before about a member of the opposite sex, and he had no idea what to do about it. He had never really dated and had always seen himself as a happy bachelor, living out his life on the farm where he had grown up and subbing for Sycamore Creek Schools. Now he was flummoxed, and he found it to be a position in which he was not at all comfortable.

Mr. Sidebottom had left a couple of worksheets for the students to complete in his absence, which gave The Rat plenty of time to sit and ponder his predicament.

"Good afternoon, students," he said once they were settled in their seats.

"Hi, Mr. Ratkowski," said Joey, who was in three of Cyndarria's classes. "How they hangin'?"

"I hardly think that's an appropriate question for the classroom, Joey."

"Sorry, Mr. Ratkowski," said Joey, his expression of regret obviously insincere.

"Now then," Mr. Ratkowski continued, "Mr. Sidebottom has left you a couple of worksheets to do. You are allowed to work with a partner, but you should both hand in your papers."

With that brief explanation, he handed them out and retired behind the teacher's desk. He picked up the latest issue of *The Philatelist,* determined to read, but found he was distracted by thoughts of Heloise and her Mahatma Gandhi stamp. And those hazel eyes.

Cyndarria looked at him curiously and wondered why he sat mooning at some non-existent sight out the window. She had never really seen him gaze at anything so dreamily before.

And then she remembered Heloise. "I think he's smitten," she thought, and, despite what an odd fellow he was, she felt kind of happy for him.

CHAPTER 17

THE FIRST PART of the day had gone quickly, but social studies class dragged because there wasn't anything to do except a couple of boring worksheets that Mr. Sidebottom had actually used once before. Finally, the bell rang and The Rat released them to their next class.

Cyndarria headed for science, hoping maybe Mr. Cassius would be gone today as well. No such luck. He was standing behind his desk watching the students come in, looking vaguely pleased with himself.

Everything about Mr. Cassius was big, starting with his nose. Cyndarria was sure she'd never seen such a large one. He was tall and barrel-chested and had unnaturally long arms with huge, thick, hairy hands attached. He always wore a sport coat, usually the same one. Mr. Cassius didn't talk; he boomed.

Despite his imposing size and voice, Mr. Cassius struggled with discipline. He had come to teaching later in life and never quite gotten the hang of gaining the students' respect. When he became frustrated, which happened on a daily basis, he would wring his hands and groan loudly, "WHAT did I DO to deSERVE such a CLASS?!"

Today, however, he was looking quite confident. The bell rang, and Mr. Cassius said, his voice ringing with pride, "Today, I have something special to show you!"

He turned and picked up a huge jar from behind his desk. He held it up. "Does anyone know what this is?"

"Looks like a snake," said one of the boys.

"Gross!" said the girl next to him.

"It is, indeed, a snake. Thank you, Harvey. And what kind of snake do you suppose it is?" he asked, hoping to show his superior knowledge.

"Well," offered Alison, who sat beside Cyndarria, "it's blue."

"Yes, indeed, it is blue!" exclaimed Mr. Cassius, clearly delighted that he still had the students' attention. "This," he fairly bellowed, "is a blue racer!"

He opened the jar, reached inside, and grabbed the unsuspecting snake, which had appeared to be napping. He held it up, and the startled reptile began to writhe and squirm furiously. Slowly Mr. Cassius's triumphant smile began to fade as he attempted unsuccessfully to grab the struggling snake by its middle. Then, with one final effort, the snake managed to escape the clutches of its captor and dropped to the floor.

Sudden screams filled the classroom as students jumped up on their desks. The snake, oblivious to the noise, slithered with surprising speed toward the door, which had been left open. Within seconds it had made its escape and was off down the hall, with Mr. Cassius and several of the students in hot pursuit.

"Stop!" Mr. Cassius screeched. The snake, of course, which did not speak Human, ignored the command and continued streaking down the corridor. At the end, it slithered around the corner and headed straight for the principal's office.

"Oh no!" shouted Mr. Cassius and increased his speed, hoping to catch the snake, which was clearly living up to its designation as a racer, before it got there. Oraleen Jackson, Mr. Johansson's secretary, looked up when she heard Mr. Cassius's desperate cry. She stood and walked hurriedly toward the office door, arriving there at precisely the same time as the determined reptile.

"Well, my stars!" she exclaimed and in an instant reached down and grabbed the fleeing snake. "A blue racer! This one's a beauty."

She had it by the head and quickly grasped its middle as well, achieving with ease what Mr. Cassius had failed miserably to do. He puffed to a stop in front of her.

"Mrs. Jackson," he exclaimed, out of breath, "you have saved the day!"

She eyed Mr. Cassius with only a mildly disappointed look on her face. "Glad to have been of service," she said, carefully handing him the snake. "Perhaps after this you should just leave it in a jar."

"Quite right," he agreed, almost meekly. He turned then and, regaining his voice, boomed, "Back to the classroom, kids!"

After all that excitement, the rest of the class was an anti-climax, but at least more interesting than worksheets in social studies, Cyndarria mused. She and Alison stood when the bell rang and headed for Community Service, their last class of what had turned out to be quite an eventful day.

When they got to the classroom, it was empty, but their teacher, Mrs. Maxwell, had left a quick note on the board. "Be right back." She arrived a few minutes later, a little breathless.

"Oh," she exclaimed, "I'm so excited!"

This was not an unusual mental state for Mrs. Maxwell, who seemed to get excited about almost everything. Her extreme excitement sometimes led her to be a bit scatterbrained, but Cyndarria liked her because she was nice and her enthusiasm was genuine.

"I've just talked with Mrs. Doolittle, the head librarian downtown, and she has a project that she would like us to help with," said Mrs. Maxwell. She looked eagerly at the students, hoping that their enthusiasm would equal her own. "Actually, two projects," she corrected herself. "The first one is this coming Friday, for lunch."

The students' ears suddenly perked up, their faces beginning to show a hint of the enthusiasm that Mrs. Maxwell was hoping for.

"Are we going out for lunch?" asked Laurie Jacobs, a pretty girl who carried about 30 pounds of extra weight. "That would be fun."

Mrs. Maxwell looked a bit disappointed; then she brightened. "Well, you might say that."

"Oh good," beamed Laurie. "I love eating out!"

"Yes, well, let me explain," said Mrs. Maxwell. "You won't exactly be eating."

Laurie's face fell; her eager smile disappeared.

"Although, actually, maybe you will. I'll have to consult Mrs. Doolittle."

"So what's the project?" asked Simon Tibble, a scholarly boy who had little patience for any lack of clarity or precise organization. He peered over his glasses with a challenging look.

"There's to be a ladies' luncheon on Friday. It's to raise money for the library's endowment fund, and they need some students who will act as servers. The ladies will eat, and then there will be a speaker, a local author named Ruth Rogers. I've heard her speak, and she's really very good. Very funny."

Mrs. Maxwell seemed about to go on with her praise of the author but was interrupted by Simon. "So we're going to be waiters. We'll need permission to miss class. Have you spoken with Mr. Johansson about it?"

"As a matter of fact, Simon," Mrs. Maxwell said, a hint of triumph in her voice, "I have, and he's very supportive. He very much likes the idea of our students providing community service.

And, of course, that," she added with some pride, "is what this class is all about."

Simon sat back, temporarily satisfied.

"How long would we be gone?" asked Tammy Mason who, when she wasn't skipping school, was looking for other ways to miss class.

"You would leave at the beginning of third hour, so you can assist with set-up, and return more or less at the end of fifth. I think Mrs. Doolittle would like you to help with clean-up as well."

"But that means we would miss our lunch!" Laurie sounded alarmed.

"I'm quite certain Mrs. Doolittle would allow you time to eat during the presentation of the guest speaker."

"I'm in," called a boy from the back. "Sounds good to me."

"Before we decide, I think we should know what the other option is," said Simon, once again intent on knowing every detail before making a decision.

"I'm so glad you asked, Simon," said Mrs. Maxwell. "Mrs. Doolittle wants to start an after-school reading program for three- through eight-year-olds. Tentatively, it will run on Wednesday afternoons from 3:30 to 4:30, at least during the school year, and she would love for some of you to be the readers."

Cyndarria was immediately interested. That age group would include both her brothers, and that appealed to her.

She raised her hand. "Yes, Cyndarria," said Mrs. Maxwell, happy at least one of her students had remembered that classroom courtesy, although the truth was with discussions like these, she didn't really object to the kids simply asking questions and offering ideas more freely.

"Would we start right away?"

"Probably not. Mrs. Doolittle still needs to work out some of the details and consult with the rest of her staff for their input. She's thinking she'd like to begin later in the spring and run the program through the summer. So," she said in summary, "those are the two options. Who's interested?"

Several of the students raised their hands to serve at the luncheon, but only a couple, Cyndarria and Simon, volunteered to read.

"Ali," said Cyndarria to her friend, "don't you want to read to the little kids? It would be fun."

Alison hesitated. "I know, but it might interfere with track practice. I'd have to talk with Coach Sam."

"I'll make you a deal," said Cyndarria, a little surprised at what she was saying. "I'll go out for track if you read with me. I'll have to check with my mom first, but I think probably she'll be okay with it."

Alison grinned. "You're on."

And that was how Cyndarria's unexpected track career began, a career which was to hold some rather interesting surprises and one very scary one.

CHAPTER 18

"DAD!" SHOUTED CYNDARRIA from the top of the stairs when her father walked through the door after work. "Guess what!"

Toad smiled when he heard the eager voice of his oldest offspring. "Let's see. Your hair turned green from eating too many vegetables." He looked up and saw Cyndarria. "Ooops, I guess not."

"No, seriously, Dad. Guess."

"Hmmm. We got a mysterious letter in the mail saying all I have to do is send in my social security number, and we will win a million dollars."

"Dad!!"

"Okay, okay, I give up. What has you so excited?"

Cyndarria came bounding downstairs and held up her English essay for Toad to admire. "Check this out!" she exclaimed.

"Wow! That's great, honey. I guess Mrs. Wackenstein must have liked your essay a lot more than you thought she would."

"Actually," admitted Cyndarria, "I think it was Grandma Rose's cookies."

"Well, that's better than your old man ever did, so congratulations!" He gave his daughter an affectionate pat.

Later, dinner was baked chicken, mashed potatoes, corn and sliced tomatoes. Belle garnished the platter of chicken with a sprig of parsley.

"Aren't we fancy," observed Toad. "Nice touch."

"It just brightens the plate up a little," said Belle. "And I have to use that parsley before it goes to seed."

Belle tended her small kitchen herb garden with meticulous care. She grew parsley, sage, rosemary, and thyme because, she said, it reminded her of the old Simon and Garfunkel song of that title, a song she particularly loved. In addition, she grew basil and oregano.

"Speaking of parsley," said Cyndarria, "Mrs. Wackenstein assigned us a story called *The Parsley Garden* to read for tomorrow. I just finished it before dinner."

"You know, I think I might have read that one when I was in her class," recalled Toad. "Something about a kid who steals a hammer, and his mother has a parsley garden. I don't remember what the connection is."

"Yeah, Al Condraj, and he finally ends up going back to Woolworth's, where he stole it, and working for a day to kind of make up for what he'd done. The manager offers to pay him a dollar for his labor, but Al says he'd rather have the hammer, which only costs a dime."

"I'd take the dollar," said J.J.

"Me too," agreed Toby. "And I would buy a candy bar and put the rest in my piggy bank."

"Smart kid," said Toad.

Toby beamed.

"I kind of get why he went back to the store to work for a day and why he took the hammer, because at the end he makes his mother a bench for her garden. I liked that part."

"So it's a story of redemption," said Belle.

Cyndarria frowned. "I'm not sure what that means."

"Well," Belle explained, "that he redeems himself or atones for his mistake, which is more or less what you said earlier."

"Okay, yeah. I understand that part; what I don't get is the title. Mrs. Wackenstein is always asking us to explain the title of a story, but I can't really figure this one out. Is it just that the mother has a parsley garden, and that's where the story ends?"

"Well," said Belle, "it could be that. Actually, I kind of like the title."

"Mom, you just like anything that has to do with herbs," Cyndarria said.

Belle smiled. "That's true, I guess, but I had another thought. You know, parsley is a biennial plant, which means it needs two years to actually bloom. It's like it gets a second chance to complete its cycle."

Cyndarria nodded thoughtfully. "Sort of like Al in the story. He kind of gives himself a second chance by going back to the store and working for a day and then doing something good with the hammer that he earned."

"Seems like a possibility," said Belle.

"I think maybe William Saroyan is a smarter writer than I gave him credit for," said Cyndarria. "I never would have thought about using parsley that way. It's like he uses it as, I don't know, kind of a symbol."

"It's an interesting idea," mused Belle. "You might ask Mrs. Wackenstein what she thinks about that interpretation."

"Good idea," said Cyndarria, suddenly much more enthused about the following day's discussion. "If I say the word 'symbol,' she's gonna think I'm a genius!"

After dinner, Cyndarria helped with the dishes, then retired to her room to write her response to *The Parsley Garden*. Her thoughts seemed to flow more easily after having talked about it over dinner. Her page finished, she decided to call Henri to see if he had completed the assignment.

Henri picked up the phone on the third ring.

"Hi, Henri. It's Cyndarria."

"Hello, Cyndarria. How are you?"

"I'm good. I just finished writing my essay for English. Have you written yours yet?"

"Yes, and now I'm reading the article that Bread and Water gave me in Spanish today. It's pretty interesting."

"Have you gotten to the part about blood and gore yet?"

"Cyndarria," Henri said in a mock serious tone. "You must speak about these things correctly. It was ritual sacrifice, not blood and gore, and had significant religious meaning for the Aztecs."

"Saaahreee!" said Cyndarria. "So what have you learned so far that's so interesting?"

"Well, they played on a field that was usually somewhat larger than a football field, and they used a ball made of rubber that weighed about nine pounds. They weren't supposed to let it touch the ground during play, so they would throw themselves around a lot to keep that from happening. Because the ball was so heavy, players came out bruised and bloody, even though they wore protective gear. Once in a while, they might even get killed if the ball hit them hard in the head.

"They weren't allowed to use their hands during play, so they used their hips a lot. The object was to get the ball through a stone hoop, but it was up so high, like as much as 15-20 feet, that it was almost impossible to do that."

"Were there really human sacrifices after the game?"

"I guess in some places. So like maybe the captain of the losing team or even the whole team might be sacrificed after the game. But in Aztec society being sacrificed to the gods was considered an honor, so it might have been the winners who died. Or the article also says that sometimes captives were forced to play, and they were the ones who were sacrificed."

"Hmm," said Cyndarria, "with rules like that, I wonder why people even played."

"Good question. I haven't finished the article yet. Maybe they talk about it later."

"I haven't even started reading my article. Bread and Water said I might want to try making *mole*. I won't have to do my report till next Monday, so I would have time over the weekend to make it if I decided to give it a try. Maybe you could come over and help me out."

"Of course, Cyndarria," Henri said in his most courtly manner. "Your wish is my command."

"Were you on one knee and bowing in my direction when you said that?" Cyndarria asked with a chuckle. "You're too much, Henri. I've gotta go. See you tomorrow morning."

"Goodbye, Cyndarria."

The two friends hung up, and Cyndarria headed downstairs to see what was happening with the rest of the family. She found her father and brothers deep in concentration on an early Detroit Tigers game. Belle was in the kitchen.

"What're you making, Mom?" Cyndarria asked.

"Oh, I thought I'd take in some cookies for my classes tomorrow. It kind of perks them up to have something to eat."

"Want me to help?"

"Thanks, honey, I'm almost done. One of your Grandma Rose's old recipes."

Belle formed the stiff dough into balls, rolled them in a cinnamon and sugar mixture, dipped her finger in water and dribbled a tiny bit on top of each ball, then popped the final sheet of cookies into the oven.

"Yum," said Cyndarria. "Snickerdoodles. C'n I have one?"

"Sure, there are plenty."

Cyndarria took a bite out of a cookie. "Snickerdoodles is such a funny name. I wonder where it came from."

"Well, according to your grandma, it came from a German word which I can't pronounce that means snail noodles. Or maybe it was just kind of a fun nonsense word someone came up with."

"They don't really look like snails," said Cyndarria, "but they do kind of make me snicker or at least smile when I eat one, so I think maybe I'll go with that explanation."

"Works for me," said Belle.

"Mom, I've been thinking about this summer, you know, maybe helping out in the migrant program."

"So have you made a decision?" asked Belle.

"I'm kind of feeling that I'd like to do it. I like working with kids, and Sophia said she might want to help out too, if you needed another aide."

"That would be great. I'm sure there would be plenty to do for both of you. I think you'd find that you really enjoy it. It's very gratifying."

"Okay, well, I'm going to go upstairs and read for a while. Oh, Mom, I almost forgot. Do you think it would be okay if I tried running track this spring? I'd have to practice after school."

"Track?" Belle gave a little chuckle. "Did I ever tell you about my illustrious track career?"

"I didn't know you ran track. Were you a champion?"

"Hardly. It was the first year my school offered track for girls, and I thought I'd give it a try. I'm not sure why I decided to do pole vault. I think maybe I imagined that it would impress the coach. He was young, and I thought he was pretty cute."

"Mom!" Cyndarria felt a little embarrassed. She hadn't thought about her mother ever being interested in anyone other than her father.

Belle smiled. "Well, he was, and he was very nice and also very engaged. Anyway, at the first track meet, I took a bad fall on my second attempt to clear the bar and broke my arm. That ended the season for me. I didn't try out the next year."

"Wow, that's too bad." Cyndarria hesitated. "So do you think that it would be all right if I tried out?"

"I don't see why not. I'll check with Mrs. Stevenson next door. I'm pretty sure it would be okay with her if Toby and J.J. stayed there for a while after school. She likes having someone for her kids to play with. I could always come home a little early some days. I don't really have to do all my paper work at school; I could bring it home."

"Thanks, Mom." Cyndarria gave her mother a peck on the cheek, grabbed another cookie, and headed up to her room.

Belle looked after her firstborn as she left the kitchen. Cyndarria was changing, and mostly in ways that left Belle feeling reassured. She still found it hard to believe that her daughter was a teenager.

Belle remembered her own years as a teen, which had been filled with tremendous insecurities and considerable pain, caused mostly by her step-mother and step-sister. Agatha, her step-mother, had died of a sudden stroke when Belle was 17. Some-how, Belle couldn't bring herself to grieve the loss, except that it left her father alone again. He never admitted it to her, but she sensed that he, too, felt as though a burden had been lifted with Agatha's passing. Agnes had left their house by then, and for the next year, before Belle went off to college, she and her father experienced a certain peaceful contentment, for which Belle gave thanks on a regular basis.

Now he was in another home, and she feared that she might lose him sooner than she wanted. She wasn't ready to say goodbye.

"Hang in there, Paddy," she thought. "I'm coming to see you again this weekend."

A couple minutes later, Belle took the last batch of cookies out of the oven, then went into the living room to join Toad and her sons.

CHAPTER 19

FOR THE FIRST time she could remember, Cyndarria was actually looking forward to English. She felt good about her response to *The Parsley Garden* and was eager to hear Mrs. Wackenstein's reaction to her thoughts about the title.

She met up with Sophia outside the classroom before the bell. They were talking about Mrs. Wackenstein's assignment, and Cyndarria told her about parsley being a biennial plant and how that might help to explain the title.

"So in a way," she finished. "Parsley could kind of symbolize the second chance Al had."

"Wow," said Sophia. "I never thought about that."

Just then the bell rang. "See you later," Cyndarria said.

Only a few other students were in the room when she entered. Jodi and Christina, of course, and Sara, who sat busily writing. Mrs. Wackenstein was at her desk paging through a pile of papers. Five minutes later, the tardy bell rang, and just afterward Joey Bellow slid through the door and scooted to his seat.

Mrs. Wackenstein frowned. "Mr. Bellow," she said, "I'm very disappointed to see that you are continuing your irresponsible pattern of tardiness."

Joey tried unsuccessfully to look chagrined. "I'm really sorry, Mrs. Wackenstein," Joey said with utmost insincerity. "I'm late because I had to redo my assignment this morning after I got up because, uhh…" Joey was clearly struggling.

A sudden look of satisfaction appeared on his face. "Because my cat had her babies all over it during the night."

"That's disgusting," said Sara.

Mrs. Wackenstein sat perfectly motionless for a moment. "I see," she said finally. "And if I call your mother after class, I assume she will confirm your story."

Joey hesitated briefly. "Oh yes, ma'am. She helped me clean up the mess."

"Of course she did," said Mrs. Wackenstein.

"How many kittens?" asked Jodi.

"Three. We're gonna give 'em away. You want one?"

"That will be enough conversation about cats for the hour. Today we are going to discuss *The Parsley Garden*. I would like a few of you to read your written responses aloud."

Nobody volunteered, so Mrs. Wackenstein called on a handful of people. Cyndarria hesitated. She wanted to read hers but was a little nervous. What if her teacher didn't like it or thought her idea was stupid?

After various students had read, Mrs. Wackenstein looked around the room. Her gaze settled on Cyndarria. "Miss Thornwell," she said, "please share your thoughts with us."

"Here goes nothin'," Cyndarria whispered to Henri, then began reading.

"At first I thought I wasn't going to like this story. The title seemed boring and didn't really make me want to read it. After I finished it, though, I liked it better, because Al sort of redeemed himself by working at the store and earning the hammer that he had stolen the first time. I also liked that he made a bench for his mother because she worked so hard. And I liked the parsley garden, which was fresh and cool and seemed like a pleasant place to be on a hot summer evening."

"I liked that part too," interrupted Joey, obviously wanting to get back in his teacher's good graces.

"That will be enough, Mr. Bellow," ordered Mrs. Wackenstein. "Continue, Miss Thornwell."

Cyndarria nodded. "I was trying to figure out the meaning of the title and talked with my mom about it. She has an herb garden with different plants, and parsley is one of them. She told me that parsley is a biennial plant, which means it needs two years to complete its growth cycle. It doesn't flower the first year, but the second year gives it another chance. When I thought about it, it seemed as though that was kind of like Al. The second time around he got another chance, and that time he did what was right. At the end, he was no longer angry or humiliated about his first mistake. He felt better about himself, and did something really nice for his mother right out there in the parsley garden by using the hammer to build her a bench."

Undeterred by Mrs. Wackenstein's previous warning, Joey once again spoke up. "Carrots are a biennial plant, too. So are onions. Why didn't the guy call his story, *The Carrot Garden* or *The Onion Garden?*" Joey's parents were very successful muck farmers and cultivated both carrots and onions, and though he often played dumb, he knew a lot about farming because he worked long hours in the fields during the summer.

"Mr. Bellow!" Mrs. Wackenstein was irate.

"Yes, ma'am," said Joey, and dropped his head to his desk, but not before an impish grin crossed his face.

"Go on, Miss Thornwell."

Cyndarria resumed reading. "So I wonder if parsley might be sort of a symbol, and if it's something the author thought about. Did Saroyan know that parsley is a biennial, so he chose that plant on purpose? I don't think a lot of readers are aware of that fact, and the whole idea would be lost on them. Does that matter? Is that something authors even think about, or do they just write what they want and if people get it, fine, and if they don't, fine? I don't know the answer to that question."

Cyndarria stopped and waited hopefully. Mrs. Wackenstein seemed to be pondering her response. At last, she said, "Very good, Miss Thornwell."

Cyndarria couldn't believe what she had just heard her teacher say, but she managed to respond, "Thank you, Mrs. Wackenstein."

She looked at Henri, who grinned and gave her a thumbs up. "Way to go, Cyndarria," he whispered.

Sara raised her hand and was acknowledged by Mrs. Wackenstein. "It's funny," she said, "but I had the same thought about the title. It seemed pretty obvious to me."

Cyndarria gritted her teeth and grimaced. Of course Sara had to try to steal the spotlight.

"Even so," Sara continued in her most patronizing voice, "it does seem to be a rather abstruse title."

"What the heck does that mean?" asked Joey, who had little tolerance for what he considered to be Sara's pretensions.

"Mr. Bellow, you will raise your hand and wait to be called upon," warned Mrs. Wackenstein.

Henri raised his hand.

"Yes, Mr. Rousseau?"

"It means hard to understand or incomprehensible."

"No kidding!" muttered Joey under his breath.

Henri closed his pocket dictionary, which he always carried in his book bag.

Christina looked at Jodi and whispered, "What kind of weirdo carries a dictionary around?"

"The ones from Haiti," Jodi said, and the two girls muffled a snicker.

"Thank you, Mr. Rousseau. You are quite right."

Mrs. Wackenstein was silent for a moment, as though trying to decide how much further she wanted to let the discussion go. The truth was she didn't much like discussions. They made her nervous because they were unpredictable. The students would often blurt things out instead of raising their hands in an orderly manner, which she found endlessly annoying. In addition, they would occasionally pose questions she had no answer for, and that was unacceptable to her.

Her decision made, she stood and said, "Please hand up your papers. We have other things to do today."

What followed was another boring grammar exercise, which students were required to do silently while Mrs. Wackenstein began to pore over their essays.

Despite that, the rest of the class passed almost in a blur for Cyndarria. She kept thinking about what Mrs. Wackenstein had said to her and feeling, unexpectedly, that maybe she didn't dislike English as much as she had always thought.

She was anxious to tell her mother about her teacher's reaction to her idea concerning the title. Mrs. Wackenstein hadn't actually commented one way or another on the questions she had raised, and Cyndarria wondered why. Still, Mrs. Wackenstein hadn't rejected what she had written. In fact, she had said two words that Cyndarria had never before heard about her work from any English teacher, let alone Mrs. Wackenstein, "Very good."

She imagined a little conversation with her teacher, "Miss Thornwell," Mrs. Wackenstein would say, "I am pleased that you are m'ntaining high standards." The thought made her giggle to herself.

Still, as she looked at the grammar worksheet without really seeing it, she felt a little tingle of pride that would last all the way to social studies class.

CHAPTER 20

THE NEXT THREE days passed more or less uneventfully. No more escaped snakes or fire drills. On Friday, Spanish reports began on the *National Geographic* articles the students had been assigned. Señor Paniagua asked them all to write down one thing they learned from each of the reports. As it turned out, Cyndarria actually found them quite interesting. They got through eleven students on Friday, so Stevie escaped what he referred to as Oral Report Hell until the following Monday.

Cyndarria stopped to talk with Señor Paniagua after class.

"I found a recipe for *mole* in a Mexican cookbook of my mother's," she said. "It's kind of a simplified version, I guess. The recipe says that chicken is usually cooked in the sauce, so I'd have to get some, but other than that I think we have all the ingredients. I was wondering if maybe I could bring it in on Monday, and everyone could try a little. I'd talk to Mr. Johansson today to make sure it would be all right," she added, remembering the last time she had brought food in without permission. "If it's okay with you, that is."

Señor Paniagua beamed with delight. "I haven't tasted *mole* for a long time," he said. "It is one of the best traditional Mexican dishes. If you're sure it's okay with your mother, I would love to have you bring it in. Be forewarned, though, *mole* has a very distinct flavor that Americans are not familiar with, so the students may not appreciate it."

"I guess I'll give it a try," said Cyndarria, although she felt a small twinge of doubt. "If the kids don't like it, I'll just give it to you to take home to your family."

"That would be most satisfactory," said Señor Paniagua with a smile. "*Mole* is my wife's favorite food!"

After school, Cyndarria checked over the *mole* recipe again to make sure they had all the ingredients. There were ten: chicken broth, olive oil, onion, garlic, oregano, cumin, chili powder, flour and, the unexpected secret ingredients, cinnamon and dark chocolate. They were out of dark chocolate, plus they would need to buy a package of chicken breasts.

Her mother took her shopping after she got home, and they bought the needed ingredients, plus a few other things that Belle had on a list she'd made.

"Your father and I are going to see your grandpa tomorrow morning," she told Cyndarria on the way home from the store. "I'll need you to watch the boys."

"Is it okay if Henri comes over to help me make the *mole*?" Cyndarria asked. "He actually kind of likes to cook."

"Of course," said Belle. "J.J. and Toby love it when he comes over. He's like an older brother to them."

That evening, even though it was a Friday, Cyndarria forced herself to spend a half-hour reading her *National Geographic* article, keeping a few notes as she read, so it would be easier to include the five interesting facts she was supposed to list after her summary.

These were her facts:
1. *Mole* comes from the Nahuatl (an Aztec language) word *molli*, which means sauce.
2. There are several different kinds of *mole*, but the most popular one is called *mole poblano*, which was first made in the city of Puebla, Mexico.

3. There are many ingredients in a *mole* sauce, but chiles are always used, no matter the recipe.
4. *Mole poblano* contains cinnamon and chocolate, to give the sauce its dark color and unique flavor. It's the only *mole* that uses these two ingredients.
5. There are several different legends concerning exactly how *mole* was created. The one I like best is that it was first made sometime in the 16th century by poor nuns from the Convent of Santa Rosa in Puebla, who had to come up with a special dish for their archbishop. As it turned out, he loved the dish and the rest, as they say, is history!

The next morning Belle and Toad left at 10:00 to see Paddy. Cyndarria worked on a Lego project with J.J. and Toby until Henri arrived forty-five minutes later.

"I am here to help you make magic in the kitchen," he announced with a flourish.

"Oh, good," grinned Cyndarria "And here I thought we were making *mole*."

"Ah, Cyndarria," sighed Henri with feigned exasperation, "you have no imagination!"

"But I have the ingredients for *mole*," she replied, "so unless you brought some special ones for the magic you said you came to create, I guess we're stuck with them."

"So be it, Cyndarria. Tell me what to do first. Your wish, as always, is my command."

"You've got to come up with a new line, Henri. That one's getting old."

Having finished with their banter, the two friends set about making the *mole*.

"I think it might be easier just to cook the chicken breasts separately," said Cyndarria. "Then we can cut them up, pour the sauce over them, spread on some grated cheese and pop them in the oven to bake for a little while, so the chicken absorbs some of the flavor of the sauce."

Henri chopped the onions while Cyndarria prepared the chicken to stew. Together they added the rest of the ingredients to a separate pot. Soon the aroma of the sauce filled the air, causing the boys to interrupt their Lego project in order to see what was happening in the kitchen.

"Mmm, that smells kinda good," said J.J. "What is it?"

"It's called *mole*," said Cyndarria. "It's a famous dish from Mexico."

Toby frowned. "Where's Mexico?" he asked. "Is it by Michigan?"

"That's a very good question, Toby," said Henri. "It's good to know where places are. Mexico is a country below the United States. People speak Spanish there."

Toby brightened. "Miss Jamison taught us some Spanish words," he said.

"Cool, Toby," said Cyndarria. "What are they?"

He frowned, "I only remember two right now, *perro* and *gato*. Dog and cat. I like *perro* better because that's what Ollie is."

"I can count to ten," boasted J.J. "Do you want to hear me?"

"Absolutely," said Henri.

J.J. stood up a little straighter and began to recite the numbers, obviously pleased that he knew more words than his little brother. *"Uno, dos, tres, cuatro, cinco, seis, siete, ocho, nueve, diez."*

"Excellent, J.J.," said Henri enthusiastically, holding up his hand for a high-five.

"Do you like Spanish?" asked Cyndarria.

J.J. looked uncertain for a moment. "I guess so," he said. "It's fun to say the words."

135

"I can go *rrrrrr!*" exclaimed Toby, trilling his tongue. "That's why I like to say the word *perro*," he added, elongating the trill as long as he could.

"That's fantastic, Tobe," said Cyndarria. "It's hard for me to make that sound."

"I will teach you if you want," said Toby generously. "I'm really good at it."

"Thanks, buddy. That would be great."

Cyndarria and Henri finished making the *mole* sauce, aided by the boys, who stood on a chair by the stove in order to help with the stirring. Then they cut the chicken up into a casserole dish and poured the *mole* sauce over it. Cyndarria added a generous layer of cheese and slid it into the oven to bake for twenty minutes.

There was some of the sauce left in the pot, so they each sampled it. Toby made a face.

"It's kind of yucky," he said.

"I like it," said J.J. "It's different. Besides, it has chocolate in it."

Cyndarria wasn't sure what to think. "Well?" she said to Henri.

"It has a very strong flavor," he said. "I think it will taste better with the chicken."

"I kind of like it," said Cyndarria. "It tastes very exotic, not like anything else I've ever eaten."

While they were cleaning up the kitchen, Belle and Toad arrived home from their visit with Belle's father.

"How was Grandpa?" asked Cyndarria.

Belle sighed. "Not real well, honey. He hasn't been eating much, and he's taken to wandering. The other day Norma wasn't at her desk, and he walked right out the front door. He was in his pajamas. If one of the aides hadn't seen him heading down the sidewalk, who knows what would have happened?

"We didn't stay long because he was sleeping. He's been very wakeful at night lately, so he tends to take long naps during the day."

Belle walked over to the kitchen window and looked at her herb garden. She touched the soil, then went to get a small watering can from under the sink, poured water in it and carefully watered each plant.

"They were dry. I need to take better care of them." She tried to smile.

Cyndarria found it hard to look at her mother's face. She wasn't sure what to say. Finally, she offered, "I'll make the boys lunch."

"Thank you, honey," said Belle softly. "I think maybe I'll take a little nap."

Toad put his arm around his wife, kissed her forehead, then walked with her up the stairs.

CHAPTER 21

WHEN CYNDARRIA ARRIVED at school on Monday carrying the casserole she and Henri had made, she noticed Mr. Johansson deep in conversation with the local fire chief, Mr. Barnes, and another man she didn't know. Mr. Contreras, the head custodian, whose quick action had put out the fire, was with them. He had found it in a closet around the corner from Cyndarria's room, had run to get a fire extinguisher, and then managed to smother the flames before they spread.

Guillermo Contreras, called Memo by his friends, had been a custodian at the middle school for several years. The students loved him because he was very friendly and helpful and always attended their sporting events if he wasn't working. His wife Carmen had died giving birth to their fourth child ten years before, leaving Memo to raise a three-, eight- and nine-year-old. Maria Victoria, his youngest, was in Cyndarria's grade, though they had no classes together so didn't know each other very well.

Cyndarria stopped by the room of Mrs. Armstrong, who taught cooking and sewing classes, to ask if she might be willing to put the casserole in the oven to warm about halfway through first hour. Since it was her prep period, she had no students and was happy to do so.

"I have paper plates and plastic sporks which you can use if you like," Mrs. Armstrong offered. "Do you have a serving spoon?"

"Ooops," said Cyndarria. "I forgot to bring one."

"No problem," said Mrs. Armstrong. "I'll leave one out for you along with the plates and sporks."

"That would be great. Thank you so much."

A few minutes before the end of first hour, Mr. Johansson interrupted classes over the public address system. "Good morning, students," he said. "I would like your undivided attention, please. As you all know, we had a fire here at school last Friday. Due to the quick action of Mr. Contreras, it didn't spread, and no one was hurt. If you watched the local news Friday evening, you probably saw him interviewed. They called him a hero, and we are certainly grateful that he saved us from what could have been a catastrophe.

"Unfortunately, we do not yet know the identity of the perpetrator who set the fire. If any of you saw anything or anyone suspicious-looking last Friday, it is essential that you come to the office to give me a full report. As some of you may know, there have been two house fires in our community within the last year, and, according to fire chief Barnes, arson was the cause in each case. It's possible that the person who set those two fires set ours as well. I cannot emphasize too much how serious this is. I am asking you all to be very aware of the situation and alert to any possible problem that might occur again. Your parents will be informed of what happened and reassured that we are taking every precaution to ensure the safety of our students. Thank you. You are excused to second period."

On her way to Spanish class, Cyndarria went to Mrs. Armstrong's room to pick up her casserole along with the paper plates and sporks. She thought it smelled really good. When she entered the Spanish classroom and the other students saw that she was carrying food, they gathered around her for a look.

"Yum, tin-foil casserole," joked Joey. "My favorite!"

"Don't worry, Joey," said Cyndarria, "I'll let you have the first serving."

"Deal," he said.

Stevie, who had somehow managed to find a St. Augustine T-shirt, was first to speak. "I read an article about the St. Augustine alligator farm," he began, a nervous tremble in his voice. "Actually, it sounds like a pretty cool place, especially if you like gators." He smiled a little sheepishly. "Well, I guess that's obvious. That they have gators, I mean. They do have other animals there too, though, including snakes and birds."

Stevie checked his notes nervously, then went on. "In fact, they have what's called a southern cassowary, which is considered to be one of the most dangerous birds in the world. It has, like, this long, straight nail on its middle toe and can really do a lot of damage with it, even to humans. It actually killed a kid back in the 1920's. I've got a picture." Stevie held it up and walked part way up and down each aisle so his classmates could see the bird. Gradually, he seemed to relax.

"Course the gators are the most important thing. The alligator farm is the only place that has every kind in the world. They're called 'crocodilians', which includes gators, crocodiles and, umm, a couple others. There are 24 different species. Oh, and they have an albino, which is really cool."

Once again Stevie held up the magazine and showed the class. "So these are my five interesting facts:

1. The St. Augustine alligator farm was founded in 1893.
"Which means it's 88 years old. I did the math." Stevie grinned.
Joey chuckled. "Wow, Stevie, I'm impressed,"
2. Albino alligators come from the Louisiana bayou. A legend says that if you see one, it will bring you good luck.
3. The biggest gators can weigh up to a ton.
4. Crocodiles have pointed v-shaped snouts; gators have wider u-shaped snouts.

5. And just a little history—St. Augustine was founded in 1565 by the Spanish, which makes it our oldest city.

"So here's a question. What's the difference between a crocodile and an alligator?"

"Stevie, you just told us," said Sara. "Their snout shape."

"Nope, it's that you'll see one later and the other after while."

The class sat, momentarily mystified, then groaned collectively.

"Get it? See you later, alligator. After while…."

"We get it, we get it," said Joey. "Did you figure that one out all by yourself?"

"Nah, I read it in the article," Stevie admitted. "Anyway, that's my report."

Four other students followed Stevie, and then it was Cyndarria's turn. She summarized her article and read her five interesting facts. "So this is the part you've all been waiting for," she said dramatically. "Food! If you want to try the *mole*, come on up and I'll serve you."

Several of the kids came forward. Joey was first in line. "Fill 'er up, Cyndarria. I didn't have breakfast this morning."

Cyndarria served a large spoonful of *mole* to Joey and smaller portions to the rest of the students who were brave enough to try it. Penny was last in line.

"It smells good, Cyndarria," she said. "I really like Mexican food."

"Thanks, Penny. I hope you like this too.

"Señor Paniagua, would you like some?"

"*Claro que sí, Rosita! Of course. Gracias.*"

Cyndarria looked around the room to see her classmates' reactions, which ranged from those who eagerly scarfed the *mole* down, to those who barely tasted it, made a face, and dumped the rest in the waste basket at the back of the room. Joey, however, was enthusiastic.

"Got any left?" he asked eagerly. "I really like this stuff."

"Sure, you can have the rest, if you want," said Cyndarria, pleased that at least one person was actually enthused about the dish.

Six more students had to give their reports. Things were going pretty well until the fifth one, when Joey suddenly stood up and bolted for the door, his hand over his mouth and a desperate look on his face. He stumbled a bit and then, certain that he wasn't going to make it out of the room, he grabbed the waste basket, bent over, and proceeded to disgorge most of the *mole* he had consumed.

"Gross!" cried Jodi and Christina in unison.

Fortunately, at that point the bell rang, and the entire class filed quickly out of the room, staying as far as possible from Joey and the reeking waste basket.

Cyndarria stayed afterward for a minute to speak with Señor Paniagua. "Did you like the *mole*?" she asked hopefully.

"It was very tasty, Cyndarria. You did a good job. Thank you very much for making it."

"You're welcome. I'm sorry there isn't any left for your wife."

"She will likely use it as an excuse to have me take her to dinner at La Cucaracha," he said. "She loves that restaurant."

"Is it okay if I leave the casserole dish here? I'll pick it up after school."

"That would be fine. *Hasta mañana, Rosita.*"

"*Hasta luego.*"

"Well, that was exciting," said Alison, who had waited to walk with Cyndarria to their P.E. class.

"I feel kind of bad for Joey," said Cyndarria.

"Don't. It was his own fault. He ate so much so fast, I don't think he even chewed it."

"I guess. He'll probably never eat *mole* again."

"Worse things could happen to him. He's obviously managed to find lots of other things he likes to eat. By the way, are you ready for our first track practice after school today?"

"I'm a little nervous about it because I still don't really know what I want to do. I guess I'll just have to figure it out."

"Like I said before, Coach Sam will help you with that." Alison put her arm around her friend. "You're gonna do great, Cyndarria, and we're gonna have a lot of fun."

"I hope so," said Cyndarria, but there was a tiny part of her that wasn't sure.

CHAPTER 22

CYNDARRIA WENT DIRECTLY to the gym after her last class and changed into shorts and a T-shirt for track practice. She was the first one ready, so she sat at the bottom of the bleachers and waited for the others to arrive. She was both excited and nervous at the prospect of being on the track team.

As a child, Cyndarria had loved to run. She remembered an incident when she was in third grade, and a small group of friends were playing pom-pom-pull-away on one of the old tennis courts. All four of the other kids had been tagged and were waiting to catch her when she attempted one last run across the court.

"Cyndarria," Alison had shouted, "pom-pom-pull-away, come away or I'll pull you away."

"Come and get me!" she had yelled, then taken off sprinting at full speed, making a sudden stop or two and changing directions, just managing to escape the hands held out to tag her. She had felt an exhilarating triumph when she got safely across the court without being touched, even by Eddie Martinez, the fastest runner in the class.

At that time, Cyndarria had thought that losing her legs would be the worst possible thing that could happen to her, worse even than becoming blind or deaf, because it would mean she wouldn't be able to run anymore.

She smiled at the memory and wondered how her speed would stack up now against that of her teammates or athletes from other schools. Soon the rest of the team began to find seats on the bleachers, and both Coach McIntyre and Coach Sam stood in front of them.

The first order of business was to hand out an information sheet with the dates of track meets and other essential information for parents to read, plus a slip they were asked to sign, both giving their student permission to participate in track and confirming that their son or daughter had had a recent physical.

After the paperwork was handed out, Coach McIntyre addressed the group. "It's great to see so many students out for track this year. Some of you participated last year, but several of you are new. As of this afternoon, 23 boys have signed up and 17 girls, so this is the largest group we've had so far, which obviously makes Coach Sam and me pretty happy.

"We'll be having track practice four days a week. As a general rule, practice will last for one to one-and-a-half hours. We'll have three meets, one against each of the schools in our mini-league, which includes Cedar Ridge, Laurelton, and Chippewa Bend. A league championship will take place on the first Saturday in June. The exact times and dates of the meets are on the sheet I handed out earlier. Any questions?"

Stevie raised his hand. "Are practices inside or out?"

"Good question. If the weather is particularly cold or stormy, we'll be inside. Other than that, we'll practice on the track."

"Exactly how cold is particularly cold?" asked Sara.

"Ah, I see we have a lawyer in the group." Coach McIntyre grinned. There were always kids who demanded a precise number and then would hold him to it, as if it were the law. "Usually if it's down in the 30's or lower, we're inside, especially if it's windy. Given that it's early April, that shouldn't happen very often, but with Michigan weather, you never know. Any more questions?"

There were none.

"Great," said Coach Sam. "Girls, I want you to come with me to that end of the gym." She pointed to her left. "Guys will stay with Coach McIntyre."

And with that, track season began.

There was a lot more to know than Cyndarria had ever imagined, and each practice Coach Sam gave them a variety of exercises and activities to help them become better runners, including things like high knees, butt kicks, and high skips. They did sprints, which Cyndarria hated, and longer runs, which she found she almost enjoyed. They always finished practice with a slow jog to cool down and, finally, stretches. On three days it was warm enough to be outside, and they went for longer runs to begin to build their stamina. By the end of the week, Cyndarria was surprised to find that she was becoming more and more comfortable and started looking forward to their first track meet at the end of the month.

Plummeting temperatures and freezing rain were predicted for Friday night and Saturday. Cyndarria, Alison, and Sophia had thought they might get together to run on their own, but not in that weather.

When Cyndarria got home on Friday, her mother and brothers were already there. Belle was in the kitchen making some soup, which was her favorite meal on chilly nights. Toad wouldn't be home till much later.

"Hi, Mom," said Cyndarria. "What kind of soup?"

"Chicken vegetable. I wanted to use up that left-over chicken."

"Smells yummy."

Cyndarria walked into the living room to see her brothers kneeling on the floor coloring, and just as she did, Toby began to wail.

"Mommy," he cried.

146

Cyndarria knew that voice and the look on her younger brother's face. Clearly, he thought that he had just suffered a gross injustice.

"J.J. taked my bestest crayon, and I need it!"

"Cyndarria, can you work things out with the boys?" Belle asked from the kitchen.

"I'll try." She turned to her younger brother.

"What's the problem, Tobe?"

"J.J.'s got my crayon. It's *my* crayon, and I need it right now."

Cyndarria eyed J.J., who was studiously avoiding her gaze.

"Do you have his crayon?" she asked.

"It's not *his* crayon," J.J. said. "He doesn't *own* it."

"It is too my crayon!" Toby insisted, irate that his older brother would deny him.

"Umm, okay," said Cyndarria. "Give me the crayon, J.J."

"Cyndarria!" Now it was J.J. who was upset.

"I just want to see it. Maybe there's another color close to that one that you could use."

J.J. refused to look at Cyndarria, his jaw set stubbornly. He crossed his arms and held tight to the crayon.

"J.J., please."

"It's not fair," he said, a position which he had taken to using quite a bit lately, feeling that it protected him from having to do anything he didn't want to.

"Oh, for cryin' out loud, J.J., just show me the crayon."

"Unnhh!" said J.J., a sound Cyndarria translated as marking J.J.'s extreme displeasure at the unfairness of her request.

"J.J.!" Toby screeched. "Don't be so mean!" He started to cry.

"I'm not being mean," shouted J.J. He stood and stomped his feet, and in a moment he too was crying.

At that point, Belle walked in the living room. "Boys!" she spoke sternly. "Do you both need a time out?"

When she received no answer other than continued wailing, she walked over to J.J. and held out her hand. "Give me the crayon, J.J. Now."

"Unnhh!" he repeated, but finally handed it over. "It's not fair," he mumbled.

Belle looked at the crayon in question. It was blue and looked quite a bit like two or three other blues in the pile of crayons. She grabbed one, then put both hands behind her back.

"Okay," she said. "We're going to play a little game. Each of you will choose a hand, and you get whichever crayon is in that hand, and that will be the end of it. Understood?"

Begrudgingly, the boys nodded.

"I go first," said J.J.

"No, me!" protested Toby.

"Okay, okay, here's what we'll do," said Cyndarria. "I'm going to pick a number between one and ten, and whoever gets closest to it picks first. Just so there's no argument about who says his number first, you're each going to write your number down and hand it to Mom. I'll tell her my number, and then she'll announce who gets to pick a crayon first."

Belle rolled her eyes. "Does it really have to be this complicated? Don't answer that. Apparently, it does. Okay, tell me your number."

Cyndarria whispered it in her mother's ear and then handed a scrap of paper and a pencil to each boy. After careful deliberation, they wrote down their numbers, then handed them to their sister.

Cyndarria looked at each one. "Okay, J.J.'s number is four and Toby's number is six. What number did I give you, Mom?"

"Ten," said Belle. "Toby, you get to go first."

"Goodie!" Toby exclaimed. "I choosed my age, and it was right!" He studied his mother carefully. "That one," he said and pointed to her right arm.

"I wanted that one," objected J.J.

"A deal's a deal, J.J.," said Cyndarria. "You get the other one."

Belle handed each of her sons his crayon. Toby's face lit up with delight. "I got my crayon," he crowed.

J.J. did not look happy, but he knew when he was beaten. He looked at his crayon for a moment and then shrugged. "I guess this one's okay," he said.

"Way to be a good sport, J.J.," said Cyndarria. "So, can I color with you guys?"

"You can help me, Cyndarria," said Toby. "You can color the green part, okay?"

"Sounds good." Cyndarria looked through the crayons, picked out a green one, knelt beside her younger brother, and began to color.

Peace restored, Belle turned and walked back into the kitchen to finish making the soup.

CHAPTER 23

THE FREEZING RAIN began falling a little after Toad got home Friday evening. It fell steadily, and Cyndarria snuggled under her quilt. She found the pattering of rain on the roof to be comforting. Soon she was asleep and had a short, silly dream in which Mrs. Wackenstein opened her mouth to scold the class, and nothing came out. Frustrated, she got up on her desk and began jumping up and down, omitting a soundless scream. In the distance, Cyndarria heard the passing bell ring once, twice, three times, and the dream ended.

Moments later, she felt a hand on her shoulder and heard her father's voice. She rolled over and squinted up at him. The half-light of morning filled the room, and Cyndarria could see a look of concern on his face.

"Is something wrong?" she asked as she stifled a yawn.

Toad shook his head slightly. "It's your grandpa, Cyndarria. Your mother and I have to go to see him."

"Oh my gosh, Dad, is he okay? He's okay, isn't he?" Suddenly she felt as though she might cry.

Toad hesitated, unsure how much he should say. "Grandpa went out one of the doors that was supposed to be locked last night. He…he got lost. They found him this morning lying under a tree."

Cyndarria's hand went to her mouth. She understood without asking what had occurred. Her face crumpled, and she fell against her father's chest. He held her tight.

"Oh, Daddy," she sobbed.

"Sweetheart, we have to ask you to stay here and take care of the boys."

"Do I have to tell them?"

"No, no, no," Toad reassured her. "Just let them sleep for now. Your mother and I will talk with them when we get home."

Cyndarria nodded. "Are you leaving right away?"

"As soon as Mom finishes dressing."

"Is she…is she all right?"

"Your mother is a strong person, Cyndarria. She's going to pull through this." Toad gave her a small smile of encouragement.

He leaned forward and kissed his daughter on the forehead. "You're being very brave, Cyndarria. Thank you."

"Okay."

Toad got up and left the room. Cyndarria sat on the edge of her bed, feeling oddly empty. "Oh, Grandma Rose," she said finally. "I hope you're there with Grandpa."

The morning passed quietly. Fortunately, the boys were content to start another Lego project. After Cyndarria made them breakfast, one-eyed Egyptians again, she washed the dishes and went back up to her room, not wanting her brothers to start asking questions about why their parents had left so early and hadn't yet returned home.

It was almost 11:00 by the time they arrived. Cyndarria heard the garage door go up and hurried downstairs. She was anxious to see Belle, but dreaded what might be the look on her face. She didn't know if she could bear to see her mother cry.

When Belle and Toad came in, Toby jumped up and ran over to his father, expecting to be grabbed up and swung around while he giggled.

"Daddy!" he yelled happily, his arms up.

Toad picked up his son and walked with him over to the table where J.J. sat working on his Lego project.

"Aren't you going to swing me around, Daddy?" Toby asked.

"Not right now, Tobe." He set his son down.

J.J. looked up. "Look at what we're making, Dad. Come and help us."

"Maybe later. Your mom and I have something we need to talk to you about first."

Toby sat studying a blue Lego piece he had just picked up, trying to decide where he wanted to put it. J.J., however, noticed the tone in his father's voice and frowned. He looked at Toad quizzically.

"Okay," he said.

Toad sat down at the table. Belle came and stood beside him. Her eyes were red-rimmed but clear.

J.J. looked carefully at his mother. "Hi, Mommy," he said softly. "Are you sad?"

Belle nodded.

"Did something bad happen?" J.J. asked.

Belle didn't trust her voice to speak. She gripped Toad's shoulder. He understood.

"Yes, buddy. Something bad happened, so Mommy's sad."

Tears welled up in J.J.'s eyes. Toby saw his brother, and his own face changed. He started to cry.

"I don't want Mommy to be sad," Toby said. He looked at his mother. "Don't be sad, Mommy."

Belle felt her heart ache with love for her sons. She patted Toby's hand. "I'll get better, sweetie."

"What happened, Mommy?" asked J.J.

Belle looked at Toad. "Do you remember last year how Grandma Rose went to heaven?" he asked.

The boys nodded slowly.

"Well, last night Grandpa went to heaven too."

"So we can't visit him anymore?" asked Toby.

"No, Toby, not when he's in heaven."

"But Grandma Rose can visit him, can't she?" asked J.J. He looked hopefully at his father.

"I think she probably can," said Toad.

"Good," J.J. seemed relieved. "That way he won't be lonely."

A moment later J.J. got up. "I have to get something," he said. He ran up the stairs. When he came back down, he had a small object in his hands.

He held it up. "It's the doggie Grandpa whittled for me. I named him Oliver the Second. I think maybe he would like to sit and watch me now."

"That's very nice, J.J." Toad patted his son's head. "I'm sure that would please your grandpa."

"I think so too," said J.J.

An hour later they had left-over soup for lunch. Hoping to sound cheerful, Cyndarria said, "This always tastes better the second day."

Belle nodded. "It does, doesn't it?"

Afterward, Toad left for the restaurant, where Antoine was filling in for him, and Belle went to their bedroom to begin making arrangements for her father's memorial service.

"Your grandfather didn't want a funeral," she told Cyndarria. "He just wanted some of his friends to get together, tell some stories, and have a meal on him. Dad says we can have the memorial in the banquet room at the restaurant. It can seat 75 people, which should be just about right. That will make feeding everybody a lot easier."

"Can I do anything to help, Mom?" asked Cyndarria.

"Not right now, honey. Thank you. I'm going to make some calls. I'll need to talk to your Aunt Agnes, of course, and there are several others I should contact. I'd appreciate it if you'd take care of the boys. If you'd like to invite Henri over to keep you company, that would be fine."

"Thanks, Mom. Maybe I will."

Cyndarria sat with the boys and worked on their Lego projects with them for a while. They were subdued, but she could see they were okay. Once in a while J.J. would say something to Oliver the Second, explaining to him what he was doing on his project.

"You guys," she said, "I think maybe I'll invited Henri over to help us out. Would that be okay with you?"

"I like it when Henri helps us," said Toby. "He's good at Legos."

"Hi, Henri," said Cyndarria when he answered the phone.

"Hello, Cyndarria. How are you this wet and stormy day?"

"Not so good, Henri. My…my grandpa passed away last night."

Henri was silent for a moment. "Oh, Cyndarria, I am so sorry. What can I do?"

"Would you want to come over?"

"Of course, Cyndarria. Give me fifteen minutes. I have to finish helping my father with something first, and then I'll be over. I'm sure it will be fine with him."

"Thanks, Henri. I, umm, I...thanks."

An hour later Belle came downstairs. She sat at the kitchen table looking at some papers from her students but found she couldn't concentrate. She went into the living room where Cyndarria, Henri, and the boys were now playing dominoes.

"I'm going to look through our family pictures and pick out some of your grandpa," she said. "I'd like to have a few to display at the memorial service."

"Do you want me to help?" asked Cyndarria.

"Not right now, sweetie, thank you. Maybe later."

Belle went back upstairs, and the four kids remained on the living room floor carefully placing dominoes end to end till they had used them all, then sat quietly, not quite ready to pick them up and start over again. Cyndarria held out her hands to her brothers, and for a while, she, J.J., Toby, and Henri held hands and bowed their heads.

CHAPTER 24

BELLE AND TOAD, with Agnes's blessing, decided to hold Paddy's memorial the following Saturday at noon. With Cyndarria's help, Belle put together a nice display of family pictures and also collected a few small items that were representative of her father—some of his fishing lures, a couple of the objects he had whittled, the Purple Heart he had been awarded after his service in World War II, a fancy framed certificate with the family name, O'Brien, and an explanation of its meaning, and his high-school senior picture.

Toad would prepare a lunch of Paddy's favorite foods: meat loaf, baked potatoes, broccoli with cheese sauce, gelatin salad with fruit cocktail, and raw-apple cake for dessert.

Belle contacted several relatives and a few of his old friends, who said they would get in touch with several others. She talked with Reverend Gallagher, the pastor of the church Paddy had attended, and asked him to say a few words.

"I heard about Paddy's passing," he said. "I'm so sorry. I always liked and admired your father, Belle. His life was sometimes very difficult, but he persevered and, for the most part, managed to keep that wry Irish sense of humor of his. It would be an honor to speak at his memorial."

Saturday morning dawned clear and chilly. Toad left early to begin preparations at the restaurant. Belle dressed carefully—a gray suit and a string of pearls that her father had given her when she graduated from high school. Cyndarria wore the dress her parents had bought her especially for the father-daughter dance back in February. It was a deep maroon with long sleeves and a pretty lace trim.

After she was dressed, Cyndarria went to check on her brothers. J.J. was ready, but Toby was struggling with a moment of indecision. He held up the two shirts he was trying to choose between.

"Which one would Grandpa like better, Cyndarria?" he asked.

"They're both fine, Toby. Which one do you like best?"

"This one," he said, holding up a blue-and-white checked shirt. "Do you think Grandpa would like it?"

"You know, Toby, I think Grandpa had a shirt almost exactly like that one. I'm sure he would love it."

Toby looked relieved. "Okay."

"So do you need any more help? Mom wants to leave pretty soon."

"No. I can finish by myself."

"Okay, buddy. See you downstairs in a while."

Fifteen minutes later, everyone was ready, and they made the 10-minute drive to the restaurant. In the banquet room, the tables were covered with white tablecloths. Juliette had created small floral centerpieces for each one and a larger one made up of lilies and red roses for the serving table. Off to one side was a podium for the use of the speaker. Belle wasn't sure if anyone besides Reverend Gallagher and herself would want to speak, but she planned to invite those in attendance who had a story they wanted to share to come forward.

Agnes arrived early and, fortunately, was not wearing the purple and orange coat she had worn for her last visit. Instead, she was dressed almost entirely in black, with the exception of the rather sizable purple feather which adorned the black cloche she was wearing and which she left on after removing her coat.

Belle approached her step-sister and embraced her. Agnes sniffled and dabbed her eyes, which manifested no sign of tears.

"I'm so glad you're here," said Belle. "It would mean a lot to Dad."

"Of course I'm here," said Agnes. "Do you think my hat is suitable? It's new."

Belle was certain that Agnes was not so much concerned about the appropriateness of her headwear as she was about eliciting a compliment.

"It's lovely," said Belle.

Agnes preened. "It is, isn't it? I fell in love with it as soon as I saw it."

Belle led Agnes to the front table. "This will be the family's table," she said. "Why don't you have a seat?"

Agnes seemed happy to comply. She much preferred to sit and watch and not have to mingle with people she didn't know. The truth was she wasn't all that fond of most of her relatives either, so she simply remained seated.

Others began to arrive, and Belle embraced them all and thanked them for coming. She was happy that so many had turned out to honor her father. When everyone was seated and all of the food was on the serving table, it was a little past 12:00. Reverend Gallagher stepped behind the podium to say grace. His prayer was short and eloquent, and then Toad invited everyone to come up and serve themselves.

"Paddy wouldn't want anyone to go hungry, and he never wasted anything, especially food," he said, "so you are obligated to eat everything we've prepared."

"Gladly!" Cedric Blunt, one of Paddy's oldest friends, said loudly.

A friendly chuckle rippled through the audience.

Much to Toad's satisfaction, those present seemed to take his admonition seriously, and there was very little left over. The raw-apple cake was particularly popular, so much so that Belle and the children ended up sharing one piece.

"I want my own," said Toby plaintively.

"Dad will make one tomorrow, just for us," Belle assured him.

"Okay," he said. "I guess."

Once everyone was finished eating and had a second cup of coffee or tea, Reverend Gallagher rose to address the audience.

"Belle asked me to say a few words today, and I am happy to honor her request to do just that. To say a few. I know she plans to address the group and she, of course, knew her father best, so it is appropriate that I cede the floor to her in just a moment. About Paddy I would say simply that he lived up to his family name, O'Brien. He was a strong and honorable man and carried himself with a humble nobility of bearing that I always admired.

"He was a devoted husband and a loving father, who dedicated himself tirelessly to the care and well-being of his family. Paddy suffered the loss of both his beloved wives, which left him to care for his daughters by himself and, after they were gone, to find a way to live a contented and meaningful life alone. Looking at his grandchildren today, Cyndarria, J.J. and Toby, it's clear that the qualities he imparted to Belle have been passed on to the next generation. I'm sure Paddy would be filled with pride at seeing them now."

Reverend Gallagher smiled and nodded at Belle. "I think that should be sufficient to fulfill my quota of words," he said. "Thank you for inviting me to be here and to share in the celebration of your father's life, Belle. The floor is now yours."

Belle stood and stepped behind the podium, grateful that Toad had been thoughtful enough to place it there, perhaps knowing that she might need something to help support her as she spoke.

"Thank you so much for your generous words, Reverend Gallagher. And thank you again to all of you who came today to share in this celebration as well. I know my father would be humbled by your presence. We served the meal first today because that is what he would have wanted, and he would have been delighted to see you eat your fill. This second part, what he would have called 'speechifying', he would not have been so happy about. He was a modest man and would have been embarrassed to hear so many kind words spoken publically about himself.

"So I'm sorry, Dad, but this is the way it's going to be today."

Several people smiled and nodded. A couple said, "Hear, hear!"

"Some of my favorite memories of my father are from my youth. He was a man who understood what children love, and it pleased him to provide it. One of the best things he did was to build me a tree house in a big old box elder in our back yard. I can't begin to count the hours my friends and I spent there during the summer. It was our own special, private, little world, and we loved it. Actually, it was the place where a boy first held my hand."

"I'm shocked!" said Toad loudly, and everyone laughed.

"He also hung a heavy rope from another tree which had a thick knot on the bottom for me to put my feet on. I could climb up into the crotch of the tree with the rope and launch myself into space. It was glorious. Kids from all over the neighborhood would come to swing on that rope. The superintendent's son came over once, somehow managed to fall from the rope, and broke his arm. Dad was afraid he might be sued, but I think the superintendent was a very wise man. He understood what a wonderful gift my father had given to so many kids, and never held his son's broken arm against Dad.

"When I was five, he taught me how to bait a hook and cast. The first fish I caught was a six-inch bass. He kind of laughed and said, 'That little guy is almost as small as you are. I guess maybe we'd better throw him back.' Which we did. Actually, I was relieved because I really didn't like the idea of having to clean a fish.

"When my step-mother Agatha passed, her daughter Agnes was already grown and had left home. The last couple years my father and I spent together before I went off to college are ones that I'll never forget, and for which I am immensely grateful. We loved taking turns reading the paper to each other, and then we would work together on the daily crossword. We weren't able to finish it very often, but we had fun trying.

"Now that he's gone..." For the first time, Belle's throat constricted. She waited a moment. "Now that he's gone, I see even more clearly what an extraordinary father and man he was, what an enduring blessing he was and continues to be in my life. I feel so fortunate to have had him with me for so long. I am beyond grateful that my children had the privilege and pleasure of getting to know him."

Belle was finished. She smiled. "At this time, if any of you would like to share a story about my father with us, please come up and do so."

And share they did.

CHAPTER 25

THERE WAS A quiet buzz in the room for a few moments, and then an older gentleman came forward. He was slender and still had a nice head of white hair. His cheeks were ruddy, and his blue eyes behind wire-rim glasses crinkled when he smiled. He wore a worn wool sport coat that had clearly seen better days, a slightly wrinkled white shirt, and a tie. He had a limp and walked with a cane but held himself erect.

"Good afternoon," he said when he arrived at the podium. "My name is Cedric Blunt. My momma always told me I did too good a job of livin' up to my last name, but I told her, 'Momma, I'm just followin' yer example.' She didn't like that too much." He grinned and the audience chuckled appreciatively.

"Well, in all seriousness," he continued, "Paddy was a great friend of mine. For a lot of years, we'd meet Saturday mornin's at Betty's Coffee Shop for a cup a' joe—that's coffee for you youngin's who aren't familiar with that particular expression, and one of Betty's famous cinnamon rolls.

"Paddy had a lot of stories, and he loved to tell 'em. One of his favorites was when some fellah from the electric company came to his shop and told him that he hadn't paid his bill, and he was gonna have to cut off his service if Paddy didn't take care of it right away.

"Paddy told the fellah he didn't have his checkbook with him, but would write a check that night and send it out the next day. The guy didn't believe him and got pretty angry, but old Paddy just sat and looked at him. Finally, the guy threatens him and says, 'If you don't give me a check for what you owe right now, I'm going to go outside, climb that pole, and cut off your service.'

"So Paddy says, 'Wait a minute. It's my lunchtime. I'm just gonna grab my sandwich, and I'll come out and watch you do it.'

"The guy knew he was beat. He just growled at Paddy, 'To hell with you,' and turned around and left."

Again the crowd chuckled.

"Paddy loved stories like that. He'd laugh along with us whenever he told one. I'm glad he was my friend. I'm going to miss him."

Cedric walked slowly back to his seat. When he got there, another man who had been sitting at the same table got up. He was shorter than Cedric, but clearly outweighed him by at least 50 pounds. He had a shiny, bald pate with a few long, gray hairs combed over the top and wore a plaid flannel shirt and bib over-alls.

"I'm Sylvester MacPherson, but everybody calls me Mac. I'm thinkin' you can probably guess why. Sylvester is kind of a silly name. I don't know what possessed my mother to give it to me."

The audience members smiled, clearly enjoying Mac as much as they had enjoyed Cedric.

"One of my favorite memories of Paddy had to do with fishin'. He liked to take his boat out and troll for muskie. One afternoon him and me went out together. He had just got this new lure called a Mister Twister, and he was pretty excited to try it out. After we'd been fishin' about half an hour, he got a big bite. He was havin' trouble reelin' it in. We was real close to shore, so he jumped out and waded up to the beach, pullin' the fish with him.

"When he landed it on the sand, we could see it was a big old muskie, and he looked mean. He was floppin' around, and we

163

was both a little nervous about grabbin' him. Finally that fish managed to break the line, and off he swam. Old Paddy looked pretty unhappy.

'Don't worry, Paddy', I sez, 'we'll get another one.'

'I don't care so much about the dang fish,' he sez, just miserable. 'He got my Mister Twister!' "

Mac shook his head and grinned. "I'm not sure he ever got over losin' that lure. He told stories about it for years afterward.

"Paddy was the best fishin' buddy I ever had, and I'm hopin' the Lord has a big old pond up there and gives him another chance to catch a muskie."

It seemed that no one else was going to speak, and Belle was about to rise to thank everyone again for coming when J.J. stood and approached the podium. When he got there, he stood on tiptoe and still couldn't see over the top. Toad went to the podium and picked up his son.

"Thanks, Daddy," whispered J.J.

There was a microphone that none of the other speakers had needed, but Toad held it up for his son.

"I'm J.J.," he began. "My grandpa liked to whittle. He was really good at it. He said when I got a little older, I could have a jack knife of my own and he would teach me." J.J. frowned and seemed momentarily to lose his voice. Toad found himself holding his breath, waiting for his son to collect himself and continue.

After a moment, J.J. pulled a small object out of his pocket and held it up. "My grandpa made this for me. It's a dog. It looks kind of like our real dog at home, so I named him Oliver the Second. I used to keep him in a box in my room, but now I put him under my pillow and keep him there. Well, except for when the tooth fairy comes. I think she might be scared of dogs.

164

"I love Oliver the Second and I love my Grandpa. I miss him."

J.J. stopped talking. "I'm done, Daddy," he whispered.

Toad set his son down gently. J.J. held up his hand. Toad took it, and they walked together back to their seats.

Everyone in the audience seemed content to end things on that note. Cyndarria got up and walked over to the table where Henri and his father were sitting. The happy memories and funny stories of the memorial had begun to lift the weight of sadness she had felt all week, and now that it was over, she felt a kind of gentle release.

"Thank you for coming, Dr. Rousseau. Thanks, Henri. It means a lot to have you here."

"You are welcome, Cyndarria," said Emmanuel. "It was a very nice memorial. Your mother spoke beautifully. I'm sure your grandfather would have been pleased."

"I think so too," said Cyndarria.

She turned to her friend. "Henri, Ali and Sophia and I are thinking about running tomorrow afternoon. Coach Sam encouraged us to do that on weekends if we had time. Would you like to run with us?"

"You are very dedicated, Cyndarria. I'm impressed. What time are you planning to run?"

"I think about 3:00. We thought we'd go over to the track and run there."

"Would that be okay, Father?" Henri asked.

"I think that sounds like a very good plan," said Emmanuel.

"Great!" said Cyndarria, happy to once again be able to look forward to and enjoy her normal activities.

"Okay," said Henri. "See you tomorrow."

"Bye, Dr. Rousseau," said Cyndarria, then went back to join her family.

When she got there, she found that Aunt Agnes had already departed, apparently pleased with the small box of leftovers Toad had retrieved from the serving table and given to her.

A half hour later, the last guest had left. "Time to go home," said Belle. "Your father will come after he finishes here."

On the way, Cyndarria sat quietly. She was glad that the memorial service had helped her to feel better. She looked at J.J. and felt a surge of pride in him. When she got home, she would go upstairs, sit in Grandma Rose's chair, and tell her all about it.

CHAPTER 26

THE NEXT MORNING Toad made a raw-apple cake for the family, as promised. Cyndarria sliced the apples and chopped the walnuts for the cake while her father mixed the batter, adding the vanilla and cinnamon, which would fill the kitchen with a delicious aroma as it baked. While it cooled, he made a butter-cream icing, which he would spread on far too thickly for Belle's taste.

"Too sweet and too many calories," she always objected, but that didn't deter Toad.

"The kids love it this way," he would respond, but the truth was his own sweet tooth was as much to blame for the excess.

Like his siblings, Toby was delighted that they would get a whole cake to themselves. "C'n I have a piece right now?" he asked even before it was out of the oven.

"Nope," said Toad. "Yah gotta wait till after dinner."

"Awww, all right," said Toby. "But then I get an extra big piece!"

"We'll see how many vegetables you eat first," said Toad.

After dinner, Cyndarria went up to her room to do a science worksheet her class had been assigned as homework. She and her friends had agreed they would meet at her house and then go over to the track together later that afternoon. Alison and Sophia arrived a little before 3:00.

Belle opened the door for them. She smiled. "It's nice to see you, girls," she said. "I understand you're going to do a little running this afternoon."

The girls nodded. "I was really sorry to hear that Cyndarria's grandpa had died," said Alison. "She always said nice things about him."

"I met him once a few years ago," added Sophia. "He gave Cyndarria and me some money for ice cream. I wish my grandpa would do that!"

"Thank you, girls," said Belle. "You're very sweet."

Just then the front doorbell rang again. It was Henri, who smiled broadly when he saw his friends. "Hi, Ali. Hi, Sophia. Are you ready to run a few miles?"

"Oh, at least 10," said Sophia. "Maybe 15 or 20."

"Oh yeah, for sure," agreed Ali. "What do you think, Henri?"

"I think you are crazy!" Henri grinned.

Belle had gone to call up the stairs for Cyndarria, who came bounding down ready to go.

"Bye, Mom," she said. "We'll be back by 5:00. Do you think maybe you could order us a pizza? We're gonna be starving!"

"I'll see what I can do," said Belle, who felt relieved to see Cyndarria back to her normal self. "Any special requests for toppings?"

"How about pepperoni and mushrooms?" she asked her friends.

"Sounds good," said Ali. The others agreed.

Their post-practice feed established, the four friends left the house and headed for the school track.

The day was somewhat warmer than Saturday had been, definitely feeling more like spring. They saw pussy willows along the way, and the crocuses and forsythia had begun to bloom. The girls skipped happily along and Henri jogged beside them.

168

When they got to the track, they were doing some stretches when Cyndarria noticed a dark shape lying on the other side of the field.

"You guys, look!" she said. The dark shape moved and seemed to try to sit up.

"Oh my gosh!" exclaimed Ali. "Who is that?"

They ran across the field and were stunned to see Maria Victoria Contreras sitting with her head in her hands.

"Maria Victoria! What happened?" asked Sophia, clearly unnerved. "Are you okay?"

Maria Victoria looked at them. She appeared to be a little woozy. "I…I think so," she said. "I'm still just a little dizzy."

She tried to stand, but fell back down.

Henri knelt down beside her. "You must sit for a few minutes, Maria Victoria. Can you tell us what happened?"

"I'm not really sure," she said. "It all happened so fast."

"Are you sick?" asked Ali. "Do you need to go to the hospital?"

"No, no, I think I'm okay. I came here to run for a while, like Coach Sam suggested. I was stretching when a guy came up kind of out of nowhere. He had on a hoodie pulled down around his face, so I couldn't really see what he looked like. He asked me my name, and when I told him…"

She hesitated. "I guess I shouldn't have done that because then he asked if I was the daughter of the guy who put out the school fire, the one who had been on TV. I said yes, and I really thought he would say something nice about it, but he just kind of looked at me weird and said that's too bad.

"And then he slapped me hard and punched me in the stomach. I guess I fainted. That's all I remember. I don't know how long I've been out."

"We didn't see anyone else around when we got here," said Cyndarria. "He must've run off right away. What a coward!"

169

"Why do you think he did it?" asked Sophia. "Do you think he could have been the one who set the fire?"

"I don't know," said Maria Victoria.

"Whatever the reason, he's a real sicko," said Cyndarria. "We have to report it right away. Like today."

"We can walk you home if you think you can walk," said Henri. "Or I can run over to your house and tell your father, and he can come pick you up. You live on Beech Street, don't you, across from the church?"

"Yes, but my dad's not at home right now. He had to run an errand over in Cedar Ridge."

"Well, then come to my place," said Cyndarria. "We can put some ice on your lip, and you can rest. You can tell my mom and dad what happened. They'll know what to do."

After Maria Victoria had recovered enough to walk, they headed back to Cyndarria's house. When Belle saw them, she was immediately concerned. She got ice to put on Maria Victoria's lip, which had stopped bleeding, but was quite swollen. She called to Toad, who joined them in the living room. The boys were next door playing, much to Belle's relief. She didn't particularly want them listening to anything scary.

"Can you tell us what happened, Maria Victoria?" asked Belle. She noticed the girl appear to shrink back briefly. "Take your time, sweetie. We're here for you."

Maria Victoria began hesitantly, feeling a little uncomfortable talking to adults she didn't know. The other four helped her out from time to time with details she had already told them and asking questions they hadn't thought of before. Finally, the story told, she sat back and looked at Belle and Toad.

"Well, it's clear we need to report this to the authorities right away," said Toad. "This guy is obviously dangerous. I'll get hold of Mr. Johansson. I imagine he's already working with the police, and he'll likely have someone he can contact."

"Good," said Belle. She turned to Maria Victoria. "Would you like to call home to see if your father is back? We can take you there if he is. If not, you can just stay here and have pizza with us later."

"Thank you, Mrs. Thornwell. I'd like to call him after Mr. Thornwell talks to Mr. Johansson."

Toad dialed the Johanssons' home phone. "Hello, Gerritt," he said when Johansson answered. "This is Toad Thornwell, Cyndarria's father. There's been an incident over at the track this afternoon, and you need to know about it."

Toad explained in some detail what had occurred, listened for a minute, then hung up. "He's going to call a special investigator from the police department who's been working on a couple other arson cases that have occurred in Sycamore Creek over the past year. They're pretty sure it's the same guy." He turned to Maria Victoria. "Your description will be the first thing they've had to go on."

"I don't know if I can be much help," she said.

"Probably more than you think," Toad reassured her. "You remember what he was wearing, that he was fairly slender and not too tall and probably had dark hair. Also, he looked scruffy and came across as pretty young. That's a start."

"Is it all right if I call my dad now?" asked Maria Victoria.

"Of course," said Belle. "Go right ahead."

"Hi, Papa," Maria Victoria said when her father answered. "I'm at Cyndarria Thornwell's right now because something happened. Yes, yes, I'm okay. Mrs. Thornwell said she would take me home. I'll tell you about it when I get there. Don't worry, Papa. I'm fine."

Maria Victoria hung up. Belle already had the keys to the car.

"I'll go along," said Sophia, who was the one who knew Maria Victoria best. "Then I'll come back. Do you guys still want to run?"

"I'm kind of out of the mood," said Ali.

"Me too," agreed Cyndarria. "Why don't we just stay here and do something? We can still have pizza later."

"I think that is a very good idea, Cyndarria," said Henri. He turned to the others. "Would you like to play Yahtzee?" he asked.

"I love Yahtzee!" said Ali. "I'm in."

"I'll get the game out," said Cyndarria. She looked at Sophia. "We'll wait for you as fast as we can," she added, remembering one of her grandpa's funny old expressions.

"Ha, ha, Cyndarria. You're such a twit!" said Sophia. "See you guys in a few."

"We've got juice, pop, or I can make us some hot chocolate," Cyndarria said to her friends after her mother had left with the two girls. "Preferences?"

Ali and Henri looked at each other. "Hot chocolate," they said in unison.

"Okay. Sophia will be back by the time it's made, then we'll see who's the Yahtzee champ."

Cyndarria smiled, surprised that she was actually feeling rather content, despite the events of the afternoon. The good thing was that Maria Victoria was safe and, with any luck, what she would be able to share with the special investigator might help him to find the arsonist. Then they would all be a little bit safer.

What she couldn't know was how, in an unexpected and frightening way, she would become involved in the case.

CHAPTER 27

THE ENTIRE NEXT week at school Cyndarria felt distracted by thoughts of the arsonist. She found herself waiting for an announcement that he had been caught, the case solved, but none came.

Maria Victoria had done her best to provide the police with a description of the guy who had attacked her, and they created what they hoped was a good likeness of him. Copies of the picture were plastered on the walls around school with a warning to be on the lookout for anyone whose appearance was similar. It was even shown on TV, in hopes that some viewer might recognize him and contact the police. Nobody did, the upshot being that by Friday the police and special detective Reynolds were no closer to finding the culprit than they had been on Monday.

By the weekend, Cyndarria was ready to relax and think about something else. Sunday was Easter, and she was looking forward to celebrating it. Toby, who still believed wholeheartedly in both Santa Claus and the Easter bunny, could hardly contain his excitement. J.J. was skeptical, but not quite ready to admit that two of his favorite mythical heroes didn't exist.

"Cyndarria," Toby said, "I want to see the Easter bunny. Let's hide behind the couch tonight, and when he comes, we can jump up and say hi. Do you want to?"

"Sounds like fun, Tobe," agreed Cyndarria, confident that he would be asleep long before her parents set the filled Easter baskets in front of the fireplace in the living room.

"Me too!" chimed in J.J. eagerly. This way, he figured, he would find out the truth about that bunny once and for all.

Saturday afternoon was devoted to coloring Easter eggs, which would be hidden around the house in preparation for the big Easter egg hunt early Sunday morning. Cyndarria loved coloring eggs and enjoyed experimenting with different colors and designs. The year before she had made a special gift of her best ones to each of her parents.

Belle admired hers, kept it in the fridge for a couple days, and then, along with most of the others, turned it into deviled eggs. Toad, on the other hand, for reasons Cyndarria never quite understood, took his upstairs and put it in his underwear drawer. However, it became buried too deep in his tighty whities, and he promptly forgot it was there until the smell of rotten eggs permeated the entire drawer.

"Gross, Dad!" said Cyndarria when he carried the offensive smelling, though still colorful, ovoid into the kitchen and put it down the garbage disposal. "Why did you keep it in your drawer?"

"Hmm," said Toad. "Good question." He looked at his daughter affectionately. "You made it, and it just seemed like a good thing to do."

"That's sweet, Dad, but next time it might be better if you ate it."

Late Saturday afternoon found two dozen brilliantly colored eggs in a large bowl in the middle of the dining room table. Many had the name of their creator written on them with a wax crayon.

"I like my blue one the bestest!" exclaimed Toby. "Which one do you like, Cyndarria?"

"The one that looks kind of like a church window," said Cyndarria, who had used a fancy new coloring kit which produced various colors that somehow managed to remain separated in one

174

bowl. "I'd give it to Dad, but he'd probably put it in a drawer and forget it was there—and we all know what happens when he does that."

"P. U.!" said Toby, and pinched his nose.

"El stinko," agreed J.J. "Better give it to Mommy."

That night, with the help of Toad, the boys pulled the couch out far enough from the wall that three sleeping bags could fit behind it. At 9:00 Belle ordered them to bed.

"Cyndarria too!" demanded Toby.

"I'll be there in a little bit. You and J.J. get your jammies on now. I'll read you a story if you like."

"Goodie!" said Toby, satisfied that his big sister would be joining them in their quest to surprise the Easter bunny.

Cyndarria chose her favorite children's book, *Hailstones and Halibut Bones.* "Which colors shall we read about?" she asked after the boys had changed into their pajamas and were sitting on each side of her on the couch.

"Blue!" said Toby. "It's my favorite color."

"Green," said J.J. "For Michigan State." He was a diehard MSU fan and was the proud owner of three different green-and-white t-shirts which boasted the Spartan logo.

"I'll take purple," said Cyndarria. "It's very regal."

"What's regal?" asked Toby.

"Royal, like something a king or queen would wear."

Cyndarria read the poems full of sensory images about each of the chosen colors.

"Do another one!" said Toby, after she had finished.

"Okay, one more each, and then you go to bed."

"I want black, like Ollie," requested Toby.

"White," said J.J. "To go with the green. Green and white, fight, fight!" He grinned.

"Okay, I'll take pink," said Cyndarria. "I like how the author describes it as the little sister of red and the great granddaughter of purple."

"Blue's a heron," said Toby, remembering the poem.

"Green's a grasshopper. And a pickle," said J.J. "I like pickles!"

"I'll read the others, and you can tell me what you like best in each one, okay?"

When she finished, she said, "Well?"

"Licorice!" exclaimed Toby. "And boom, boom, boom! The sound black makes."

"Snowflakes and vanilla ice cream," said J.J. "Yummy!"

"I like that she said sometimes Easter bunnies are pink plush. And speaking of Easter bunnies, it's time for you two to hit the sack. Did you brush your teeth?"

The boys nodded. "Okay, good. I still have to put on my pajamas and brush mine, and I'll be back down, all right?"

"Okey dokey, Cyndarria," agreed Toby. "C'mon, J.J., let's hide!"

By the time she returned to the living room, both boys were fast asleep. Since she had promised she would join them, she lay down, listened to their soft, rhythmic breathing and soon drifted off to sleep herself. An hour later, Belle and Toad hid the Easter eggs and placed the filled baskets in front of the fireplace, gazed at their three children, then walked hand in hand up the stairs to bed.

Toad left early the next morning to finish preparing the Sunday brunch. They expected a sizable crowd after church services were over, and he wanted to make sure everything was ready and that the entire restaurant looked especially festive and inviting.

Toby was the next one awake. He immediately jumped up from behind the couch, hoping still to be able to catch the Easter bunny in the act. His disappointment was short-lived when he saw the Easter basket awaiting him. He grabbed his basket and immediately began digging through it.

A large chocolate bunny, yellow marshmallow baby chicks, and jelly beans of every color filled the basket. There was also a small gift wrapped in paper with pink bunnies on it and a plastic egg which, when opened, revealed a handful of shiny silver dimes. Unable to resist, Toby tore the paper off his present and found a box of colorful new Lego pieces.

"Yippee!" he exclaimed. "Cyndarria, J.J., look what I got!"

Cyndarria sat up and yawned. J.J. continued to snore softly. She stretched and walked over to where Toby sat, examining each new Lego piece, all of which he had unceremoniously dumped on the carpet.

"Look, Cyndarria! I got a truck and a train engine—and all this other stuff!"

"Nice, Tobe. I missed the Easter bunny. Did you see him?"

Toby made a face and harrumphed. "No. I falled asleep and I didn't wake up. I think the Easter bunny is very quiet and sneaky. Like Santa."

"Maybe we can try again next year."

"Okay," agreed Toby, content to start playing with his new Legos.

There was a muffled snort from behind the couch.

"That you, J.J.?" said Cyndarria. "Come look what Toby got in his Easter basket."

J.J. moaned sleepily. After a minute, he got up and wandered over to the fireplace. "I missed the Easter bunny," he said. Secretly, he was almost relieved because it meant that he could continue to believe in Mr. Bunny, and that made him happy.

J.J. went through the contents of his basket. "Dimes for my piggy bank. Yea!" Of the three siblings, J.J. was the most successful at keeping his bank generously filled with coins. He picked up his present and opened it.

"I got Legos too! Mine is like a farm. Look!" There was a barn, a tractor and various animals pictured on the box: a cow, a pig, a horse, a chicken, a sheep, and a duck.

"What did you get, Cyndarria?" J.J. asked.

"I don't know. I haven't opened it."

"Well, aren't you gonna?" demanded Toby.

"Sure." Cyndarria picked up her gift. It was in a small box. She shook it.

"Can you guess what it is?" asked Toby.

"Hmm, I don't know. Maybe some kind of jewelry because it's pretty small."

"Maybe it's a diamond ring!" exclaimed Toby.

"I kind of doubt that, Tobe," laughed Cyndarria. She opened the gift carefully, trying not to tear the paper.

On the box was a picture of its contents. "Oh my gosh, it's a Tinker-Bell watch!" Cyndarria was delighted. She was enchanted by the story of Peter Pan and was particularly fond of the tiny fairy. "I love it!"

"Put it on, Cyndarria," J.J. said, almost as excited as his sister. He, too, liked the story of the boy who never grew up, but his favorite character was Captain Hook.

"Okay." She opened the box, removed the watch from the bands that held it in place, and put it on. She held it up for her brothers to admire.

"It's nice," said J.J. "Not as nice as Legos, but it's nice."

Toby nodded in agreement.

Just then Belle appeared. "I see you've managed to find your Easter baskets," she said. "What did the bunny leave?"

Belle oooed and aahhed as the children showed her their gifts and the other goodies that filled their baskets. "Pretty nice," she observed afterward. "I think the Easter bunny outdid himself this year."

"C'n we have the Easter egg hunt now?" asked Toby. "I think I'm going to find the most this year!"

"Absolutely," said Belle. She looked at the clock over the fireplace. "Your father is expecting us for brunch this morning, so how about after you find all the eggs, everyone gets cleaned up and ready to leave?"

There was a special afternoon service in the church they attended for those who couldn't make it in the morning, and Belle planned to take the children then. The pastor, who understood all the other things children wanted to do on Easter morning, had decided to add this service in the hope that youngsters would understand and appreciate the day for more than just baskets full of sweets. Much to his satisfaction, the service turned out to be attended better than he had dared hope. The father in him appreciated the innocent delight of children at this holy time, but the man who served God still wanted them to come to love Him as much as they loved the Easter bunny.

This was a joyful time, a holy time, and a day when Cyndarria would think about Grandpa Paddy and Grandma Rose and probably a little bit about Jesus too. She felt her heart fill with a mixture of sadness and happiness. And gratitude. She would think about that, especially. Grandma Rose had always said, "It's good to count your blessings every day, not just on Thanksgiving."

Cyndarria knew she was right and planned to do just that.

CHAPTER 28

PAUL TURNBULL STOOD in front of the mirror in his sister's bathroom and looked himself over. He liked the changes he saw. Missy, his sister, was in what she liked to call beauty college and was learning to cut and color hair and do manicures. She attended classes at night and worked in a local fast-food place and as a maid in a nearby hotel during the day and on weekends in order to be able to pay the rent on the rather shabby apartment she and Paul shared.

She liked to practice what she was learning on Paul, and he didn't mind. Her last experiment had been her boldest yet. The cut was short and simple, but she had also changed his hair color, bleaching it and then tinting it a nice light brown. She had even bleached and colored his eyebrows, so he looked like a whole new person.

For his 19th birthday, Missy had taken him shopping at the local Goodwill outlet and bought him a serviceable pair of khakis and a lightly-used denim jacket. "If you dressed nicer, you could probably find yourself a job," she had told him.

Paul didn't like it when his sister said that, but he let it slide because she treated him well and let him stay in her apartment after his folks had kicked him out of the house.

Missy Turnbull and Paul were both high-school drop outs. Missy struggled in school, flunking most of her classes, and finally got so discouraged that she gave up. Their aunt taught at the school Missy was now attending and convinced the owner to give

Missy a chance. So far, it had worked out well, and Missy was excited to think that someday she might even have a beauty shop of her own. She already knew what she wanted to call it: Missy's Cut and Curl.

Paul, on the other hand, was shrewd, in a street-smart way, and lazy. That and his penchant for getting into trouble were the reasons he had been kicked out of school and then out of his parents' home. He smoked when he could get his hands on a cigarette and occasionally succeeded in talking his sister, who was sweet and very loyal to her younger brother, into buying a six-pack of beer, which he consumed entirely by himself.

To complete his new look, Paul had bought himself a cheap pair of fake wire-rim glasses. He put them on now and studied himself further. He smiled, just a slight upturning of his lips, no teeth, because he felt it gave him a more sophisticated look. "Perfect," he thought.

The next week passed quickly for Cyndarria. The last Saturday in April was to be their first track meet at Cedar Ridge, then home against Laurelton a couple weeks later, away against Chippewa Bend after that, and this year the league championship on the first Saturday in June was to be on their home track.

Cyndarria was looking forward to finally being able to compete. With Coach Sam's help and Cyndarria's natural inclination, she had settled on the half-mile, an 880-yard run, and also being on the mile-relay team with Sophia, Penny and Maria Victoria.

At last the long-anticipated day arrived. The team rode the bus to Cedar Ridge, arriving at 10:00. Parents and other family members drove and sat on the bleachers. The meet would last a few hours, and people came prepared with coolers full of food and drink and blankets for cover if the spring wind got too chilly, or to sit on if they got what Cyndarria referred to as "bleacher butt."

Toad had to work the lunch shift, so Belle had invited her friend Lovelie to go with her and keep her company. Lovelie had never attended a track meet before but remembered that Haiti had been embarrassed in the track-and-field events at the 1976 Olympics. The Haitian president, known as Baby Doc, had chosen the athletes from among his personal friends, and the results had been predictably disastrous.

She recalled that Dieudonné LaMothe, who ran in the 5000-meter race, recorded the worst time in Olympic history. Lovelie found it ironic that his name, Dieudonné, meant God given. She figured the Lord had short-changed him considerably when it came to God-given athletic talents.

Emmanuel Rousseau waved to them from his seat on the bleachers when they arrived, and they went to join him. J.J. and Toby didn't want to sit. They had met up with a couple of school buddies and joined them in exploring the world under the bleachers, which offered the occasional interesting find—something that had been dropped and never recovered. Within the first half-hour, J.J. had found 78 cents and Toby an apple, which looked good until he turned it over and saw a worm snugly ensconced in the apple's flesh.

Toby studied the worm for a moment. "I think this worm is pretty happy living in this apple," he said, and placed it carefully back on the ground.

Emmanuel greeted Belle and Lovelie with a smile. "I'm glad to see you again, Belle," he said.

"It's nice to see you too, Emmanuel. I want you to meet my friend, Lovelie. This is her first track meet."

"I'm happy to meet you, Lovelie. Do you have a son or daughter on the team?"

"Belle has told me many wonderful things about your son Henri. I'm pleased to meet his father. But no, actually I have no children, although Belle often tells me I should marry and have a family."

Emmanuel smiled again. "It is good to have children, even when one is forced to become a single parent. I think I would be very lonely and sad without Henri. He is a fine son, and I am proud of him."

"What events is Henri participating in?" asked Belle.

"The 120- and 330-yard hurdles."

The field events got underway before the races began. In the distance, they could see Joey. Judging by his reaction, they could tell he was clearly not satisfied with his first attempt at the shot put.

Neither Cyndarria nor Henri ran during the first half-hour, although Belle was particularly interested to see how Alison did in the 100-yard dash. She knew Alison had been league champion the previous year and was hoping to repeat this spring. As it turned out, the race was not especially close, and she won easily.

After the boys' 100-yard dash, the 120-yard hurdles was announced. This was Henri's first time running the hurdles in competition. From what they could tell, he looked very focused, but relaxed. The starter's gun went off, but one of the boys made a false start and everyone had to be called back.

The idea of having to jump obstacles while running so fast made Belle nervous, and she felt herself tense up as the race began. Henri was running second and looked strong until halfway through the race when his shoe clipped the top of a hurdle and he went down. He immediately leaped up and continued running, but by then the race was lost. His teammates patted him on the back and applauded him for finishing the race, even though he'd had no chance to win.

Cyndarria could tell Henri was disappointed in himself. "Don't feel bad, Henri," she said. "That was your first time in a race; you'll do better next time."

Coach McIntyre approached. He looked at Henri's knee and the palm of his hand. "See the trainer," he said. "He'll clean you up and put something on those scrapes, and you'll be as good as new."

"Thank you, Coach. I'm sorry I disappointed you."

Coach McIntyre shook his head. "I would only have been disappointed if you'd given up," he said. "Any runner clips a hurdle once in a while. You're still learning, and your technique is actually looking good. Don't worry. You'll be fine."

Coach Sam called Cyndarria over. She was consulting her clipboard. "You're up after this next event. Any questions?"

"Do I have to do 50 push-ups if I come in dead last?" Cyndarria joked.

"Probably 100." Coach Sam grinned. "Actually, your times have been really impressive, and I think you've got a good chance of winning. I can remember only one other runner from last year who was faster—a girl from Laurelton. She's in the eighth grade this year, so you'll see her at the next meet. Better make sure you're stretched and ready to go."

"Don't worry, Coach," said Cyndarria. "I've already stretched so much this morning, I've probably grown an inch."

Coach Sam gave an exaggerated eye roll. "Funny girl." She patted Cyndarria on the back. "Go get 'em," she said.

"I'm gonna try."

A couple minutes later, the girls' 880 was announced.

Belle watched her oldest child at the starting line and felt her heartbeat increase and her palms grow sweaty.

"Ready, set." Belle's heart jumped when the starting gun went off.

The runners would circle the track twice, and pacing them-selves was important. Cyndarria had experienced a nervous flut-ter at the starting line, but as soon as the race began, she settled down and felt only the steady beat of her heart and the deep even

184

breathing of her lungs. She was content to run behind the girl who started fast and maintained the lead the first time around the track. At about 600 yards, however, the girl was clearly tiring. Cyndarria passed her almost effortlessly, but suddenly she heard heavy footsteps coming up behind her, and another runner from Cedar Ridge took the lead.

Belle's stomach was in her throat. She jumped up, and even though she knew her daughter probably wouldn't hear her, she found herself yelling, "C'mon Cyndarria! Go, go, go!"

With 150 yards to go, the girl from Cedar Ridge had her by a yard. "It's now or never," Cyndarria thought, and she accelerated. Coming down the stretch, the two girls were even. Cyndarria gave one final gut-wrenching kick and lunged across the finish line barely in front of her competitor.

She was vaguely aware of loud cheering, but what attracted most of her attention was her stomach, which was reacting violently to the effort she had just expended in the race. She bent over, gasping, and began to wretch.

Sophia and Alison held back for a moment, but as soon as Cyndarria stood up, they rushed over and gave her a huge hug.

"Cyndarria!" exclaimed Sophia. "That was amazing! Way to go!"

"Running like that you have a chance of becoming league champ," enthused Alison.

Cyndarria looked at her friends. "I think it's a little early to be making predictions like that." But she grinned and felt a surge of pride.

Coach Sam ran up and gave her a hug as well. "Great race!" she said. "I knew you had it in you." She looked over to where Cyndarria had been when she threw up. "I see you've, uhh, fertilized the grass. That's happened to me a few times. Drink some water and sit down for a bit. You should be okay for the relay because it doesn't come up for quite a while."

Cyndarria looked up in the stands and saw her mother, Lovelie, and Emmanuel. She waved, then called to them. "I'll come up and talk to you in a minute. I'm going to get a drink of water."

Belle gave her a thumbs up. She took a deep breath. The first race was over. Now she could relax for a while.

Cyndarria walked over to the water fountain by the food stand. She noticed a guy standing there who seemed to be looking at her.

"That was a heck of a race you just ran," he said as she approached the fountain.

"Thanks," said Cyndarria.

"What your name?" he asked and gave her a friendly little half-smile.

"Cyndarria Thornwell."

"I'm Patrick. I go to Cedar Ridge High School, but I'm here watching my little brother compete."

"My grandpa's name was Patrick," said Cyndarria, "but they called him Paddy."

"I'm just plain Patrick," he said.

"What's your last name?"

At that moment the loud speaker came on announcing the 330 hurdles.

"Gotta run," said Cyndarria. "A friend of mine is in that race. Oh, what did you say your last name is?"

"Scofield. Maybe I'll see you around."

Cyndarria shrugged. "Cedar Ridge is quite a ways from Sycamore Creek, so I kinda doubt it."

"You never know," said Patrick.

As it turned out, he was right.

186

CHAPTER 29

THE MEET AGAINST Cedar Ridge turned out to be a victory for Sycamore Creek. All of Cyndarria's friends had done well, at least placing in each of their events. Stevie, the smallest guy on the track, had won the mile run. Even Sara, who Cyndarria had assumed never really exercised any part of her body but her brain and her mouth, managed to place third in the long jump.

On the ride home, the team was tired but happy. Coach McIntyre asked the bus driver to stop at a Dairy Queen on the way, so all the kids who were hungry could get something to eat. That, of course, meant everyone. Cyndarria ordered her favorite—a medium cone dipped in chocolate, which she licked contentedly the rest of the way back to school.

"Who was that guy I saw you talking with over by the food stand?" asked Alison. "He was kinda cute."

"Patrick something. I forget his last name. He's goes to Cedar Ridge High School and was at the meet to watch his brother."

"Seemed like he looked pretty friendly." Alison lowered her voice conspiratorially. "Maybe he'll ask you out." She giggled.

"Not interested," said Cyndarria. "Besides, my mom and dad don't really want me dating anyone till I'm in high school."

"Actually, my parents feel the same way," Alison admitted. "It's kind of fun to think about, though."

The bus pulled into the school parking lot at 3:30, and the kids all piled off.

"See you Monday, Sophia," Cyndarria called. "Bye, Alison."

Henri joined her for the walk home.

"Good job today, Henri," said Cyndarria. "I was really happy you got second in the 330 hurdles, especially since you fell in your first race."

"Thanks, Cyndarria. You did great too. I think you're going to end up doing very well this season."

"What I really hope is that we win the league championship. The whole team could celebrate that, and it would sure make the coaches happy."

"Coach McIntyre said he thought we'd have a better idea about that after the meet at Laurelton. They had a really strong team last year, and a lot of those kids are back."

The two friends walked along in silence for a while, then Cyndarria asked, "So have you found any more pennies lately?"

"I haven't, but actually my father found one the other day. He had just bought some of his favorite cookies at the bakery and was going to put them in the cookie jar. When he opened it up, there was a penny inside."

"That's so cool. What does he think that means?"

"He's thought about it a lot. He says he just kind of gets the feeling from this last one that maybe it's my mother's way of saying that she wants him to do things that make him happy—like the cookies do.

"I have no idea if that's the case, but I do know, in her life, that was something my mother wanted. She just loved seeing my father happy. She was always telling him not to work so hard, that he should take time to relax and enjoy himself more.

"I think one of his happiest times was when we took a trip to Orlando. We went to Disney World, which was the best part for me. There are many Haitian refugees who have settled in Orlando, and one night we went to a Haitian restaurant for dinner.

The food, the music, the waiters, and most of the customers were from Haiti.

"My father was almost like another person. He laughed and he talked with practically everyone in the restaurant. He sang with the music, and he even got my mother out on the little dance floor they had to dance the *kompa.*"

"What's a *kompa*?" asked Cyndarria. "I've never heard of it."

"It's kind of the national dance of Haiti. It's slow and very graceful. I didn't know my dad could move like that!"

"I don't think my dad can!" Cyndarria laughed. "My mom says he has two left feet."

"When my father came back to the table after the dance, he actually had tears in his eyes. He said he was so happy to reconnect with his native culture. I've always remembered that. I want to go to Haiti sometime, but not while Baby Doc is in power. He is corrupt, and he and his father have been responsible for the torturing and killing of thousands of Haitians, including one of my father's best friends, who was only 17 when he died.

"It was because of Baby Doc's father, Papa Doc, that my dad came here. He finally realized after his friend was murdered that it wasn't safe for him to stay in Haiti. That is one of the reasons he loves this country so much. He knows he is safe here. And he knows that I will have opportunities that I never would have had there. He says he feels blessed every day to be a citizen of the United States."

"My Grandma Rose would have liked your dad if she had ever met him. She was always telling people to count their blessings. She would really have appreciated your father's attitude."

"I think my father would have liked your grandmother as well. And I'm sure he would have loved her cookies! I do too," he added. "I think maybe that's a hint." Henri grinned.

189

"Gotcha," said Cyndarria. "I'm not so sure you deserve any, but your dad does. Maybe I'll make up a batch tomorrow. If you come over in the afternoon, you can help, and I'll send a bunch for him home with you."

"You're on!" said Henri. "He'll be so happy!"

They had arrived at the Thornwell home, and Henri said good-bye.

"See you tomorrow," said Cyndarria. "Why don't you come over around 3:00 or 4:00?"

"Sounds good. I'll check with my father, but I'm quite sure he'll be fine with it, especially if we're making him some cookies!"

When Cyndarria went in the house, she found her father sitting on the living room floor with her brothers, who were once again deep in Lego construction, this time using the new ones they had received from the Easter bunny. Her mother was on the phone.

"Hi, you guys," she greeted them. "Did you have fun at the track meet?" she asked her brothers.

"I found a dollar and three cents under the bleachers!" boasted J.J. "I already put it in my piggy bank."

"Did you find any money, Toby?" asked Cyndarria.

"No, J.J. finded it all."

"But guess what he found," said J.J., seemingly enthused about his brother's great find. "An apple!"

"With a worm in it!" exclaimed Toby.

"You didn't eat it, did you?" asked Cyndarria. "That would be gross!"

"Cyndarria!" Toby looked mildly offended. "It was the worm's apple!"

Cyndarria stifled a laugh. "Good point, Toby."

"Right," observed Toad. "Possession is nine-tenths of the law."

"What does that mean, Daddy?" asked Toby.

"Just what you said, Tobe. "The worm was living in the apple, so it was his. You didn't really have any right to take it away from him."

Toby nodded, pleased to have his position confirmed.

"Your mother tells me you did great at the track meet," said Toad. "Congratulations!"

"Thanks, Dad. It was fun. I'm already excited about the next one. Coach says Laurelton has a really good team, though, so it's going to be a lot tougher to do as well as we did today."

"I'm sure you'll be up to the challenge."

"Hope so."

"At least you didn't fall and break anything," said Belle as she came into the room. She smiled. "I was really proud of you, honey."

"Thanks. So, did Lovelie enjoy the meet?"

"I think she did. She also seemed to enjoy talking with Emmanuel. They really sort of hit it off."

"Oooo, Mom, that would make you kind of a match-maker!"

"I don't think it's quite gotten to that point," said Belle, but she smiled. "It was just so nice to see them enjoying each other. Actually, it's hard for me to imagine that either of them could find a more suitable person for a relationship."

"I'm going to get something to eat," said Cyndarria, starting for the kitchen. "I'm starving!"

"Your mother has talked me into making spaghetti for dinner," said Toad. "Why don't you have something real light now, and I'll get started on the spaghetti. It won't take too long."

"Spaghetti! Yum!! Definitely worth the wait. I'll help out, if you want."

"Why don't you fix us some garlic bread, and maybe Mom will make a salad."

"I think I could be convinced to do that," said Belle.

"Sketti! Yea!! I love sketti!" exclaimed Toby.

"Me too," said J.J.

"Mommy," said Toby, "c'n we watch a Bugs Bunny video while you're making dinner?"

"Yeah!" enthused J.J. "The one with Elmer Fudd when he goes after Bugs and he says, 'Say your pwayers, wabbit!' I love that one!"

"Sure, sweetie. I like that one, too."

An hour later the kitchen smelled tantalizingly of basil and oregano as Toad poured the spaghetti sauce into a large bowl, then drained the pasta. Cyndarria cut the crispy garlic bread into thick, buttery slices, and Belle tossed the salad, bright with lettuce, tomato, green pepper, carrot and cucumber.

The boys finished viewing several cartoons of Bugs Bunny and Elmer Fudd, who was repeatedly frustrated by the antics of that "wascally wabbit." They turned off the television, and the entire Thornwell family sat down together to a delicious Saturday evening dinner, blissfully unaware of the surprise that "Patrick something" had in store for them.

CHAPTER 30

ON MONDAY AFTERNOON in Community Service class, Mrs. Maxwell announced that this Wednesday was to be the first session of the after-school reading program for three- through eight-year-olds at the public library.

"Mrs. Doolittle has received an enthusiastic go-ahead from her staff," Mrs. Maxwell explained. "She will have a selection of books to read and a special space set aside for the children, as well as a few suggestions for other activities readers can do with them related to the stories you read. Because this is a new program, she would like to meet with those who are participating tomorrow during this class to give you a short orientation and training session.

"I have spoken with Mr. Johansson, and he has approved your early departure from school. In fact, he has offered to drive you to the library. He would like to hear firsthand about the program because he has a couple grandchildren he would like to see attend the reading sessions.

"So, let's see, Cyndarria and Simon volunteered to be readers. Is there anyone else who would like to volunteer?"

Alison raised her hand. "I would, Mrs. Maxwell. Coach Sam said Cyndarria and I could miss track practice if we agreed to make up the time on our own, and we're willing to do that."

"Thank you, Ali. Mrs. Doolittle said she would like to have three volunteers, so if one or even two people needed to miss a session, there would still be someone available to read. This is excellent. I'm sure she'll be pleased. I'll let Mr. Johansson know that the three of you will be in his office at the beginning of last hour tomorrow."

Track practice after school that day had an almost festive atmosphere because Saturday had been such a satisfying victory.

"Okay, kids," said Coach McIntyre when he had them seated on the bleachers at the track, "let's all calm down. I love your enthusiasm, but Saturday was just the first meet. I'm proud of you all for how hard you've been working, and the results showed, but there are still three more meets before we can claim a really big victory. Coach Sam and I think this team is special, and you have the potential to win a championship, but over-confidence can and often does bring failure.

"The meet against Laurelton is in two Saturdays, and that should tell us where we stand and what our chances are to win it all. Till then, let's just keep working hard, and we'll see where it takes us. So...everybody ready to get started?"

"Let's go!" yelled Joey, and everyone echoed his words.

On Tuesday, Cyndarria, Alison, and Simon went to the principal's office after checking in with Mrs. Maxwell for attendance.

Oraleen Jackson smiled when she saw them. "I hear you're going to do some reading for the children at the library. I told my daughter about it, and she wants to send her little girl. Maisie, that's my granddaughter, is all excited."

"Is Mr. Johansson going to be able to take us to the library?" Cyndarria asked. "Mrs. Maxwell said that he would."

"I'll go right in his office and remind him," said Oraleen. "Sometimes he forgets these things."

A moment later she returned. "He's on the phone, but he'll be done in just a minute."

Mr. Johansson appeared shortly, and ten minutes later he and the three students were going up the steps of the library. Mrs.

194

Doolittle greeted them at the main desk. She was a short, stocky woman with a friendly smile, and she appeared to be genuinely pleased to see them.

"It's nice to meet you," she said after the students had introduced themselves. "Thank you so much for volunteering to be part of the story-hour program. It wouldn't happen without you. I hope that you'll find it to be a lot of fun. Based on reports I hear from my staff, there seems to be considerable interest on the part of the community, so you will likely find yourselves to be very popular. As you probably know, children love being read to, so the hour you spend with them should be very enjoyable."

After her short speech, Mrs. Doolittle led everyone to the reading nook she had prepared. It was set up to accommodate one, two, or three small groups of children, who could be divided up according to age. There were a few beanbags as well as some small tables and chairs. The area was covered with a nice, thick plush carpet, so the children could sit comfortably on the floor as well. There were shelves displaying some popular kids' books and on the walls, posters of Bert and Ernie, Winnie the Pooh, and James and the Giant Peach.

"This is very impressive, Mrs. Doolittle," said Mr. Johansson. "You've created a very inviting space for the children."

"I love it," said Alison. "Winnie the Pooh is the best!"

"My brother Toby's favorite book is *James and the Giant Peach*," said Cyndarria. "He's going to want a poster like that."

Simon nodded. "Yes," he agreed. "This is very satisfactory."

Mrs. Doolittle looked delighted. "I'm so glad you approve," she said. "We've worked very hard to make this an appealing space for children. So now let me explain your responsibilities to you and how each session will be organized."

Forty-five minutes later, the orientation was done. Mrs. Doolittle gave each of the volunteers a sheet containing the schedule and a few tips for maintaining interest and discipline, if the latter ever became an issue. She included the library phone number and asked them to notify her if they were going to have to miss a session.

"Does anyone need a ride home?" Mr. Johansson asked as they left the library.

"I live pretty close by," said Simon, "so I can walk."

"Cyndarria and I have track practice," said Alison.

"Well, as it turns out, I'm heading back to school," said Mr. Johansson with a smile. "I should be able to get you there just about on time."

Practice went well. Coach Sam spent quite a bit of time working with the relay teams on their hand-offs, which were frequently shaky.

When Cyndarria got home, she told her mother about the orientation at the library. "Mrs. Doolittle has a really cool space set up for the kids. I think they're going to like it."

"Like what?" asked J.J. as he came into the kitchen.

"The reading nook at the library," said Cyndarria. "Wednesday is the first story hour. Do you think you want to come?"

"Come where?" demanded Toby, who was never far behind his older brother when he went into the kitchen hoping for a snack.

"To the library for a story hour. Would you two like to go? It's going to be fun."

"Will you be there, Cyndarria?" asked Toby.

"Yes, I'm one of the readers."

"Goodie!" exclaimed Toby. "I like stories!"

"How about you, J.J.? Do you want to come?"

"Are there snacks?" asked J.J., who generally measured the worth of any after-school activity by how well it would satisfy his stomach.

"I'm not sure," said Cyndarria, "but there might be. Mrs. Doolittle seems to know what kids like."

"Okay," said J.J. "I guess I'll try it."

"Good." Cyndarria turned to her mother. "Alison's mom wondered if maybe the two of you could take turns driving us. Would that be okay?"

"Sounds perfect," said Belle. "I'll call her tonight and let her know."

Cyndarria was looking forward to Wednesday afternoon. When they arrived at the library, there were already several children there. J.J. and Toby immediately saw friends from their classes and went to join them. The three students had spoken briefly with Mrs. Doolittle and had agreed that if there were enough kids to divide into small groups, Simon would take the seven- and eight-year olds, Ali the five- and six-year-olds, and Cyndarria the youngest ones.

Much to Mrs. Doolittle's delight, 14 children showed up for the first story hour. She told parents who had brought them that they were welcome to sit with their child this first time if they wanted to, or if not, she would be delighted to host them for coffee in the small kitchen in the back of the library. Then she turned and picked up a large purple laundry basket from behind a bookshelf. It was filled with small stuffed animals.

She smiled at the children, who were sitting on the floor. "I thought some of you might like to have a friend to sit with you today."

A light, excited ripple passed through the children; a couple of the girls clapped. "If you would like to hold a friend, you can come up and choose one when I say your name."

Mrs. Doolittle nodded to Cyndarria, who stepped forward. "This is Miss Cyndarria," she said. "Maisie and Zach can come up and pick out a friend now; then you will go with Miss Cyndarria for a story."

Cyndarria was a little disappointed that there would be only two children in her group, but decided that since this was her first time, maybe it was a good thing. Maisie jumped up and came forward, but Zach hung back a little.

"Zach, do you want to choose a friend?" asked Mrs. Doolittle. She held out her hand toward him. Zach nodded and slowly approached her.

Cyndarria knew that Maisie was Oraleen Jackson's granddaughter, and she was pleased that she would have Maisie in her group. Looking at her, it struck Cyndarria that she was maybe the most beautiful child she had ever seen.

She had long blond hair, which looked as though it had been curled especially for the occasion, and the largest, deepest blue eyes Cyndarria could imagine. Her skin was light except for her rosy cheeks, and she seemed to have a perpetual smile. She was dainty and wore a pink dress, white socks with little flowers on them, and black patent-leather shoes. She definitely looked like she was going to a fancy party, and her infectious smile seemed to suggest that, for her, story hour was exactly that.

Unlike Maisie, who embraced the occasion with delight, Zach was hesitant. Maisie chose a purple bunny from the basket of stuffed animals, but again Zach held back. Maisie seemed to sense his shyness. She looked the basket over carefully, and then picked out a small teddy bear with a plaid ribbon around its neck and held it up.

"Do you like this one?" she asked.

Zach nodded and Maisie handed it to him.

198

"Okay," she said, then looked up at Cyndarria and held out her hand. Cyndarria took it and held out her other hand for Zach to take. He hesitated briefly but then took it. Cyndarria felt an odd moment of pride, and right then decided that she would try to be the very best reader and storyteller ever.

"Let's sit over there," she said and took the two children to a table in the corner right by the poster of Bert and Ernie. "We have a book that I think you're really going to like."

CHAPTER 31

IT WAS EARLY May, and Cyndarria felt content. Her classes were going well, even English with Mrs. Wackenstein. She was enjoying track with her friends and found herself looking forward to story hour on Wednesdays, which would last throughout the summer. Summer! One more month! She couldn't wait.

Saturday, May 9, the date of the Laurelton track meet, arrived. It was cloudy and threatened rain, which could make it a really long day at the meet. The team knew that if there were lightning, everyone would have to take cover and wait for at least a half-hour without another flash. Coaches generally expected them to run in the rain if it wasn't too heavy, but lightning was too big a risk. It was a hard and fast rule.

Team members had all heard Coach McIntyre's stories of deaths caused by lightning. He seemed to have made a study of it. He even owned a copy of the *National Summary of Climatological Data* for 1959-1979 and would quote statistics from it.

"In Michigan alone, there were 54 fatalities from lightning strikes during that period and 404 injuries. In Camp Grayling, 45 National Guardsmen were injured when lightning struck their mess tent in June of 1979. So we don't take any chances with lightning. Ever."

It sprinkled early, but then the sky started to clear and seemed to promise a better day. Belle had once again invited Lovelie to join her, and when Cyndarria checked the stands, she saw them there with Henri's father. Lovelie sat between him and Belle, and both she and Emmanuel looked quite happy.

Cyndarria grinned. Her mom, the matchmaker. She went over to Henri and tapped him on the shoulder. "Look who your dad's sitting next to."

Henri gazed up in Emmanuel's direction. His smile matched his father's. "I am happy for him," Henri said. "He has been very lonely. It is time for him to have a nice friend."

The meet began less than auspiciously for Sycamore Creek. Everyone seemed to be struggling. Cyndarria wasn't sure why, but she hoped it wouldn't affect her. She knew the runner from Laurelton was really fast, and Cyndarria would have to run a perfect race to beat her.

The sun was gone again, covered by dark storm clouds, and it began to rain just as the girls' 880 was called. Cyndarria lined up next to Laurelton's best runner. The girl was tall with long legs that looked like they could cover twice as much ground as Cyndarria's in a single stride. She turned to Cyndarria, seeming to size her up.

"I'm Brandi," she said. "Good luck."

"Yeah," said Cyndarria, surprised that the girl had said anything to her. "You too."

The rain began to come down harder. Cyndarria looked over at Coach Sam, who was talking with Coach McIntyre. She wondered if they might suspend the meet for a while.

"Ready!" the starter called. "Set!" His gun went off.

The runners surged forward. Brandi held back, forcing some other runner to lead. After 400 yards, Cyndarria found herself passing the pace-setter, who had tired. She knew Brandi couldn't be far behind. By now the rain was coming down in torrents, and Cyndarria was having trouble seeing. Half-way around the track for the second time, she noticed a small hole that had filled with water and swerved to avoid it.

At that point the unthinkable occurred. Just as Cyndarria moved to avoid stepping in the hole, Brandi closed in to pass her. Cyndarria's sudden move caused her to bump hard into Brandi, throwing Brandi off her stride, and almost making her fall. Cyndarria felt sick. She wanted desperately to stop and apologize, but knew she couldn't, so in the downpour, soaked to the skin and already feeling miserable, she kept running.

Cyndarria crossed the finish line first and immediately turned to look for Brandi. She was far behind, refusing to stop, but limping. Coach Sam approached.

"Cyndarria, what happened? I saw you swerve and crash into Brandi."

"I didn't see her. I was trying to avoid a hole full of water."

Just then, Brandi managed to cross the finish line. Cyndarria went up to her. "I'm really sorry," she said. "I didn't realize you were there."

The Laurelton coach ran up, clearly angry, before Brandi could say anything. "Your girl is disqualified," she said sharply to Coach Sam. "She did that on purpose!"

There was nothing to be done. Whether or not she had bumped Brandi on purpose, it had happened, and it was Cyndarria's fault. In just her second race, she was disqualified. She had let the team down, and she had disappointed herself.

At that point, the meet was suspended until the rain would let up. Parents had long since cleared the stands, and both teams ran for cover. Coach Sam appeared with towels for team members to use to dry themselves off as well as they could. Cyndarria stood off to one side, still feeling bad and not wanting to talk to her teammates.

A voice from behind her said, "Tough break on that race."

Cyndarria looked around and, much to her surprise, saw Patrick, the guy she had met before. "Oh, hi," she said. "Yeah, I got DQ'ed."

"Sorry about that," said Patrick.

"Me too." She looked at Patrick, wondering why he was there. "I thought you said you were from Cedar Ridge. Why are you here, especially on a day like this?"

"I like to scout other teams for my brother. And I thought maybe I'd see you again."

"Oh," said Cyndarria and didn't know what else to add. She was starting to feel a little uncomfortable because Patrick was looking at her very intently.

"I have to go," she said finally. "I need to talk to my coach."

"You're not going to be running again for a while. Stick around." Patrick reached out and took hold of her arm. "I like talking to you."

A nervous thrill ran through Cyndarria. She looked at Patrick's hand. She managed a sheepish smile. "Okay, sure," she said.

Cyndarria saw Alison approaching and felt a wave of relief.

Alison was grinning. "Who's this?" she asked. "A new friend?"

"Uhh, yeah. This is Patrick...I'm sorry Patrick. I forgot your last name."

"Well, that's embarrassing," said Ali, obviously enjoying Cyndarria's discomfort.

Patrick gave a small smile. "Scofield," he said. "Patrick Scofield."

"Nice to meet you, Patrick Scofield." Alison extended her hand in a dramatic gesture.

"Yeah, you too," said Patrick.

"Well," said Alison. "Gotta go. I need to talk to Sophia."

"Wait, Ali," Cyndarria said, but her friend had already turned and run off.

"So, I'd really like to see you again," said Patrick. He backed her up against the building wall, his arms on each side of her. She felt trapped.

"I'm sorry, but I don't think so, Patrick. I'm really busy with school and, and…my friends."

"I could be your best friend. C'mon, I'm a nice guy." He took hold of Cyndarria's arm again and squeezed a little too hard.

Cyndarria's stomach tensed. She was starting to feel a little desperate. She didn't want to scream for help. That would be ridiculous. She just wanted to get away from this guy she didn't really know, who was scaring her.

At that moment, she heard Coach Sam's voice. "Okay, ladies," she called. "Time to huddle up. The rain's starting to let up, and there are a few things I want to talk with you about."

"That's my coach," said Cyndarria. "I really do have to go."

Patrick let go of her arm reluctantly. "I'll see you again soon," he said.

"Not if I can help it," thought Cyndarria.

She ran over to where Coach Sam was talking to her teammates. She looked at Cyndarria. "You okay?" she asked.

Cyndarria shrugged. The truth was she wasn't sure how she was feeling. First there was the disqualification and then the run-in with Patrick. She just wanted the day to be over, so she could go home where she would feel safe and protected.

Three hours later the day was over, and the score was abysmal. Laurelton had trounced them badly. As much as they had felt ecstatically high after the Cedar Ridge meet, they felt equally low now. Even Joey, who usually had something funny to say, was glum.

Cyndarria found her mother waiting in the car for her. "I drove Lovelie and the boys home earlier," she said. "I'm afraid the weather kind of took a toll on everyone's enthusiasm. I guess you guys didn't do so well, huh? Want to talk about it?"

"Maybe later," said Cyndarria. "I just want to go home and take a nap now."

Belle patted her daughter's knee. "It'll get better, honey. We all have bad days."

"I know, Mom," said Cyndarria, but inside she wasn't so sure.

CHAPTER 32

WHEN THEY ARRIVED home, Cyndarria went directly to her room. She sat down in Grandma Rose's rocker. "Today was awful, Grandma," she said. "I got DQ'ed in my race, and we lost the meet. Bad, really bad. Plus this guy named Patrick was there. This is the second time he's shown up, sort of out of nowhere. He won't leave me alone. I don't know what to do."

There was a knock on the door. Belle opened it and stuck her head in. "Okay if I come in?" she asked.

"Sure, Mom."

Belle sat down on Cyndarria's bed and studied her daughter. "What's wrong, honey? I know you're bummed because of the meet. Is there anything else bothering you?"

Suddenly Cyndarria's throat constricted and she teared up. "It's just everything," she said. "I got DQ'ed, and I'm not sure if Coach Sam believes that I didn't bump Brandi on purpose. I hate that she doubts me."

"You can talk with her again on Monday. I think she'll be convinced."

"Plus we lost the meet so bad, and here we thought we were going to do really well this season."

"Well, you have a couple more meets, including the league championships. There's still time."

"I know, Mom. It's just...I guess I'm just feeling really discouraged right now."

"That happens to all of us. You're a good runner, Cyndarria. Your team has a lot of potential. When something like this happens, you have to learn from it, then put it behind you and focus on the next meet. I'm sure Coach Sam will tell you the same thing."

Cyndarria shrugged. She nodded. "Thanks, Mom."

Belle waited a moment. "Anything else you want to talk about?"

Cyndarria looked at her mother. Belle met her gaze. She gave Cyndarria a small, sympathetic smile.

"There's this guy," Cyndarria said. "Patrick Scofield. He goes to Cedar Ridge High School and he....I don't know....He just keeps talking to me, and today he grabbed my arm when I said I had to go. He said he'd see me again soon. Mom, he gives me the creeps."

Belle frowned. "I think we need to talk to your father about this."

"Okay," said Cyndarria, relieved. Her father would know what to do. He would protect her.

When Toad got home an hour later, he was in high spirits. "Pizza night!" he called as he came in the door.

"Yea!" cried J.J. "Did you get pepperoni on it?"

"One with pepperoni and the other with vegies, to please your mom."

"I want pepperoni!" said Toby. "It's my favorite!"

Belle came downstairs and gave her husband a kiss. "Pizza, huh? That will be great because I have absolutely nothing planned for dinner."

"Where's the daughter unit?" asked Toad, who was a big fan of the Coneheads.

"Upstairs resting. She had a really bad meet today, and something else happened that we should talk about later."

Toad looked quizzically at his wife. He nodded. "Okay, sure."

Belle tossed together a quick salad, and the family sat down to eat. Cyndarria was quiet, but the boys talked happily about their day.

"We got all wetted at the track meet!" exclaimed Toby. "It was fun!"

"J.J. jumped in a big puddle," reported Belle. "His mother was not pleased."

"Sorry, Mommy," he said. "I won't do it again."

Belle gazed fondly at her middle child. "Why do I find that a little hard to believe?"

After dinner, Cyndarria helped clear the table, and Belle loaded the dishwasher. The boys settled in front of the television to watch a Speedy Gonzales video.

"So what happened today that we need to talk about?" asked Toad, when he finished putting the left-over pizza in the refrigerator. "Is there a problem?"

"Why don't we go upstairs to talk?" said Belle. "I'd rather the boys didn't hear about it."

Toad looked immediately concerned. "Sounds serious."

"It could be," said Belle. "I'm not quite sure, but it makes me uncomfortable."

"If you're uncomfortable, I'm uncomfortable," Toad reassured her.

They started upstairs. "It's about Cyndarria," said Belle.

"Cyndarria? Did she get in trouble?"

"I'll let her tell you."

When they were seated in their room, they both looked expectantly at their daughter. "What's up, kiddo?" asked Toad. "Something wrong?"

Ten minutes later, Cyndarria finished telling him about what had happened with Patrick Scofield. "He just makes me feel really uncomfortable," she said.

"I can understand why," said Toad. "I think maybe I'll contact Cedar Ridge High School on Monday and see what the story is on him."

Sunday passed quietly. Ali and Cyndarria went running in order to make up the practice time they had missed on Wednesday. Cyndarria pushed herself extra hard, experiencing a certain catharsis from the effort.

"So this Patrick Scofield seems pretty interested in you," Alison said.

"I'm not interested in him. He's creepy."

"How so?"

Cyndarria told her friend the details of what had happened.

"Did you tell your mom and dad?" Ali asked.

"Yeah, my dad's going to contact Cedar Ridge High School tomorrow."

Monday morning before he headed to the restaurant, Toad was on the phone. The principal's secretary listened briefly to his concern, then said, "Mr. Sheridan is in his office. I'll connect you right now."

"This is Ben Sheridan," said the voice that answered. "What can I do for you?"

"Mr. Sheridan, this is Toad Thornwell. My daughter attends Sycamore Creek Middle School, and there was an incident involving one of your students at last Saturday's track meet."

"I see. Who's the person in question?"

"A guy named Patrick Scofield. He was harassing my daughter."

"Hmmm…Scofield did you say? Patrick Scofield?"

"That's right."

There was a moment of silence. "Mr. Thornwell, are you sure the young man was from Cedar Ridge?"

"That's what he told my daughter."

"I've been here for 15 years, and I can tell you flat out that there are no Scofields who even live in the area, let alone attend this high school. However, the fact that this guy said he was from here is very concerning to me. Unfortunately, I'm not sure what more I can tell you."

"I'm not either, at least not right now," admitted Toad. "Thanks for your help."

"Good luck, Mr. Thornwell. Don't hesitate to contact me if anything else comes up where I could be of service."

"I appreciate that," said Toad.

He hung up and sat at his desk, thinking. At this point, he felt there was real reason to be concerned. Why would the kid lie about attending Cedar Ridge High School? And if he lied about that, had he lied about anything else?

One thing Toad knew for sure: he would be at Cyndarria's next track meet. He had no idea why the kid had chosen her for his unwanted attention, but he meant to make certain it stopped.

CHAPTER 33

CYNDARRIA WAS LOOKING forward to the next story hour. When Wednesday arrived, she was happy to see that both Maisie and Zach were there again, and she had a new four-year-old named Molly, who seemed very excited to be there.

She sat the three children down at the same table she had used before. "We have another fun book to read today, and then we're going to draw a picture. After that, I think maybe we get to have a snack. How does that sound?"

Molly and Maisie both clapped their hands. Zach looked at them. He had yet to say anything in Cyndarria's presence, limiting his communication to nods and shakes of his head. He reminded her of her little brother. She hoped she could make him feel comfortable enough that he would open up a bit.

"Today we have a counting book," Cyndarria said, smiling enthusiastically. "Who knows how to count?"

Molly and Maisie raised their hands eagerly. "I do!" exclaimed Molly. "Do you want to heaw?"

"I'd love to, Molly," said Cyndarria.

Molly sat up a little straighter and seemed to compose herself for this important moment. "One, two, fwee, fouw, five, six, seven, eight, nine, ten." She looked at the others triumphantly.

"That was great, Molly!" exclaimed Cyndarria.

Zach was looking a bit oddly at Molly and appeared almost to relax a little.

"How about you, Zach? Can you count for us?" Cyndarria asked.

He nodded tentatively. He looked around the room, seeming to check to see if others were listening. He took a small breath. "One," he said, then stopped.

"That's good, Zach. Can you tell us what comes after one?"

"I know!" said Maisie eagerly.

"You can count next, Maisie. It's Zach's turn, okay?"

"Okay," said Maisie.

Cyndarria turned back to the little boy. She smiled and waited.

Zach pressed his lips together. "One," he said again. "T-t-t-two."

"Aahh," thought Cyndarria. "That's it."

Zach seemed to be waiting for a reaction.

Cyndarria nodded encouragement. "Good, Zach. One, two…"

Zach gathered himself. "Three, four, f-f-f-five, six, seven, eight, nine, t-t-t-ten."

Maisie clapped. "Good, Zachie, my turn!"

Cyndarria smiled at the child. "Okay, Maisie. Let's hear it."

Maisie counted happily.

"Wow, you guys are so good," said Cyndarria. "I think you all deserve a high five." She held up her hand.

Zach seemed especially pleased as he slapped Cyndarria's hand. "Good," she thought. "This is going to work."

"Okay," she said. "Let's look at our book." She held it up. "It's called, *Counting with Animals*." She opened the book to the first page. "What do we have here?" she asked.

"It's a fwoggie!" exclaimed Molly, delighted. "It's gween!"

"Good job, Molly. You're exactly right. It's one green frog. What does the frog say?"

"Wibbit, wibbit!" said Molly.

"Right again. Let's look at the next one. Zach, can you tell us what this is?"

He nodded. "A b-b-b-bunny."

"Two bunny wabbits!" said Molly, almost beside herself with excitement.

"Do you guys know who hunts wascally wabbits?" Cyndarria asked.

"I do! I do!" said Maisie. "Elmer Fudd! But these bunnies don't look wascally. They're just little and cute."

Cyndarria nodded. "I think you're right, Maisie."

They went on with the book: three yellow ducks, four red-and-black ladybugs, five bluebirds, six white kittens, seven brown puppies, eight orange foxes, nine gray mice, and ten purple butterflies.

"Which one did you guys like the best?" Cyndarria asked when they had finished.

"Kitties! I love kitties," said Maisie. "I have one at home. She's all black, and her name is Midnight."

"I wike the bunnies," said Molly. "I gave them names."

"I'm sure they would like having names," said Cyndarria. "What are they?"

"Maisie and Zachie!" Molly exclaimed. She clapped and looked at the others to see if they were as delighted as she was.

"Okay," said Maisie. "I'm a bunny." She put a hand on each side of her head and wiggled her index fingers. "Maisie bunny. Do you want to be a bunny, Zachie?"

Zach shook his head. "A f-f-f-fox," he said. "They're smart."

"So we have a bunny and a fox," said Cyndarria. "What animal would you like to be, Molly?"

"I think a buttewfwy," said Molly. "It would be fun to fwy."

"Yes it would," agreed Cyndarria. "Okay, I have some paper and some crayons, so you can draw and color the animal you'd like to be."

"What animal do you want to be, Miss Cyndarria?" asked Maisie.

"Maybe a doggie. We have a dog at home named Oliver. I think I would like to be his friend."

For the next fifteen minutes, the three children sat and painstakingly drew and colored their pictures, with occasional help from Cyndarria. She was surprised at how seriously they worked. The girls had some trouble staying inside the lines of their drawings as they colored, but Zach was another story. He was completely focused and very patient. The fox he drew was surprisingly good, and he took his time coloring, carefully staying within the lines of his drawing. When he was done, he put his crayon down, and looked his work over critically.

"Okay," he said.

"How about if we tell a little bit about our drawings?" said Cyndarria.

"You start, Miss Cyndarria," said Maisie.

Cyndarria held up the dog she had drawn. "Here's my doggie," she said. "Her name is Olivia, and she's Oliver's friend. They like to play together. Who's next?"

"Me!" said Molly. "This is my buttewfwy. I think she's nice."

"What's her name?" asked Maisie.

"Hmmm, Betsy. Betsy is a good name."

"I like that name too," said Cyndarria. "Do you want to go next, Maisie?"

"Okay. This is my bunny. Her name is Bunnylicious. She's my friend."

"Thank you, Maisie. Zach?"

Zach held up his drawing. "Fred the f-f-f-fox," he said. Zach set his drawing back down on the table.

"He's a very handsome fox, Zach. Do you think he could trick a hare?"

Zach nodded. "He's v-v-v-very smart."

"What's a hare?" asked Maisie.

"It's a cousin to your bunny," said Cyndarria.

"Well, my bunny is smart too, so no tricks, Zachie!"

"Okay," said Zach.

"Are you guys hungry?" asked Cyndarria. "I think I just saw Mrs. Doolittle bring in the snack."

"Yes!" the girls shouted.

Zach settled for nodding his head.

"All right," said Cyndarria. "Why don't we go over and check out the snacks?"

When they got to the snack table, there were already several other children lined up. Toby came over to Cyndarria.

"Hi, Cyndarria," he said. "This was fun. Alison read us a story about Alexander's terrible, horrible, no good, very bad day. It was funny."

"I like that story," said Cyndarria. "What was the worst part of his day?"

"Kissing on TV," said Toby. "Yuck! And his friend was mean to him."

"Yeah, that would be the worst part," agreed Cyndarria. "But he had to eat lima beans for dinner. That's pretty bad too."

Toby nodded, then went over to talk to J.J., who had just joined the line.

Mrs. Doolittle stood in front of the group. She held up her hands and looked at the children. She put one finger to her lips.

"Shhhh," she said. "It's time to listen. Did you have a good time today?"

"Yes," the children chorused.

"Did you enjoy your stories?"

"Yes," they repeated.

"Are you hungry for a snack?"

This time the answer was much louder and punctuated by clapping. Molly jumped up and down. "I'm hungwy!" she exclaimed.

"Okay," said Mrs. Doolittle. "You can form two lines and choose your snack, but first, how about if you tell Miss Cyndarria, Miss Alison, and Mr. Simon thank you for reading to you today?"

"Thank you," the children called obediently, then eagerly formed two lines.

Cyndarria stood in back with Alison. "This was the most fun I've had in a long time," she said. "I'm glad we get to do it all summer."

"Me, too," said Alison. "The kids are great, and it makes me feel good."

"Yes, it does," agreed Cyndarria. Since the previous Saturday, this was the first time she had felt relaxed and happy. "It's good, she thought, "to feel good."

CHAPTER 34

PRACTICES THAT WEEK and the following one suddenly became more intense, even without the coaches' urging. Team members were frustrated with themselves because they knew they hadn't performed as well as they were capable of performing the Saturday before.

Among the boys, Joey was particularly vocal. He began each practice with a loud yell. "Let's go, you guys! We can be champions!!"

His energy and drive became infectious. Kids no longer complained about running sprints, endlessly practicing their hand-offs, or taking extra jumps till they reached their goal for the day. Voluntarily, the distance runners ran more laps. At the end of every practice, they huddled up in one huge circle and yelled what had become their mantra, "WE CAN BE CHAMPIONS!"

May 23rd, the date of their meet with Chippewa Bend, dawned sunny and warm. The temperature was predicted to be in the 70's with low humidity—the best kind of Michigan spring weather and perfect for a track meet. Toad drove Belle and the boys. Emmanuel invited Lovelie to accompany him, and she happily accepted. They sat together in the stands. Belle put sunscreen on the boys and let them run free with their friends.

The team had arrived in high spirits. The last couple weeks of intense practice had them feeling better about themselves and confident they would do well against Chippewa Bend. Before getting off the bus, Joey had yelled, "What can we be?"

"WE CAN BE CHAMPIONS!" was the rousing cry, shouted and, at that moment, believed by everyone on the team.

Alison started them off with a win in the 100-yard dash. On the other side of the field, Joey recorded his longest shot-put of the season, and Chippewa Bend's best shot-putter, who had been the league champion last spring, fell just short.

"This is a very good sign," said Henri, who was standing beside Cyndarria, waiting for the 120 hurdles to be called. "Joey really wanted to beat that guy."

"Good luck today, Henri. It's time you won one."

"I will do my best," said Henri. "Coach McIntyre has been working with me a lot on my technique. I feel more confident."

A few minutes later the announcement came over the loudspeaker. "Hurdlers in the 120, you're up next."

"We're all rooting for you, Henri," said Sophia, who had joined Cyndarria on the sidelines.

"Thank you, Sophia."

Henri lined up with the others. The race would be short, well under twenty seconds, and didn't allow for any mistakes. Emmanuel and Lovelie both watched intently. The starter's gun went off, and Lovelie gripped Emmanuel's arm.

"C'mon, Henri!" she yelled.

Emmanuel held his breath without realizing it as he watched his son skim cleanly over each hurdle. At the finish line, Henri leaned forward hard as Coach McIntyre had taught him, and by a head he had his first victory.

Lovelie and Belle both leaped up cheering, their arms held high. Emmanuel stood, his face a mixture of joy and parental pride.

Toad shook his hand. "Congrats, man, your son just won his first race!"

"Yes, indeed he did," said Emmanuel. "Indeed he did."

The rest of the day was filled with one celebration after another. Cyndarria won the 880, and this time she didn't throw up afterward. Her relay with Penny, Maria Victoria and Sophia would be the final event of the day, so she could relax for a while.

"I'm gonna go buy a Gatorade," she said. "My mom gave our last one to Henri."

She jogged over to the food stand and stood in line. While she was waiting, she heard a familiar voice behind her.

"I told you I'd see you soon."

Cyndarria closed her eyes and said nothing.

"Hey," Patrick said, "aren't you going to tell me how glad you are to see me? I came all the way over here from Cedar Ridge, just to watch you run. You did great today."

"Uhh, thanks, Patrick." Cyndarria was at the head of the line. "I'd like a Gatorade, please. The blue one."

"I've got that," said Patrick, and handed the vendor a dollar bill.

"No, I've got money," objected Cyndarria. "I don't need yours."

"Hey, it's my pleasure," said Patrick. He smiled.

"Well, thank you," Cyndarria said. "I've got to go. My relay is coming up soon."

"I've seen the schedule," Patrick said. "Your race isn't for at least half-an-hour. Stay and visit awhile. I just bought your Gatorade. The least you can do is talk to me for a few minutes."

Cyndarria looked over toward her parents. She saw Toad stand.

"I've really got to go," she said.

Patrick looked annoyed. He grabbed her arm as she tried to push past him. "You're not being very grateful," he said. "I just want to talk for a while."

Cyndarria pulled on her arm, but Patrick's grip tightened. "No!" she said.

Patrick looked almost as though he might hit her. He raised his hand, and at that moment, Cyndarria heard her father's voice.

"Take your hands off her!" Cyndarria had never heard her father sound so angry.

Patrick turned and glared at Toad. "Yeah? Who're you to tell me what to do, old man?" Patrick's voice had changed too. It was almost a snarl.

"I'm her father. Let go of her." Toad's voice was steely, and his eyes didn't leave Patrick's.

Patrick continued to grip Cyndarria's arm, even when she tried again to get loose. He stared back at Toad, daring him to do anything more.

Cyndarria made one final effort, and she almost fell over when Patrick released her arm. Toad immediately pushed her behind him.

"Do not ever touch my daughter again." Toad's voice was low and menacing. "Do not talk to her. Do not try to see her."

Patrick's anger had been building. Suddenly he ran at Toad and pushed him hard into Cyndarria, causing her to fall. Toad turned to pick her up, and Patrick kicked at him.

"I'll do what I want," he screamed. "You can't stop me!" He turned then and ran off.

Toad wanted to pursue him, but he was more concerned about his daughter. "Are you okay, Cyndarria?" he asked, his face full of anguish.

"I think so. Thanks, Dad. I don't know what would have happened if you hadn't come up."

Toad put his arm around his oldest child and walked her back to her teammates. "Are you going to be all right to run?" he asked.

"I have to be," said Cyndarria, but she felt shaken and sick to her stomach. "Don't worry, Dad."

220

Toad returned to the bleachers where Belle sat, looking traumatized.

"Oh my God, Toad, what happened? Is she okay?"

"It was that Patrick kid. It shook her up. She says she's all right to run, but I'm not so sure."

"What did he do?"

"I'll tell you about it later," said Toad, "when we get home. He's gone, and I don't think he'll be back. That's the main thing."

The mile relay was finally called. Cyndarria, as their fastest runner, ran anchor. Penny ran first, then Sophia, followed by Maria Victoria. Sycamore Creek had a comfortable lead when Maria Victoria handed the baton off to Cyndarria.

Cyndarria gripped it tightly because her palms were sweaty, and her heart was already pounding. Her stomach felt queasy. She finished the first 200 yards still ahead, but the Chippewa Bend runner was gaining on her. On the far side of the track, the feeling of nausea overwhelmed her, and she bent over and began to throw up. She felt dizzy, and almost without knowing what was happening, she found herself on her knees. She heaved again, and then began to cry uncontrollably. She tried to get up, but went down again and finally sat on the track and wept.

Before she knew it, Coach Sam was at her side. She put her arms around Cyndarria and held her tight.

"I'm so sorry," Cyndarria whispered between sobs. "I'm so sorry."

"Don't worry. It's not a big deal. We've had a great day. The most important thing right now is for you to be okay."

Cyndarria managed to nod, then let her head fall on Coach Sam's shoulder and allowed herself to be comforted.

221

"Do you want to ride home with your mom and dad instead of on the bus?" Coach Sam asked. "That might be better today."

"I think so," said Cyndarria, relieved that she wouldn't have to face her teammates and be pestered by their questions.

The ride back to Sycamore Creek was quiet. Even Toby and J.J., who sensed that their sister was upset, were subdued. When they got home, Cyndarria looked at her father. "Thanks, Daddy," she said.

Toad felt his throat tighten. He nodded.

"I'm going to take a nap," she said. Cyndarria walked upstairs to her bedroom and quietly closed the door. She dropped her gym bag, pulled off her shoes, lay down on her bed, and began to cry softly.

CHAPTER 35

IT WAS THE last week in May, and it was clear that teachers as well as students were eager to finish the school year and begin to enjoy summer vacation. In English class, Mrs. Wackenstein assigned them a final essay: "The Most Important Thing I Learned This Year." Cyndarria wasn't sure what to write about, but after thinking about it for a while, she decided to describe her track experience, avoiding the negative aspects, and rediscovering herself as a runner.

Like her teammates, she hoped that the track season would end with Sycamore Creek winning the league championship. The team talked about it at every practice, and the coaches even got everyone a T-shirt with the motto, "We Can Be Champions!" printed on the front. The shirts were red and white, the school colors, and were worn daily at practice. If enthusiasm and motivation could win championships, the Sycamore Creek Middle School track team had a better than even chance of pulling it off.

Wednesday at story hour found Maisie, Molly and Zach eagerly awaiting Cyndarria's arrival. She greeted each of them with a big smile and a hug. She was delighted that Zach continued to be willing to talk—not a lot, but some. The girls both encouraged him with their infectious laughter and clapping whenever he added something to the conversation. He smiled more often, and even when he was quiet, seemed to be enjoying himself.

During snack time, Cyndarria was approached by a woman she had noticed the first day but had never met. The woman smiled and held out her hand.

"I'm Anna Russo, Zach's mother," she said.

"I'm so happy to meet you," said Cyndarria. "I've really enjoyed having Zach in my group during story hour."

"You know, he was very nervous about coming the first time. I almost couldn't convince him to try it."

"He was really shy at first," agreed Cyndarria, "but he seems to have come out of his shell a lot. And he's very talented artistically. He draws way better than I do!"

"He does love to draw. That's probably the only area where he's truly confident."

"He kind of reminds me of my little brother Toby. He doesn't like to talk a whole lot either, but he's really good at arithmetic."

"Actually," said Anna, "the reason I wanted to speak with you was to thank you for all you've done for Zach. He looks forward to coming to story hour now, and he likes to talk about it. That's never happened before."

"Thank you, Mrs. Russo, but I can't take a lot of credit for that. The two little girls who are in his group, Maisie and Molly, have been the difference makers. They're both very friendly and expressive and always applaud Zach when he participates. And, to be honest, I think working with those three kids makes me happier than it does them."

"Will you be continuing in the program this summer?"

"I absolutely will. In fact, it's one of the things I'm most looking forward to."

"I'm sure Zach will be pleased to hear that. Despite you not wanting to take much credit, it's obvious to me that Zach likes you and enjoys being in your group."

"I really appreciate that, Mrs. Russo, and, honestly, the feelings are mutual."

Wednesday was the hottest day of spring so far: 85 degrees with 80 per cent humidity. More like mid-July. It didn't cool off much that night. Cyndarria tossed and turned in bed. She was wearing shorty pajamas and had kicked off her sheet, but she was still uncomfortably warm. She slept fitfully, and at 1:00 in the morning she woke up, her throat dry.

"I hate this weather," she grumbled to herself. She got out of bed and went to the bathroom to get a drink. She let the water run till it was good and cold, then filled her glass. She looked out the window as she often did when she got up at night. It was always peaceful, and in the winter she loved looking at the snow sparkling under the streetlight.

She was about to turn and go back to bed when she noticed a lone figure walking up the sidewalk. He was dressed in a dark sweatshirt and seemed to be studying each house as he walked by. He stopped for a moment under the streetlight and lit a cigarette. He looked vaguely familiar to Cyndarria, and she strained to see him better as he smoked.

When he dropped the cigarette and crushed it with his shoe, it hit her. "It's Patrick!" she thought. She felt a moment of panic, but realized quickly that she was in her house and perfectly safe.

Patrick pulled the hood of his sweatshirt up over his head and removed something from a backpack he was carrying. He walked quickly, then stopped in front of her house and checked the name on the mailbox. He pulled out his lighter again and lit what appeared to be a fuse coming out of a bottle and, to Cyndarria's horror, threw it at the house. As soon as he let the bottle go, he turned and ran.

Cyndarria saw it arcing toward the house, almost in slow motion, and waited for a crash as it broke through the front window. Instead, it hit the side of the house just to the right of the large picture window and dropped down into the bushes, immediately igniting a fire.

For a second she stood paralyzed, unbelieving, and then she screamed and ran for her parents' bedroom.

"Mom! Dad!" she shrieked. "Wake up! There's a fire! Wake up!"

Toad sat up and was immediately fully awake. "Cyndarria, what are you talking about? A fire? Where?"

"Out in front. In the bushes."

Toad turned to his wife, who was still a little groggy. "Belle, get the boys, and all four of you get out of the house now! Go out the back door! I'll get the fire extinguisher."

Belle stood up quickly. "Cyndarria, go wake up J.J. I'll get Toby. Hurry!"

She turned to her husband. "Should I call 9-1-1?"

"Let me see what I can do first. Give me a couple minutes."

J.J. woke up quickly when Cyndarria shook him. "J.J., we have to get outside right away. There's a fire."

He looked confused for a moment, then he grabbed Oliver the Second from under his pillow. "Okay," he said. "We need to get Ollie too."

"We will," said Cyndarria. "Hurry!"

Belle ran into Toby's room, gathered him in her arms, and carried the sleeping child down the stairs. She thought she could smell smoke when she reached the main floor. There was no evidence of fire, but she could see flames in front of the window.

"Out the back," she ordered.

When they were out, she gave Toby to Cyndarria and ran around to the front of the house to see if Toad had the fire under control. Despite his best efforts, the flames were spreading to other bushes and threatening the shutters on the house.

"Better call 9-1-1," he yelled. "I can't seem to stop it!"

Belle ran back around and into the kitchen. She dialed the emergency number. "Our house is on fire," she said, trying to speak calmly.

"Okay, ma'am," said the dispatcher. "Are you at 647 Pine?"

"Yes."

"Is everyone out of the house?"

"Yes, we're all okay, thank God. I'm in the kitchen right now, but I can get out safely."

"Very good, ma'am. We're on our way. We should be there within five minutes."

"Thank you. Please hurry."

"We'll do our best."

In just under six minutes, the Sycamore Creek fire truck, sirens piercing the night air, careened around the corner onto Pine, just a block from the Thornwell house.

By then, Belle and the three children were standing in front on the sidewalk, still unable to believe what was happening. J.J. gripped Oliver fiercely.

"Toad," said George Barnes, the fire chief, "we'll take over now."

Toad nodded. "Thanks, George. Glad you're here."

With the arrival of the firemen, the flames were extinguished within five minutes. The bushes in front of the house were destroyed, but the house itself suffered minimal damage to the siding and shutters. After the fire was out, George and Pete Sanborn, one of his men, examined the ground around the burn area carefully and found a broken bottle.

"Looks like a Molotov cocktail, Chief," said Pete. "I'm thinking this must be the work of our friendly local arsonist. This is the first time that we found direct evidence so quickly."

"Good chance you're right. I'm going to talk to the family. See if anybody saw anything."

Toad, Belle and the children were still huddled together on the sidewalk. When Chief Barnes approached, Toad held out his hand. "Thanks, George. Really appreciate that fast response."

"I've got a good group of guys working with me," said George. "We found a broken bottle that looks like it could have been used for a Molotov cocktail. Any possibility someone saw it happen?"

"Cyndarria got us up," said Toad. He turned to his daughter. "Did you see anything before the fire started?"

Cyndarria nodded. "I know who it was," she said. "I saw him throw it."

Belle was stunned. "You know who it was? Who?"

"Patrick Scofield. I wasn't sure at first, but he stopped to smoke a cigarette under the streetlight, and I got a good look at him. I know it was Patrick."

"Reynolds isn't going to believe this," said George, referring to the special investigator who had been working on the arson case. "He's been trying to solve this thing for months. He's going to want to talk to you tomorrow." He turned to Toad. "Can you take her into the police department around 10:00?"

Toad looked at his daughter. Cyndarria nodded. "She'll be there, George. We know this kid for other reasons. I won't be sorry to see him locked up."

"Me neither," thought Cyndarria. "Me neither."

CHAPTER 36

THE FOLLOWING DAY Belle called the middle school to excuse Cyndarria from her morning classes.

"Is she ill?" asked Oraleen, who was always concerned about the students' welfare.

"No," said Belle. "Someone threw a Molotov cocktail at our house last night, and Cyndarria saw who did it."

"Oh my goodness!" exclaimed Oraleen. "Is everyone okay? Was much damage done to the house?"

"Fortunately, we were all able to get out safely, and between Toad and the fire department, the house suffered minimal damage."

"Thank the good Lord for that!"

"Believe me, I have!" said Belle. "Anyway, because Cyndarria actually knows this guy, she has to talk with the police this morning. They think it's probably the same one who was responsible for the other two house fires in the last year and likely for the fire at the school."

"Mr. Johansson is going to be so pleased to hear this," said Oraleen. "He's been very worried. Do you mind if I tell him?"

"That's fine," said Belle, "but I think it would be better not to say anything to anyone else for the time being."

"Of course," agreed Oraleen. "I'm so glad no one was hurt."

"Thank you, Oraleen."

Toad and Cyndarria arrived at the police station a little before 10:00 and were sent to speak with Detective Reynolds. He sat and listened carefully, taking a few notes, as Cyndarria told what had happened.

"Are you certain of the identity of this guy?" he asked when she had finished.

"I've had a few run-ins with him recently, so yeah, I'm certain."

"We'll still want to do a lineup, just to have you identify him officially. Of course, the first thing is to pick him up."

"There may be a problem with that," said Toad. "I talked with Ben Sheridan, the Cedar Ridge High School principal, and he told me there's no Patrick Scofield there now, and there never has been. In addition, there are no Scofields who live in that district. So where does that leave us?"

"We'll check with other schools in the area," said Reynolds, "and see what we come up with. If we find nothing, we may have to consider the possibility that he lied to Cyndarria about his identity. In a case like this, which involves harassment as well, that would not be unusual. Unfortunately, it would also make finding him considerably more difficult. As a last resort, we may have to hope that he shows up at her next track meet, and we could nail him there."

"I hope it doesn't come to that," said Toad. "I don't want him anywhere near Cyndarria again."

"I understand. I'll get some people on it and keep you posted. Thanks for coming in today."

"Sure thing," said Toad. "Good luck."

Cyndarria found herself on edge for the next few days. There was no word from Detective Reynolds, and she was beginning to get nervous about another run-in with Patrick, or whoever he was, at the league championship. She didn't want anything distracting her that day.

Saturday morning there was a surprise call. Belle answered the phone.

"Is this the Thornwell residence?" a voice asked.

"It is," said Belle. "May I ask who's calling?"

"This is Ben Sheridan. I'm the principal over at Cedar Ridge High School. I spoke with your husband a few days ago. Is he around?"

"Yes. Just a moment, please. Toad," Belle called, "It's Ben Sheridan. He'd like to speak with you."

"Mr. Sheridan, hello," said Toad.

"Good morning. I'm sorry to bother you on a Saturday, but I've been mulling our earlier discussion over in my mind, and I've had a thought that may be of interest."

"Anything you can tell me would be helpful. This guy who calls himself Patrick Scofield threw a Molotov cocktail at our house the other night. Cyndarria actually saw him, and she's certain it was Scofield. Fortunately, not much damage was done to the house, but he's also continued to harass her. We talked with the police, and they're going to see if they can find any Scofields in the area, but they're also considering the possibility that the kid may have lied about his identity."

"Interesting you would say that because I've had the same thought. There was this kid named Paul Turnbull who got kicked out of school two, three years ago. A real trouble maker. His parents kicked him out of the house at about the same time. He had a nasty temper—started a fire in a waste basket once and also abused his girlfriend. Stalked her when she tried to break up. Her parents finally had to take out a restraining order against him."

"Do you have any idea if he's still in the area?"

"Not sure. I checked the phone book, and there's no Paul Turnbull listed. There is a Melissa Turnbull. That would be his older sister. She dropped out the year before Paul did, just kind

231

of gave up. There's an address and phone number listed for her. She might be able to tell you where Paul is."

"It's worth a shot," said Toad. "Give me the address and number. I'll get in touch with Detective Reynolds and have him check it out. Thanks a lot, Mr. Sheridan."

"Ben. Please."

"Thanks, Ben. I'll let you know what happens."

"I'd appreciate that. Glad I could be of help."

Reynolds had given Toad his home phone number and told him to call anytime, so Toad dialed him up immediately.

Reynolds answered on the second ring. "Reynolds," he said, his usual greeting at work and at home.

"Detective, this is Toad Thornwell. I just got a call from Ben Sheridan over at Cedar Ridge, and he gave me some pretty interesting information. I thought I should let you know right away. It may be the break you've been hoping for."

"Fire away," said Reynolds. "We haven't been able to find any likely Scofields in the area. An old guy who lives alone and a young, widowed mother with two daughters. No help there."

"Sheridan thinks it might be a kid named Paul Turnbull. High-school dropout. Trouble maker. Fire bug. Abused his girl-friend. I have the phone number and address of his sister, Melissa. Sheridan's feeling is that she might know where he is."

"This sounds like a real possibility. Give me what you have, and we'll check it out today."

"Great. Let me know if we can do anything."

"If we get the kid, we'll round up a few others and have your daughter come in and look at the lineup. Hopefully, she'll be able to identify him."

"I'll let her know," said Toad.

The rest of the morning and early afternoon, Cyndarria felt as though she existed in suspended animation. She couldn't think about anything else, just waited for the phone to ring. Finally, at 4:00 it did.

Toad answered on the first ring.

"We got him," said Detective Reynolds. "He tried to sneak out the back when he heard me talking to his sister, but fortunately, I had somebody waiting for him there. We've put together a lineup. Can you come in now?"

"We'll get there as soon as we can," said Toad.

He turned to Cyndarria, who stood waiting to hear what had happened. "They got him. Detective Reynolds would like us to go in, so you can look at the lineup right away."

"I'm ready," said Cyndarria.

Toad told Belle what was going on; then he and Cyndarria left.

When they got to the police station, Detective Reynolds was waiting for them. "We've had a little talk with Mr. Turnbull," he said. "He waived his right to an attorney. Won't say anything but that he's innocent, although his language was much more colorful than that. I'm going to take you to the room where you will look at the lineup. Don't worry; it's one-way glass. Nobody will be able to see you."

"Okay," said Cyndarria. Now that it was about to happen, she felt nervous. "Is it all right if my dad comes with me?"

"No problem."

Detective Reynolds led them to a small room with three chairs. A minute later, five guys about the same height and age as Patrick/Paul entered the small room opposite. Each one held a number.

"Take your time, Cyndarria. I want you to be very sure you're identifying the right guy," cautioned Reynolds.

Cyndarria looked at all five carefully and felt a surge of relief. He was there, she was sure. "He's number four," she said.

"You're absolutely certain," said Reynolds. "No doubts at all."

"Yes sir," said Cyndarria. "I'm sure."

Reynolds seemed to look as relieved as Cyndarria felt. "That's Turnbull," he said. "He fits the profile, and Cyndarria's ID makes it a slam-dunk. Looks like we got our boy."

He stood and held out his hand. "Thanks for bringing her in, Mr. Thornwell. And thanks, Cyndarria. If this goes to court, and it won't if there's a plea deal, you'll be asked to testify. We can fix it, so he can't see you. We generally do that for minors, so you don't have to be afraid."

Cyndarria nodded, though the possibility of having to testify made her nervous. "Okay," she said.

On the drive home, Toad took Cyndarria's hand and gave it a squeeze. "I'm really proud of you, kiddo. You did great."

"Thanks, Dad. I'm glad it's over. I hope I never see Paul Turnbull again."

"I think you can probably count on that," said Toad.

CHAPTER 37

FINALLY, SATURDAY, JUNE 6, the day the entire Sycamore Creek Middle School track team had been eagerly awaiting, arrived. The league championship would be the final athletic event of the school year, and Principal Johansson had encouraged the whole student body to attend.

Track didn't generally draw many fans, but today there was a good crowd. Students were feeling particularly rowdy and celebratory because classes would end the following Wednesday. Many of those in attendance had one or more friends on the track team, and they were determined to make their cheers heard.

As the home team, Sycamore Creek had the most supporters.

"This is so cool," said Sophia, as she waved to one of her friends. "I wish we had crowds like this all the time."

"Me too," said Cyndarria. She was stretching and running in place, even though the 880 wouldn't be called for at least 45 minutes. She had butterflies in her stomach because today would be her toughest race and had the most at stake. She had seen Brandi across the field when the team from Laurelton arrived. She stood out from the others because of her height and seemed to carry herself with a confidence that Cyndarria wished she were feeling right then.

Before the first event, everyone huddled up, and Joey led them in their team cheer: "We can be champions!"

Ten minutes later, the day started well for Sycamore Creek when Alison once again earned the 100-yard-dash crown.

The Sycamore Creek fans erupted in cheers. "Alison! Alison! Alison!" they chanted. Most of the girls on the team surrounded her for an excited group hug.

Coach Sam approached and chided them. "Okay, ladies, that's enough celebrating. It's going to be a long day, and that was just the first race."

The group hug ended, but the enthusiasm that Alison's victory had engendered did not.

"Way to go, Alison," said Coach Sam after the girls had left. "I'm proud of you."

"Thanks, Coach," replied Alison. "I'm really happy."

Time was passing quickly. Cyndarria was so focused on her own race and trying to tame the butterflies in her stomach, she missed seeing several of the events. She knew Henri had done well in the 120-yard hurdles, placing second. His best race was the 330 though, and she hoped he would win that one.

When the 880 was called, Cyndarria went over to line up. There were eight lanes with two girls from each school. Brandi had the fastest time of the season, so she was given lane one. Cyndarria was in lane two.

Brandi nodded at Cyndarria when she saw her. "Good luck," she said.

"I'll try not to bump you this time," said Cyndarria. She smiled sheepishly.

"I know you didn't do it on purpose. We're cool."

"I'm glad," said Cyndarria.

The starter, a grandfatherly type who had been doing this for years, interrupted them. "If everyone is done talking, we're going to get started here," he said.

Immediately the eight runners assumed the ready position. "Ready! Set!" The starter's pistol went off.

Like Brandi, Cyndarria preferred to let another runner set the pace. She settled into third place; Brandi was a couple runners back. Cyndarria knew that her best time was very close to Brandi's—only a couple seconds slower—and she was hoping, with the extra running she'd been doing, she might be able to surpass her.

The first half of the race went smoothly, and Cyndarria was feeling confident. The lead runner had tired and dropped back, so Cyndarria found herself in second place, just one stride behind the leader, a girl from Chippewa Bend, whom she had beaten earlier that season.

With two-hundred yards to go, Cyndarria sped up and passed her, not yet running full out. She felt good, her strides long, her breathing deep and even, her heart beat strong. At one hundred yards, she could hear footsteps pounding behind her. She knew without looking that it was Brandi. She'd been saving a final kick, and now she accelerated, but Brandi was gaining. With fifty yards to go, the two girls were even, and then Brandi did something that astonished Cyndarria. She found yet another gear and suddenly was leading by a full stride. Cyndarria tried, but she had nothing left. Brandi crossed the finish line first and raised her hands triumphantly in the air in celebration.

She came up to Cyndarria. "Good race," she said. "I thought you had me there for a while."

Coach Sam, who had been at the finish line, gave Cyndarria a hug. "Don't feel bad," she said. "That was your best time all season. I couldn't ask for anything more."

As the meet continued, it became clear that the two strongest teams were Sycamore Creek and Laurelton, only five points separating the two, with Laurelton in the lead. The best news was that Joey had placed first in shot put and simultaneously set a new school record of 48 feet 3 inches. He couldn't stop beaming and now went around encouraging all his teammates.

237

He led the entire middle-school cheering section in chanting, "We can be champions! We can be champions!"

But the result that made Cyndarria happiest was that Henri had won the 330 hurdles, all his hard work paying off. He had run up into the stands afterward, where his father and then Lovelie embraced him.

"You have made me very proud, son," said Emmanuel. "You have achieved for yourself and, more importantly, for your team. Now go down and cheer the rest of your teammates on."

"You did great, Henri," said Lovelie, near tears. "I am so happy for you. I know how hard you worked."

"Thank you, Father. Thank you, Lovelie. I have a good feeling about today. I think Joey is right. We can be champions."

The mile relay was the last event of the day. On the one hand, Cyndarria hoped that the championship would be decided by then; on the other, she wanted the final result to depend on that race, imagining that somehow Sophia, Penny, Maria Victoria, and she would win the day, giving the championship to Sycamore Creek. She wanted to be a hero, but on another level it terrified her. What if she failed? She had really wanted to win the 880, but she had lost to Brandi. Maybe she just wasn't good enough.

Going into the final relay, Sycamore Creek was leading by three points. As agreed upon, points awarded for first through fourth place would be 10, eight, six and four. All Sycamore Creek had to do was place second, and they would be champions. That took considerable pressure off Cyndarria because she knew her main competition once again would be Brandi in the anchor leg.

The four girls formed a huddle before the race. Coach Sam let them talk amongst themselves. She had done what she could do. Now it was on them.

"Okay, you guys," said Sophia. "It's up to us. We can do this."

"I believe in you guys," said Cyndarria. "We've worked so hard all spring. It's our time."

And right then she believed it.

Cyndarria held out her hand, and each of the girls placed hers on top, one at a time.

"What can we be?" cried Maria Victoria.

"We can be champions!" they all shouted. "Let's go!"

The mile relay was an event that took over four minutes. Even so, no team could drop too far off the pace, or they would be doomed. Generally, schools had their fastest runners go first and last, hoping for both a strong start and a strong finish.

After the first two runners, Laurelton had a slight lead, with Sycamore Creek close behind and Chippewa Bend another couple yards back. Cedar Ridge had fallen well off the pace and now trailed by five yards. Cyndarria felt her heart pounding as she watched Maria Victoria, who ran third, come down the stretch to where she would hand the baton off to her. She had run a terrific third leg and now was leading by a full yard. Cyndarria began running as Maria Victoria approached, and she gripped the baton firmly on the hand-off.

Cyndarria felt almost ecstatic as she started to run. It was possible. They were in the lead. They could be champions! Despite her excitement, Cyndarria paced herself, knowing the worst thing she could do would be to run out of steam before the end of the race.

The first 200 went well. Cyndarria was still in the lead, but she could tell that Brandi was gaining on her. That was okay. She wanted to win, but knew second would still be good enough.

"We can be champions," she thought again and again, and one step coincided with each syllable.

She was on the backside of the track running comfortably when it happened. Suddenly, she felt her toe catch and, before she could stop herself, she went sprawling. Her palms scraped the track; both knees stung with the fall. She heard urgent shouts and screams in the background, but her mind didn't register the words' meaning.

In a flash, she heard her Grandma Rose say, "Well, you've gotten yourself in quite a pickle. I suggest you do something about it!"

She scrambled to her feet, her palms bloody and smarting, her knees hurting. "I will, Grandma," she thought. "Watch me!"

And she began to run as she had never run before, throwing caution to the wind, not worrying about a final spurt of energy at the end. Just running, tears streaming down her cheeks.

She had lost a few yards before she managed to get up, and the Chippewa Bend runner was ahead of her now. For an electric moment, she saw herself as a third-grader playing pom-pom-pull-away, tearing across the tennis court, outrunning all the other kids who wanted to catch her, making it safely to the other side. Panting. Triumphant. Almost giddy with pleasure.

She remembered the little engine that could and his mantra, "I think I can, I think I can," and, in her mind, it became her own. It calmed her and focused her effort as she pounded down the track.

"I think I can! I think I can! We can be champions!"

With 100 yards to go, she was close. She could tell the Chippewa Bend runner was pushing herself desperately, her arms almost out of control.

"I think I can! We can be champions!"

Suddenly, she was aware of the faces of teammates on the sidelines, cheering, urging her on, begging her to push harder. She heard loud cries from the stands. Someone shouted her name. "Cyndarria!" Was it her father?

Fifty yards and a guttural scream emerged from her lips. She felt it propel her forward. She would not lose! She would not lose!

Twenty-five yards. She was almost even with the Chippewa Bend runner. She could see Brandi was near the finish line. Second place. That's all she needed.

The entire cheering section was shouting, "We can be champions! We can be champions!"

Cyndarria was gasping; she felt she would throw up. Somehow, deep within herself she found something, and every bone, every muscle, every ounce of strength left in her body pushed her forward. The finish line was there. Cyndarria leaned forward desperately, then sprawled once again on the track. She didn't know if she had beaten the Chippewa Bend runner. For a moment she couldn't see or hear, only feel the agony of her body, which was beyond exhaustion. She felt sick and knew she was going to heave again. She got to her knees and her churning stomach emptied its contents.

And then her teammates were there, jumping up and down and screaming. What were they saying? Maria Victoria had tears in her eyes. Why was she crying?

For an instant, Cyndarria heard her Grandma Rose again. "You did well, Cyndarria. I'm proud of you."

Things finally came into focus. Coach Sam was there, helping her to stand. "Congratulations, champ," she said. "You just helped us win league championship."

Sophia, Penny, and Maria Victoria hugged her at the same time and blubbered, all of them overcome with emotion, "We are the champions!" And at that moment, Cyndarria felt that she had never been happier.

CHAPTER 38

THE FOLLOWING MONDAY after school, the track team had a party to celebrate their first league championship. Coach McIntyre and Coach Sam provided snacks. Team members were still jubilant, the girls hugging, the guys exchanging high-fives.

"Okay," said Coach McIntyre after 15 minutes of sheer celebration, "how about if you all take a seat? Coach Sam and I each have a special recognition for one of our team members."

Everyone sat down on the grass and waited expectantly. Coach McIntyre continued. "First, I want to say that all of you were terrific this season and I, for one, couldn't be prouder."

Coach Sam nodded in agreement. "Amen," she said.

"Each of you did your part, and as your coach, I appreciate all your effort and willingness to hang in there when things got a little tough. Still, Coach Sam and I both felt there was one person on each of our teams who deserved special recognition. Among the guys, this person gave us a lift every day with his enthusiasm and can-do attitude. He even gave us a slogan and led the way to a league championship while also setting a school record. I'm sure all of you know who I'm talking about. Joey, come on up here."

A cheer arose from the entire team and Joey, who seemed surprised and was uncharacteristically tongue-tied, came forward.

"Wow," he said when the coach handed him a framed certificate, "I don't know what to say. I just...I...Thank you so much. This is awesome!"

Everyone clapped, and Joey returned to where he had been sitting, grinning all the way.

Coach Sam stepped forward. She smiled at everyone. "Like Coach McIntyre, I am so proud of this entire group. Your work ethic was phenomenal, the best I've ever experienced in working with a team. As your coach, I was supposed to be the one who inspired you but, in all honesty, there were many times when you inspired me. There are several girls I could give this certificate to and feel good about it. However, I decided to choose the one who demonstrated particular courage and heart at a moment of adversity when it mattered most. We would not have won the league championship without her gutsy performance."

Suddenly all the girls began clapping and chanting, "Cyndarria! Cyndarria! Cyndarria!"

Coach Sam joined the team in applauding. Cyndarria felt simultaneously thrilled and embarrassed. "C'mon, girl!" said Coach Sam, holding out her hand.

Cyndarria got up and walked forward. Coach Sam gave her the framed certificate and hugged her.

"Thank you, Coach," said Cyndarria. "I'm not sure I deserve this, but I'm glad...I'm glad you think so."

She turned to the group. "Back in March when we started practice, I wasn't sure I was going to like track. I almost quit a couple times. To be honest, I kinda hated all those sprints."

The rest of the team laughed and applauded. "So did I," yelled Joey, once again the clown.

"Whaddah yah mean, Joey?" shouted one of his team-mates. "Your body is still a stranger to sprints. You wouldn't know a sprint if it came up and bit you!"

Joey raised his hand and nodded. "Yah got me there," he said, and everyone laughed.

"Anyway," said Cyndarria. "Track turned out to be one of the very best parts of my spring. I had almost forgotten how much I love to run."

She looked around at everyone. "You guys have all been terrific, and I'm really...I'm really grateful to have had all of you as teammates. Thanks."

The last couple days of school were mere formalities. Teachers had given up on trying to teach the students anything. Testing was over, and it was a question of handing in missing assignments, which a few teachers still begrudgingly accepted, and turning in textbooks.

Tuesday afternoon the entire student body attended the annual basketball game between the teachers and the students, fondly referred to as "Flunkers versus Dunkers." The crowd boisterously rooted for the students and booed the staff, which the teachers cheerfully accepted. When Penny, the smallest player on the floor, made a quick move around a panting Mr. Cassius and hit a shot, the students erupted in unbridled delight. The Dunkers won, but it was close—50-48, one painfully close, last-second, three-point shot away from victory for the Flunkers.

Wednesday was a shortened day, with only 20 minutes in each class. Some teachers brought in treats; many contented themselves with sitting around visiting with their students and wishing them a happy summer.

At the end of English class, Cyndarria told Henri to go ahead, then stopped at Mrs. Wackenstein's desk. She knew she wanted to say something but wasn't quite sure what. Mrs. Wackenstein looked at her expectantly.

"Yes, Miss Thornwell? Did you have a question?"

"Umm, no. I just..." There was an awkward silence. "I just wanted to tell you that I hope you have a nice summer and ...and I learned a lot this year. I didn't really expect to—I've never been very good at English. But I did. Thank you."

Mrs. Wackenstein looked at her thoughtfully. "I appreciate that, Miss Thornwell. Good luck in high school. I hope you continue to m'ntain high standards."

"I'll try," said Cyndarria. "Good-bye, Mrs. Wackenstein."

"Good-bye, Cyndarria," Mrs. Wackenstein replied, a small hint of a smile on her lips. "I wish you well this summer."

Cyndarria left her English room for the last time, feeling quite different than the first time she had walked in. "Hmm," she mused. "How about that? She called me Cyndarria."

At 10:25, Mr. Johannson came on over the public-address system.

"Attention students: I want to take this opportunity to thank you all for another great year at Sycamore Creek Middle School. Congratulations once again to our fantastic track team, who won the league championship last Saturday. Stay safe this summer and have fun. I'll see many of you in the fall. For you eighth-graders who will be entering high school next year, I wish you the very best as you continue your education. It is my sincere hope and belief that we have prepared you to succeed. With that, I wish you all a terrific summer. You are dismissed!"

Cheers went up from every classroom, and students flooded out into the hallways and headed for home. In the office, Mr. Johannson turned to Oraleen Jackson. "As always, thank you for everything, Oraleen. Honestly, I don't know what I would do without you. I've discovered that being a successful administrator requires two main things: being a good listener and having a great secretary."

"Thank you, Gerritt. There's no one I'd rather work for. I think we make a pretty darn good team, if I do say so myself."

Cyndarria and Henri walked home together, as usual. They talked little, content to enjoy the June sun and soft breeze.

"I'll see you this weekend," said Cyndarria when they arrived at her house. "I can't believe I'm turning 14 on Sunday."

"I'm looking forward to it," said Henri. "I love having brunch at Toad and the Frog's restaurant. It's cool that you invited the others too."

The others included a few members from the track team: Alison, Sophia, Penny, Maria Victoria, Joey and Stevie. Her father had offered to treat her and as many friends as she wanted to invite to a special brunch on her birthday, and Cyndarria had happily accepted.

"No presents," she had told them. "Just come and celebrate with me."

That afternoon was story hour at the library. Cyndarria and Alison arrived a little early in order to help Mrs. Doolittle get the snacks ready. She tried to vary them and offer the children something tasty and healthful within the constraints of her limited budget. Today there were Macintosh apples, and for a special sweet treat, which was always the children's favorite part, she filled a bowl with lollipops.

"I invited in a friend to do something special with the children the first part of the hour today," Mrs. Doolittle told the girls. "Her name is Mavis Forsythe. She's the choir director at my church. She works with both the adult and the children's choirs, and she's quite engaging. I think the kids will like her."

The children began arriving just as the snacks were finished. Mrs. Doolittle had them all sit on the floor in a circle. As she was about to speak, a small woman with flaming red hair, a face full of freckles and startling green eyes came through the library door. She was wearing a long dress covered with brilliant flowers and a necklace with several strands of bells, which tinkled happily when she walked. Her lips were painted orange, and her huge smile revealed a tiny smear of lipstick on one of her front teeth.

Mrs. Doolittle looked delighted. "Mavis! I'm so glad you made it."

"I almost didn't," said Mavis. "Trixie, that's my pet Pekingese," she explained, turning to the children, "had a little accident, and I had to clean it up before I came. But," she continued enthusiastically, "I'm ready to go now. Are all of you ready?"

The children nodded.

"Great! Today I thought it would be fun to teach you a little song. Some of you may already know it, and you can help the others. Have any of you heard of the round, 'Are you sleeping?' "

A couple of the older children raised their hands. "*Wunderbar!*" said Mavis, using what turned out to be her favorite expression. "That means 'wonderful' in German. Can you say that?"

"*Wunderbar!*" the students repeated, with mixed results.

"*Wunderbar!*" Mavis exclaimed again. "Those of you who raised your hands, come up and join me and we'll get this party started!"

The next 15 minutes were a hilarious mix of false starts, giggles, a general misunderstanding of the exact nature of a round, considerable dancing about by Mavis, and a continuous flow of *wunderbares.* Finally, she was satisfied that the children knew the words and had a modestly firm grasp of how to sing a round.

"*Wunderbar!*" Mavis sang out once again. "Let's sing!"

"Are you sleeping, are you sleeping?" the first group began, and on they went, with each succeeding group intoning the first line when Mavis signaled them to begin. At the end, the children, as well as Mrs. Doolittle, Cyndarria, Alison, and even Simon, laughed in delight at their success.

"I think we all deserve a hand!" cried Mavis. Everyone clapped and laughed some more, obviously pleased with themselves.

Mrs. Doolittle stepped forward then. "Thank you so much, Mrs. Forsythe. That was…well, it was *wunderbar!* I hope you will come back and visit us again."

"Any time," said Mavis. "I loved it!"

After all the excitement of learning the round, the rest of story hour was something of an anti-climax, redeemed only by the snacks. Alison's mother picked her, Cyndarria, J.J., and Toby up at 4:30.

"See you Sunday," said Cyndarria when she got out of the car.

"Lookin' forward to it," said Alison.

When Cyndarria entered the house, she found her mother in the kitchen. "When are the people from the nursery coming to plant the bushes and trees?" she asked.

"I just got a call," said Belle. "They'll be here tomorrow."

The week before, the burned siding and shutters on the house had been replaced, and now new bushes would be planted. With Cyndarria's help, Belle had decided on holly bushes. "The shiny leaves are pretty," she said, "and the red berries will be beautiful in the winter." Cyndarria agreed.

"You know," Belle had added. "I'd also like to plant a tree in honor of your Grandpa Paddy. I'm thinking an apple tree, a golden delicious. The blossoms are lovely in the spring and, once it's a little older, we can harvest apples in the fall. Besides, your grandpa loved apple pie."

"Can we get a tree for Grandma Rose too?" asked Cyndarria.

"I think that would be perfect," agreed Belle. "Do you have a tree in mind?"

"How about a cherry tree? I like the Stella cherry we read about because it's self-pollinating, and I love the white blossoms."

"Did you know your grandma won a cherry-pie baking contest when she was a teenager?"

248

"She never told me that," said Cyndarria, "but I'm not surprised."

"She never really talked about it. Can you guess what her secret ingredient was?"

"Hmmm," said Cyndarria. "Cinnamon?"

"Nope. Maraschino cherry juice, which replaced the almond extract. Apparently, it was quite a hit with the judges."

"She never taught me that recipe," said Cyndarria. "I'll have to see what I can figure out. That will be a good challenge this summer."

That evening Cyndarria went upstairs to her room a little early. She sat down in Grandma Rose's rocking chair and thought.

So many surprising things had happened the spring of her thirteenth year—some happy, some sad, some scary, some exciting, and some that just made her wonder and think.

As she often did lately, she felt her grandmother's presence. "Thank you, Grandma Rose," she said. "You helped me a lot this spring. I hope you're proud of me."

She rocked contentedly for a few minutes, holding Sebastian, her teddy, on her lap. There was a knock on her door. "Come in," she said.

Toby entered, carrying a book. "Will you read to me, Cyndarria?" he asked.

"Sure, buddy, whatcha got there?"

"*James and the Giant Peach*. It's my favorite. Can we read part of it now?"

"Of course. Where would you like to start?"

"I think with chapter one, when James has to go live with Aunt Sponge and Aunt Spiker. They're mean, but they're funny too."

"Sounds good, Tobe," said Cyndarria. "I always like to begin at the beginning. Here, you hold Sebastian."

Toby took the teddy and scrambled up on his big sister's lap. She settled him more firmly and gave him a little kiss on the top of his head. She turned to the first page, which showed a picture of James Henry Trotter at the age of four. He was smiling.

"Do you think I look like him?" asked Toby.

"Nah," said Cyndarria. "You're much cuter, and probably much better at math."

Toby looked pleased.

"I think maybe it's because I'm older," he said.

Cyndarria smiled, gave her little brother a squeeze, and began to read.

Later, she lay in bed thinking again about everything that had happened during the spring and wondered if the next three months would hold as many surprises as the last three had. Maybe she would have an epiphany. Now *that* would be a surprise!

Cyndarria Rose Thornwell's Mini-dictionary

For the Conscientious, the Curious, and the Lover of Words

Abysmal: extremely bad

Acknowledgment: an expression of appreciation or acceptance

Admonish: to advise, caution

Admonition: advice, counsel, caution

Adversity: misfortune, distress

Aggrieved: offended, disturbed

Alzheimer's disease: a disease of the brain that steadily worsens, leading to dementia (a severe loss of intellectual capacity)

Ambivalent: having mixed feelings

Anguish: acute distress, suffering, or pain

Anti-climax: a descent in quality, a disappointing or weak conclusion

Appalling: horrible, very bad

Ardent: eager, enthusiastic, passionate

Assiduously: done with careful attention or persistent effort

Attire: clothing

Au gratin potatoes: potatoes baked in a cheese sauce

Auspiciously: in a promising or favorable way

Aztecs: A powerful Indian tribe in Mexico, which was conquered by the Spanish, led by Hernán Cortés, in 1521. The Aztecs introduced the Spanish to corn and chocolate. They were also among the first people to make education required for everyone.

Banter: playful or teasing remarks

Beatific: blissful, saintly

Begrudgingly: reluctantly

Bette Davis: an American actress of film, television, and theater from the 1920's to the 1980's—regarded as one the greatest actresses in Hollywood history

Bewildered: confused

Bookie: a bookmaker; one who determines odds and receives and pays off bets on sporting and other events

Brandish: to shake or wave, like a weapon

Brook: as a verb, to tolerate or put up with

Catharsis: release of pent-up emotions

Chagrined: embarrassed, ashamed

Chasten: to restrain or subdue

Chide: to scold or find fault

Chortle: a blend of "chuckle" and "snort" from *Through the Looking Glass* (a sequel to *Alice's Adventures in Wonderland)* by Lewis Carroll

Cloche: a close-fitting, bell-shaped hat

Concoct: to make by combining ingredients

Contrite: sorry, apologetic

Coy: flirty, artfully shy

Courtly: polite, flattering

Culprit: person guilty of an offense or fault

Curt: rudely brief in speech

Deceived: tricked, fooled

Depart: to leave

Designation: a distinctive name

Diction: word choice

Diminutive: in grammar, used to show smallness, familiarity or affection

Disgorge: to throw up

Dismayed: upset, alarmed, discouraged

Distraction: something which amuses or entertains; something which divides your attention, makes you think about something else

Distraught: very agitated or upset

Doctorate: doctor's degree, Ph.D.

Down syndrome: a genetic disorder which causes a wide range of developmental delays and physical disabilities. In the United States today, one in every 700 children is born with Down syndrome.

Dumbfounded: speechless because of being amazed or astonished

Elicit: to bring out, draw forth

Eloquent: movingly expressive

Emanate: to come forth, originate (from)

Endowment: the funds or property that an institution has as a permanent source of income

Engender: to cause, produce

Enlighten: to instruct, shed light on

Ensconced: sheltered securely, concealed

Erudite: very knowledgeable, scholarly

Exhilarating: making you feel excited, spirited, or glad

Feign: to pretend

Flaunt: in this context, ignore, refuse to obey

Flabbergasted: surprised, astounded

Flourish: in this context, to wave or shake dramatically, to make a dramatic gesture

Flummoxed: bewildered, confused, unsure what to do

Frog: sometimes used as a teasing nickname for French people because of their love of frog legs

Gaelic: an Irish language

Garner: to get

Giddy: lighthearted, joyfully elated

Gimlet eye: sharp or piercing glance

Glum: gloomy, dejected

Gratifying: pleasing, satisfying

Greta Garbo: a Swedish-born American film actress of the 1920's and 1930's

Grimace: to make a disgusted or ugly face

Gross: extremely bad, as in the expression, "a gross injustice"

Haitian Creole: the modified form of French spoken by most people from Haiti

Harrumph: to express yourself gruffly

Heartily: enthusiastically

Illustrious: distinguished, glorious

Impending: something threatening that's about to happen

Impish: mischievous

Inaudible: incapable of being heard

Incumbent: in this context, obligatory; imposed, as a duty

Incorrigible: bad beyond correction or reform; unruly, uncontrollable

Inexplicable: unable to be explained

Ingenious: clever, inventive

Intersperse: to scatter at intervals

Interrogate: to question, sometimes seeking answers that the person might want to keep secret

Intimidate: to make timid or fearful

Irate: angry

Ironic: the opposite of what a word's literal meaning suggests

Jubilant: overjoyed, rejoicing

Laudable: worthy of praise

Leonardo: Leonardo da Vinci (1452-1519), a famous Renaissance artist, best known for painting the Mona Lisa

Literal translation: exact or word-for-word translation without interpretation of how the word might actually be used in a given sentence

Manifest: to show

Mantra: an often repeated word or phrase used by an individual or group which embodies a guide to action, similar to a slogan

Meekly: in a submissive way

Meticulous: precise, thorough

Mingle: associate with

Mischievously: in a playful but annoying or teasing way

Morbid: gloomy, gruesome

Mooning: gazing dreamily

Mull: to consider, think about carefully

Muck: a highly organic black soil

Nahuatl: the language of the Aztecs, still spoken by 1.5 million people, mostly in central Mexico. Some words taken by English from Nahuatl include chocolate, chili, tomato, and avocado.

Notorious: in this context, widely known for a particular trait

Neurologist: a doctor who specializes in diseases of the nervous system

Obscure: little known, difficult to see or understand

Oppressive: unjustly harsh, tyrannical

Outspoken: said in a frank, straightforward way; saying exactly what you think, which can sometimes get you in trouble!

Ovoid: egg-shaped object

Pate: head

Patronizing: condescending, acting in superior way

Penchant: inclination; taste or liking for something

Pensive: thoughtful in a dreamy or sad way

Permeate: to penetrate, saturate

Perpetrator: a person who commits an illegal or evil act

Perpetual: lasting a long time, continuing without interruption

Persevere: to continue despite obstacles

Persist: to keep on

Personable: friendly, pleasant

Philatelist: stamp collector

Plaintively: sorrowfully, mournfully

Ponder: think about deeply

Premature: occurring too soon

Pretension: a false show of merit or importance

Prevaricate: to lie

Pristine: having its original purity

Proficient: competent, skilled

Pulverize: to demolish, crush, defeat

Reeking: stinking

Refugee: in contrast to an immigrant, a person who has fled his or her country for safety or refuge, as in a time of war, political conflict, or personal danger. Lovelie and Emmanuel were both refugees.

Renaissance: the time of a great revival of art, literature, and learning in Europe, beginning in the 14th century and extending to the 17th century. It marked the transition from the medieval to the modern world.

Renaissance man: a man of many interests and talents, like Leonardo da Vinci

Reprimand: to scold or condemn, usually from a position of authority

Reticence: reluctance or hesitation to speak

Rotund: round, plump, fat

Ruefully: with regret, regretfully

Sacrilegious: disrespecting anything held sacred or deserving of great respect

Self-pollination: A type of *pollination* in which the pollen from the **anther** (the pollen-bearing structure in the stamen, the male organ) of the flower is transferred to the **stigma** (the sticky part of the pistil or female organ) of the same flower, as happens with the golden delicious apple tree and the Stella cherry. This means another tree of the same species does not need to be nearby in order for pollination and the reproduction of seeds to occur.

Semblance: appearance, likeness

Skeptically: doubtfully, with doubt

Smitten: charmed, in love

Smug: contentedly confident in one's own ability or superiority

Steel yourself: to make yourself strong or determined

Stoical: resigned to or accepting of whatever may come

Stricken: deeply affected, as with grief or fear

Subtle: difficult to perceive or understand

Suspended animation: the state of not moving

Taken aback: surprised

Tantalizing: possessing a quality that stimulates desire or interest

Taunt: to insult or jeer

Tentatively: in a hesitant or uncertain way

Terse: brief in an almost rude way

Toque: a tall, white chef's hat

Traumatized: frightened, feeling psychological pain

Tremor: shaking

Uncharacteristically: not typically

Undeterred: not stopped or prevented

Undiminished: not lessened

Unfazed: not discouraged or alarmed

Upshot: result

Witty: amusing, clever

Wry: cleverly, ironically, or grimly humorous

Yards vs. Meters: In Michigan, schools began moving from yards/miles to the metric system in track in 1980. In 1981, the time of this story, both were still in use. In 1986, it was mandated that the metric system be adopted statewide.

SOME THINGS TO THINK ABOUT

AT THE END of the novel, Cyndarria is thinking about what a surprising spring it has been. There have been things that were happy, others that were sad; some were exciting, others scary; a few were frustrating, and others were very rewarding. Some just made her wonder and think.

Things That Make You Wonder: One of the things that made her wonder occurred in the first couple chapters: the mysterious disappearance and reappearance of a comb and a paper she had been writing on. Have you ever experienced or heard of anything like that or like what happened with pennies to Henri and his father? How would you explain such an occurrence? What kinds of things make you wonder?

Maintaining High Standards: Early on in the novel, Cyndarria was frustrated and annoyed by Mrs. Wackenstein. Over the course of the story, however, her feelings about Mrs. Wackenstein and about herself as an English student changed. Why? One of the things Mrs. Wackenstein always emphasized was maintaining high standards. What inspires you to "maintain high standards"— that is, strive for excellence or do your best?

Bullying: Bullying is a challenging issue in many schools and can also occur among adults. In this novel, Tommy and his father, Mr. Aubrey, are both bullies. Bullies often pick on people whom they see as weaker than themselves, but when faced with someone equally strong or stronger, they show themselves to be cowards. That happened with Mr. Aubrey when Emmanuel and Toad came to Belle's defense. Have you ever experienced bullying? How is that handled in your school?

Racism: On the whole, the characters in this novel were pretty tolerant of each other, but in Chapter 13 there was an obvious example of racism when Mr. Aubrey spoke to Henri's father at brunch. Another very subtle example occurred in Chapter 19 on the part of Jodi and Christina. What happened and what did each incident tell you about the characters' attitudes? Have you seen examples of racism in your own school or community? In your opinion, what is the best way to deal with racism or prejudice against those who are different?

Teachers' Attitudes toward Students: In Chapter 14 Stevie said about Mrs. Wackenstein, "She hates me." Why did he think she would feel that way? How do you think Mrs. Wackenstein would describe her feelings toward Stevie? Do you think teachers really do "hate" some students? Do you think a teacher is ever justified in having negative feelings toward a student? Why or why not?

Author's Purpose: In Chapter 19 Cyndarria raised a question about the title of *The Parsley Garden,* wondering if Saroyan thought about parsley being a biennial plant and if the implied symbolism were intentional. What do you think authors do—write for a particular audience (and hope they understand) or write what pleases themselves (and hope that the audience likes it)? When you write, what are your concerns?

Value of Reports: In Chapter 21 students gave reports in Spanish class, and Cyndarria actually found them quite interesting. She also seemed to have enjoyed making *mole* and learning something about its history. How do you feel about doing "reports" for class? What do you think is the best way for reports to be assigned and presented? Have you ever done a report that you found interesting? If so, what was it about?

Choices: At one point Cyndarria remembered playing pom-pom-pull-away when she was a child and outrunning her friends. She recalled thinking at that time that the worst thing that could happen to her would be to lose her legs—worse even than becoming blind or deaf. In your opinion, what would be worst—losing your legs, your sight, or your hearing? Why?

Dealing with Loss: The saddest thing that happened to Cyndarria was the death of her grandfather, but she felt better after his memorial. Why do you think she felt better? If you were going to write a farewell speech about a loved one or a person you admire, what would you say? If someone were to write a farewell about you, how would you want to be remembered?

Gratitude/Making a Difference: Cyndarria's feelings about Easter are described in Chapter 27: "This was a joyful time, a holy time, and a day when Cyndarria would think about Grandpa Paddy and Grandma Rose and probably a little bit about Jesus too. She felt her heart fill with a mixture of sadness and happiness. And gratitude. She would think about that especially." What are the things you're most grateful for? Although she passed away, Grandma Rose was still very important to Cyndarria. Who are the people who have made a difference in your life? What do you do to let them know how much they mean to you? Have you been told by others how important you are to them? How did that make you feel?

Attitude and Effort: In Chapter 28 Henri apologized to Coach McIntyre for disappointing him because of losing his race. Coach McIntyre said he wasn't disappointed. Why not? Under what circumstances might a coach be disappointed in an individual player or team? Are there situations when you have felt disappointed in yourself for any reason? What have you done to feel better?

Good Teachers: Cyndarria had six teachers and one sub that you got to know: Mrs. Wackenstein, Señor Paniagua, Coach Sam, Mr. Sidebottom, Mr. Ratkowski, Mr. Cassius, and Mrs. Maxwell. Which of the six would you most like to have as a teacher and why? Which would you least like to have and why? In your opinion, what makes a good teacher?

Attitude toward America/Immigration: Both Señor Paniagua, originally from Mexico, and Emmanuel Rousseau, Henri's father, originally from Haiti, talked about how grateful they were to be Americans. People who are naturalized citizens often seem to be more appreciative of America than those who were born here. Why do you think that is? Are immigrants important to this country? Why or why not? How do you feel about being American? Do you take pride in America? If so, how do you show it?

Rewarding Activities: A couple different activities were rewarding for Cyndarria and made her happy: running track and reading for story hour. Doing better in English also made her feel good about herself. Those sorts of activities are important for all of us to experience; they're things we should seek out. What have you done in your life that has been particularly rewarding and has made you feel happy and good about yourself?

Cyndarria's Surprising Spring: What did you think about Cyndarria's "surprising spring"? Of the many things that occurred, what did you find most surprising? What surprise do you think helped Cyndarria to grow the most? If you were to have your own "surprising spring," what surprises would you want to have occur?

Grandma Rose's Oatmeal-Peanut Butter-Chocolate Chip Cookies (Yum! The Best!)

1 cup brown sugar
1 cup white sugar
1 cup butter or margarine, softened
2 eggs
1 cup peanut butter
1 teaspoon vanilla
1 cup flour
1 teaspoon baking soda
2 cups quick-cooking oats
½ teaspoon salt
2 cups chocolate chips
1 cup walnuts (optional)

Preheat oven to 350 degrees.

Cream together the butter and sugars. Add the eggs, peanut butter and vanilla and combine well. Add dry ingredients and mix completely, then stir in the chocolate chips and walnuts (if desired).

For large cookies, drop by heaping tablespoons onto greased cookie sheet and bake at 350 degrees for 14-15 minutes. Makes about three dozen.

For smaller cookies, use rounded teaspoons and bake for 13 minutes. Be careful not to overbake! Makes around five dozen.

Let cool, then share with friends. They will love you for it! ☺

These cookies can be stored in plastic bags in the freezer for up to a month, but they probably won't last that long!

NOTE TO THE TEACHER

If you are a teacher who has purchased multiple copies of the book to use with your entire class, you are eligible to receive supplementary materials free of charge which include:

—Vocabulary practice exercises based on the Mini-dictionary

—Vocabulary quizzes

—Chapter questions, both short-answer and discussion

—Chapter quizzes, based on clusters of chapters

—A test over the entire book, including objective and essay questions

—Suggestions for projects based on the book

You will be able to download all materials and make as many copies as you need. If you wish to receive these materials or if you have questions or comments for the author, contact her at:

mkmrpublishing@gmail.com

ABOUT THE AUTHOR

Mary Roessler spent her entire professional life as a teacher of Spanish and English. Now retired, she continues to work as a volunteer ESL teacher for Lansing-area refugees and immigrants. She loves her work and the people she teaches.

Mary's husband Mike was a middle-school social-studies teacher and then a professor of education. Their daughter Kate, an elementary-school teacher, and her husband James have three children—Gus, Ruby, and Lola, whose picture appears on the cover.

Mary and Mike make their home in Dimondale, a very small town near Lansing.